RUSTED SYNAPSE

ELWOOD STEVENS

ISBN: 979-8-9916727-0-2

Contents

Acknowledgments

I would like to thank the following people for their contributions (intentional and unintentional) to the creation of this book:

Mimi, for force feeding me Rodgers and Hammerstein musicals as a youth till the songs were permanently seared into my brain.

Phillip K Dick and Ridley Scott, for collaborating to make Blade Runner, a work that was foundational to the neo-noir and cyberpunk aesthetic I decided to play with.

William Gibson, for his myriad of novels, none of which I have read, but inspired others to create works in the cyberpunk genre that inspired me. My work stands on the shoulders of those countless creators he inspired.

Masamune Shirow and Mamoru Oshii, for their work on 1995's Ghost in the Shell, without which there could be no Vivi Rodriguez.

Hideo Kojima, for the seminal Metal Gear Solid series of videogames and numerous examples of how not to portray women in media.

The Botez Sisters, for their Youtube channel that made chess fun and watchable while researching for the book.

Chris Broad, for his Abroad in Japan Youtube channel that helped me escape to Japan vicariously after the COVID pandemic robbed me of the opportunity in 2020.

All of my beta testers, for encouraging me to create more chapters till the novel was done.

My editor, Kourtney Spak, for helping me cut away the useless fat at the edge of the novel and polish what remained to a glossy sheen.

My cover artist, Jane Kirt, for lovingly bringing Vivi and her furrowed brow off the written page and onto the front of this book.

Jeff and Masashi, for their help to ensure the Spanish and Japanese appearing in the novel doesn't look translated by a robot.

Ted, for saving literally the whole book by pointing out the most awful and glaring plot hole I somehow missed.

Andrew, for helping me understand that sometimes there's no answer that could ever be good enough.

Monique, for letting me know I properly tapped into my feminine side in writing Vivi.

Greg and Lauren, for helping me to realize the main character in your novel *probably* needs a backstory.

Lea and Brian, for getting me so disturbingly drunk at a "candle making bar" that I threw up half the rest of the night and magically came up with the entire second half of the novel while hanging over a toilet.

Lacey, Elizabeth, and Sylvie for putting up with me the ~~9 months~~ 20 months it took to birth this book.

Chapter One

An Interested Client

Vivi knew when she put her name to the contract that she'd likely die a violent death, but she never realized how boring it would be waiting around for the end once the violent part was done.

An old fluorescent tube in dire need of replacement hummed audibly above and cast only the faintest flickering light across her small hospital room, illuminating the stained tile floor below. There were exactly 276 unbroken tiles separating the space between her only window and the door to the hallway. She knew this because she had counted them at least twice this day alone. There was little else to do within the four shabby walls at the Veterans Affairs hospital except count the tiles on the floor, ruminate on what would happen after she breathed her last breath, and peer back into her memory. Only one of those options wasn't painful.

The metal sliding door to her room was bent wide open and no longer capable of closing shut. She thought it probable a former resident of the room attempted escape instead of allowing the Army to repossess their property. There was no chance of her escape, though. She had resided within the space for a long twenty days, incapable of leaving her chair by the window. A concern gnawed at the back of her mind that she was becoming a permanent fixture. A concern that her sad four walls were becoming the last home she'd have in her thirty-two years of existence.

The rest of the room hardly painted the picturesque setting one would hope to find themselves slowly dying in. A moth-eaten mattress atop a broken hospital bed she couldn't climb into and two metal chairs with an end table by the small window rounded out the space that was unfit for human habitation. No loved ones to surround her when she would finally close her eyes for the last time. Why would they? There was no one left that wanted her. Nowhere else to go except here. *A fitting place for an unwanted thing*, she thought.

One can't stop warm summer days from giving way to the cold, empty darkness of winter, and Vivi knew she had no means of removing herself from her fate. There was a long time to think about it while the bureaucracy played out, and so she resigned herself to it. Now it was only a matter of waiting for the end.

And despite that, looking down at the wall outlet barely keeping her alive, she still couldn't find the will to end things herself. The will to pull the plug. Her plug. Why? Why was she still holding on? It was so simple. It was right there. She could pull it and be done. There was only the one answer, of course.

Fear.

Vivi brought her only hand to her chest and felt it rise and fall as she inhaled and exhaled, checking yet again to make sure her lungs still drew breath, knowing it to be the reason she stayed her hand from the outlet. Her one fear and the thing she found most untenable about death: the crushing sensation of being unable to breathe. A sensation she knew all too well and dreaded to feel ever again.

So Vivi sat in her chair by the window and stared, unblinking, out into the chilly darkness of a neon-lit fog that permeated the nighttime sky above the slums of old Phoenix. She looked for anything in the fog that would help block her memories bubbling to the surface as she waited, either for the cold embrace of death, or Freddy with her fucking cigarettes. Whichever came first.

Heavy footsteps down the hallway told her which of the two was arriving before the other and broke her trance. She called out to the footsteps, "About goddamn time. How much I owe you?"

A large man in old medical scrubs lumbered in through the doorway and set a pack of cigarettes on the small table next to Vivi. "Nothin'. It's on me this time."

"Oh yeah? That's not like you." Vivi picked up the sealed pack of cigarettes with her only hand, looking up at Freddy with a doubtful eye. "Yesterday it was seventy bucks a pack plus a delivery fee. Why the change of heart?"

Freddy shrugged. "Feelin' generous tonight. Hey, you want some help with that?"

"I might only got one arm, but I think I can still manage to open a pack of smokes by myself." Vivi pulled the cigarette pack to her mouth, bit at the cellophane lip of the packaging, and tore it open with her teeth. "'Sides, you'd probably charge me a fee for the pleasure of your help, am I right?"

"Hmm. You ain't wrong." Freddy smiled. "So how 'bout it? Can I get one of those?"

"Nah. Sorry, Freddy. Dunno how many more of these I'm gonna get." Vivi opened the pack of Fortunes and drew out a white cigarette with a thin green band at the filter.

Freddy turned to leave with an air of displeasure on his face, shaking his head. "Suit yourself. You're welcome, by the way."

"Yeah... thanks," Vivi responded coldly as Freddy left the room. His heavy footsteps could be heard just outside her door, headed down the hallway and away from her tiny room. Soon the hum of the anemic fluorescent light was once again the only sound that filled the darkened space.

Vivi put the cigarette to her lips and looked down for only a moment to the table at her side for her lighter, when she felt another presence in the room. No footsteps heralded the newcomer's arrival. She looked up to see a tall man standing in the doorway, his weathered face wreathed in an almost unnatural shadow thanks to the room's dim lighting.

She brought the lighter toward her face, flicked the top cap open and ignited the end of the cigarette. Her face was momentarily illuminated in the darkness till she snapped the lighter closed and exhaled a thick plume of smoke. "Well, now I suppose I know who to thank for the cigarettes."

"Viviana Rodriguez?"

Vivi took another drag from the cigarette and exhaled another billowing stream of smoke, shaking her head at the stranger in her doorway. "Never heard of her."

The man took a silent step into the room, exposing more of his face to the light. To Vivi, his features looked as if hewn out of an old block of wood, like some kind of caricature of a seasoned war hero one might see in an old holofilm. He was dressed impeccably in a black suit with wing-tip shoes, a white shirt and white tie; his hair was combed back neatly and was not yet entirely gray. Nothing on his person was a millimeter out of place, which Vivi felt stunk to high heaven of ex-military brass.

He spoke with a stern, serious voice, "Are you sure? Because you look an awful lot like the product of a story I was told." The stranger paused for a moment in consideration before continuing, "Tell me if any of this sounds familiar: she was hired by Paulo Cruz to rip off a Herrera Cartel pharmaceutical shipment, but the job went sideways. When the Herrera's caught up with her, they tore her limb from limb and left her for dead as an example. Only real reason she's still alive is due to her brief stint in the Army that gained her admittance to this VA hospital where she's been hiding out for three weeks. The same Army she still owes fifty million dollars to for that decommissioned prosthesis she signed a ten-year contract for. Does that sound about right?"

"No. You're wrong." Vivi glared as she pulled the cigarette to her mouth, and took a long, considered drag before exhaling smoke out her nose. "Job didn't go sideways, it was upside down from the start." She sighed in annoyance, looking away. "So what, you here to collect?"

The man shook his head. "Quite the contrary, Ms. Rodriguez." He motioned to the chair across from her with a calm conservation of movement. "May I sit?"

From her seated position, Vivi could feel the stranger looking down at her with an appraising eye. She knew what she must've looked like in her current dilapidated state. It was as the stranger said, torn limb from limb and left for dead.

Starting with the hand holding the cigarette, exposed metal peeked out where the artificial skin had torn open on Vivi's knuckles. The silicon-based skin used to cover prosthetic body parts was normally quite convincing at approximating human flesh, but in its current state, ripped open, its authenticity was belied by the latticework of metal and wires visible beneath. If that were all, perhaps she could have passed as a human with a few replacement parts, however the rest of her mangled artificial body painted a clear picture for anyone willing to look: there wasn't much left of Viviana Rodriguez that was still human.

Vivi's left arm was completely torn off mid-bicep with a tangle of wire and fibrous artificial muscle hanging out. Her left leg ended just above where her knee should have been and her right leg wasn't much better, having been shorn off at the calf, leaving her carbon fiber frame and metal skeleton exposed with a mess of electronic components spilling out.

Had Vivi's appendages been intact, she would have looked to have been a perfect physical specimen, statuesque and elegant; easily mistaken as human at a casual glance, but currently, she was a pathetic heap hunched over in a chair. A broken thing. A large black stain sat atop the blue medical gown she wore, pooling damply at her upper left abdomen just beneath her rib cage. Battery acid and other chemicals oozed from the wound beneath the gown. From the wound that was slowly killing her.

The only seemingly unmarred portion of Vivi's artificial body was her face, which was pleasing enough to look at despite the dour expression that seemed permanently etched onto its olive complexion. Freckles were visible on her nose and cheeks even though they were covered under a light layer of dust and dirt. Her artificial eyes were light hazel and complemented with dark eyelashes framed by thick bangs and long hair which had been dyed indigo and draped messily over each of her shoulders.

Vivi motioned to the chair across from her. "Fine, pull up a chair. And you are?"

"An interested client."

Vivi laughed and coughed at the same time, sending up a cloud of smoke in the process. "You're a funny old man. Your eyes broken? You knew all that shit that went down with the Herrera's and you still came to chat business?"

The man sat down in the chair across from Vivi and leaned slightly toward her. "Tell me, are you or are you not in possession of a Somatech MK5 ONI combat platform?"

Vivi nodded and motioned to what remained of her body with her only hand before flicking the end of the cigarette into an ashtray on the table. "What's left of it, yeah. Why? You wantin' to use me for spare parts once my brain finally sluffs it? Cause if so, get in line. Army's got first dibs on the repo."

"No. I have a business opportunity that has need of it and its computational capabilities, not to mention an operator behind it with... wetwork experience."

"Well, in case you hadn't noticed, I'm not exactly in a position to help you," she scoffed. "Even if I had all my extremities and wasn't on death's doorstep sitting in this VA junkyard, the military locked out all the good shit when they decommissioned me." She picked up the ashtray and brandished it at the man in the chair. "This ashtray probably has more processing power than I do."

"Currently, perhaps."

Vivi slammed the ashtray down on the table beside her in annoyance as she spat back at the mysterious stranger, "Oh yeah? What, you gonna snap your fingers and magically unlock the encryption protocol locking down my hardware? Tell me, 'interested client', how many qubits does that imaginary quantum computer in your pocket got? Because unless it's in the tens of thousands, your proposition's a non-starter, irrespective of the fact I've got no legs and need five hundred thousand in repairs to keep myself out of a fuckin' grave."

The man began to lean forward, closer to Vivi, as he extended out his index and middle finger toward her left temple. "In a manner of speaking, Ms. Rodriguez, I am."

Vivi recoiled slightly in her seat with a perplexed look. "Wait, what're you—"

The stranger closed his eyes, his fingers moving ever closer to her head. "Going to snap my fingers..."

The fluorescent light in the room and the neon outside her window dimmed ominously as the man's fingers touched the side of her head. Internally, Vivi saw her processor array's temperature readings alarmingly increasing one, then five, then seven degrees before dropping back to normal levels. As her internals began to cool down, she noticed one of the locked nodes within her body's operating system became available to her again for the first time in years: Ping Network Protocol. Accessing it, she turned it on, and like a blinding light flicking on in an endless darkness that became more tolerable the longer one looked, Vivi could see a visual representation of the network running in and around the Veterans Affairs building. Every person, computer, phone, and electronic device connected to the network was visible to her in read-only mode.

Vivi shoved the man's hand away from her forehead. "Just who the fuck are you?"

The man leaned back in his chair, resting his hands on his lap. "You can call me Mr. Faust."

Vivi's mind raced. The ability to unlock a military grade hardware encryption in an instant had far-reaching implications as to the identity of Faust. Government spook? PMC mercenary? Mega Corporation operative? All were valid hypotheses. Perhaps a few of the possibilities overlapped. One thing was a given: he was a serious player. But why was he interested in her? There were plenty of other fully prosthetic former soldiers with services ready for the buying that weren't sitting in a scrap heap waiting for death. Probably sporting newer combat frames and ONI rigs too. After all, her underlying kit wasn't exactly new when her brain was shoehorned into it five years ago. Compared to newer models, her body was positively outdated by comparison.

Vivi pulled the lit Fortune in her hand to her lips again and inhaled. "Faust, huh?" She exhaled an impressive cloud of smoke out of the side of her mouth as she regained her composure and took back on her sardonic tone. "Yeah, that's a loaded name if I ever heard one. You sayin' you made a deal with the devil, or that you're him in the flesh?"

Faust chuckled. "Maybe a bit of both, Ms. Rodriguez."

"So, this business proposal of yours. You gonna tell me about it before or after my trip to the morgue?"

"Hopefully before, but not here. Tomorrow, Hotel Executor, 6pm. I'll have an associate arrange your transport."

"Mmm. That might be a bit of a problem. Like you said, I got left for dead." She pointed to the black stain on her gown. "Impaled, right through the power plant. Won't hold much of a charge anymore." Vivi turned her head to the side and motioned to the thick gauge wire extending from the back of her neck that hung down over the chair, snaked around the base and plugged into the wall. "Wall outlet's the only thing keepin' the lights on."

"I think we can accommodate you." Faust got up from his seat and smoothed over the front of his suit jacket.

She reached out as if to stop Faust from leaving. "Hey wait! This job, what's it pay?"

"Tomorrow. 6pm. Hotel Executor. You'll have your answers. Your transport will be here at 4."

"Yeah? And just how do I know it's gonna be worth my time?"

Faust smirked and shook his head. "You mean other than the fact that taking it will save your life? Hmm…" Faust looked away momentarily in thought before returning to lock eyesight with Vivi. "I'll tell you what, if you come to Hotel Executor tomorrow and decide not to take the job, I'll still provide you nicer accommodations than your current surroundings to spend your few remaining days."

Vivi only needed an abbreviated moment to contemplate Faust's offer. No place could be worse than her current surroundings, and at the very least, maybe there'd be some new floor tiles to count. She set her cigarette down on the ashtray and extended her only hand to Faust to shake. "Deal."

Faust clasped his right hand with Vivi's and shook it. Normally when she shook hands with another person, she could glean bits of information about them, but from Faust, Vivi received nothing. It was as if she were shaking hands with a blank sheet of paper. She felt his hand physically in hers, gripping her back, but it felt wrong, like she was shaking hands through a third person. If Vivi had hoped to learn anything from physical contact to Faust, she had failed. He remained an enigma.

With little fanfare, he exited the room as quietly as he entered it. Vivi didn't even hear Faust's footsteps down the hallway after he left her room.

Chapter Two

Not Dead Yet

The bed in Vivi's room had gotten no use in the three weeks since she arrived. Possessing an artificial body meant little in the way of getting physically tired of sitting in one position, and in her current state, dismembered and tethered to the wall to maintain a pulse, getting in and out of bed was not a feat Vivi could accomplish on her own. Moreover, with her entire prosthesis weighing in at close to 400 pounds of carbon fiber, metal, electronics, and wires (had all her appendages been intact), propositioning others for help to carry her from place to place would have been difficult given the low number of wheelchairs rated to hold her weight the VA seemed to possess; no doubt thanks to improper funding and ongoing budget cuts. So Vivi remained propped up in the metal chair in her room, occasionally requisitioning one of the ward's orderlies, Freddy, for cigarettes.

Annoyingly, Freddy frequently used her room as a refuge from his actual job, which had a tendency to cost her a surprising percentage of the cigarettes she paid him for. On this particular day, though, rather than shoo him away, she probed him for information about the previous day's mysterious visitor.

"So, Freddy, that old guy who bought my cigarettes for you yesterday, he say anything to you?"

Freddy shot her a confused look. "Old guy?"

"Yeah. Slicked back grey hair, nice suit, face that looked kinda like it was made outta tree bark."

"Nah. Don't know what you're talkin' bout."

"Oh, come on. This a ploy for one of my smokes? Fine, you can have one." Vivi extended out the opened pack of Fortunes to Freddy, who happily took one, lighting it.

"Wasn't no old dude. He was young, twenny-eight...twenny-nine. Black. Shaved head. Chrome fingers."

"And this guy, he say anything?"

"Just that the Fortunes for you was on him and asked what room you was in."

"And that's it?"

Freddy blew out a cloud of smoke and nodded. "That's it."

"You didn't think maybe he coulda been one of the Herrera Cartel out to finish me off?"

"He didn't look like no cartel. Sides, if he was, he'd be doin' you a favor. Said so yourself a few days ago."

Vivi spent most of the day in anticipation of 4pm, curious of what Faust's job proposal would entail. But more importantly, she wondered how he planned to keep her mangled prosthetic body alive while moving it from the VA in slums of old Phoenix over to one of the nicest hotels in the city on the north side of town.

Her answer arrived promptly at 4pm, slung under the arm of the man Freddy met the night before.

"A car battery? Really?" she asked incredulously.

The man smiled cheerfully at her. "Best I could do on short notice, but trust me, it'll work. I once kept a buddy of mine going for three days out in the field swapping in and out car batteries after he got ripped in half by a mortar."

"Yeah? Your buddy, what happened to him after the third day?"

The man looked down for a moment, muttering to himself in discomfort, before returning to his genial visage. He held out a thick-gauge charging cable connected to the car battery toward Vivi, offering it to her. "Tomas Holt by the way. Mr. Faust sent me to retrieve you."

"I kinda figured," Vivi replied in a mocking tone as she swiped the wire with her only hand.

Tomas looked tall to Vivi up close, or perhaps it was due to her seated position. He was a dark complected man with brown eyes and a handsome face with a broad jaw line and wide nose, sporting a short well-kempt goatee. The top of his head was completely devoid of hair, having looked to have been fresh shaven. As Freddy mentioned to her earlier, all eight of Tomas's fingers were shiny chrome prosthetics, leaving only his natural thumbs. He was somewhat fashionably dressed in a maroon sport coat with a white t-shirt beneath and dark jeans. He wore one thin chrome chain around his neck, which looked coordinated to match the metal of his fingers. Beneath the chain, the neural port on the lower right side of the man's neck looked to have been surgically installed slightly crooked and featured a robust port cover; suggesting to her that Tomas's neural interface was likely military issue.

Vivi couldn't help but notice when he leaned in to give her the cable that he was carrying a side arm within an inside holster of his pants. Given the man's overtly friendly posturing, she had a hard time envisioning him actually using the gun on anyone.

Vivi set about the process of twisting and unplugging the cable from her charging port connected to the VA before she replaced it with the one from the car battery.

Tomas motioned to an industrial strength looking wheelchair that looked rated to carry artificial bodies. "Do you need any help?"

"No. Just push the chair closer and keep holding the battery."

Vivi used her one arm and what remained of her thighs to scooch herself into the wheelchair. Once firmly seated, she looked over and realized she was now too far away from the end table to reach her bag. She grumbled in annoyance. "You mind grabbin' my purse?"

For the first time in three weeks, Vivi was wheeled out into actual sunlight. She waited in front of the VA hospital as Tomas went to retrieve his car: an old, beat-up, cherry red Fortaleza GT. Well, Vivi assumed it had been cherry red at one point. The car's paint job looked like it had seen better days, but that was probably years earlier.

While getting into the wheelchair might have been mostly painless, getting Vivi into Tomas's car was more of an ordeal and required the help of a few of the VA's orderlies, including Freddy after Tomas slipped him forty bucks. Connected to a car battery at the neck and shoved into the passenger seat of a crappy car in a medical gown, she was beginning to wonder if the indignities of the job offer were worth it.

Vivi looked out the passenger side window as the car's electric motors spun to life, propelling the pair through the slums of old Phoenix. Dilapidated buildings and disrepair on city block after city block were a depressing reminder of the state of urban decay under the setting Arizona sun. She reached into her purse, pulling out her cigarettes and lighter.

Tomas looked over with concern. "Woah! Ms. Rodriguez! Please don't smoke in my car."

Vivi returned the cigarette she was about to light up into the packaging and placed it back in her purse. "Sorry. I forget sometimes." She brushed her thick indigo bangs out of her face, looking back to Tomas. "Call me Vivi by the way. Management can call me 'Ms. Rodriguez' all they want, but fellow help can't. And I'm sorry, but you don't look much like management to me."

Tomas smiled back. "Okay... Vivi. And just how do you know I'm not management?"

"Well, this car. It kinda sucks."

"Heh. Maybe so. But it is mine, and I like to take good care of my shit. Why do you smoke anyway? You're full-on borg. Are you even getting any nicotine out of it?"

"Yeah actually. Body might be a bot, but my brain's still human. Still needs oxygen. Which means breathing, artificial lungs, blah, blah, blah..." She flapped her hand as if it were talking. "But it's not about the nicotine. When they first strapped me up in this thing, they told me it was important to have as many connections to my former life as possible. Smoked ever since the day I enlisted. Seemed as good a way as any to remember I'm still me."

Tomas turned his full attention to Vivi as the car began to drive itself. "So, what got you? Rust? Or complications of life at war?"

Searing hot pain bubbled up from the depths of her lungs. Her breathing shallowed as she gasped for air that her lungs refused to take in. Phantom limbs reached up to clutch at her chest, but there were no hands to do so. Both had rotted away days earlier. The stumps of what remained of her forearms were covered in dull, rust-orange colored sores of the necrosis still eating away at the flesh. They brushed in futility against her breast.

She writhed on the operating gurney and coughed up flecks of blood and spittle as she looked with a pleading eye at the surgeon looming above her and whimpered, "I- I can't breathe. Please! Please...help. Help me..."

The surgeon reached down and rested a reassuring hand on her forehead. "The service contract isn't done yet. It won't be long, though. Just try to stay calm a little while longer while it's finalized."

"Please... I can't. I wanna go home... I just wanna go home...Please!" Her world began to fade as her lungs seized up and became like a burning hot iron within the center of her chest. She tried to scream, but no sound came out. Her eyes darted around the room, looking for help, but there was none to be found. Tears streamed down her cheeks. They would be her last.

Vivi returned to the present and put her hand to her chest, double-checking to ensure she was still breathing. Her voice wavered, "Rust."

Oblivious, Tomas held up his eight chrome fingers proudly. "Yeah, that's what got my fingers too. Rust. Painful as shit, not that I have to tell you. The disease didn't spread too far on me though."

Tomas smiled and gave Vivi two thumbs up. "Got to keep my thumbs at least."

Vivi shot Tomas an antagonizing look. "Yeah, real nice," she snarled, returning a singular thumbs up with her good hand while holding up the stump of what remained of her left arm, "I used to have two thumbs too. So, what do you know about this job?"

Tomas chuckled. "Honestly, probably not much more than you, other than that Mr. Faust needs you."

"Yeah? And how do you fit into this?"

"Can't say I know. He put me on retainer two days ago." Tomas leaned back into his seat. "So far I've mostly just been his gofer."

"Gofer, huh?" Vivi leaned her good elbow against the door casually. "What kinda stuff's he had you collect?"

Tomas looked away nervously. "Other than you and the wheelchair in the trunk? I'm not sure I'm at liberty to say."

"Anything to do with that side arm you're packin'? Brave of you carryin' it around in city limits."

"This side the border?" Tomas scoffed. "You're brave not carrying one."

Vivi cocked her head to the side. "Whatever. We get pulled over, I don't know you."

Tomas rolled his eyes. "We just met. You don't know me."

Vivi turned away, looking out of the car's window again as the scenery changed from older run-down structures to larger, newer buildings with mirrored finishes that gleamed brightly in the setting sun. Graffiti and poverty gave way to pristine surfaces and monetary excess. On the radio, some talking head was bemoaning how a trade deal between Brazil and the European Union would cut off a significant chunk of GDP growth for the war economy and WCO markets. Vivi often wondered how radio was still hanging on to relevance in an age with instantaneous access to any media one could want just by thinking about it.

She leaned her head over, looking back. "Know you well enough to know you have trash taste in radio stations."

Tomas clutched at his heart, feigning a wound. "Ouch! Well excuse me for wanting to be up to date on what's going on in the world. And just what would you have me change it to?"

Vivi gave a considered look back to Tomas, responding instantly. "Desert Heat FM, of course."

Had Tomas's eyebrows gone up any further, they could have been mistaken for hair. "Hold up! Lemee get this straight. You're sitting in my car all morose, 'everything sucks, woe is me', and yet you want me to put on some booty shakin' music on the way to a serious job offer? What kind of merc are you anyway?"

Vivi let slip a tiny smile. "The not dead yet fun kind. Put it on."

"Hah! She can smile! And for that, your wish is my command." Tomas grinned as he reached over to the car's antiquated touch screen and started adjusting the radio.

The two rode the rest of the way to Hotel Executor listening to the latest, most popular dance music 2140 had to offer, interrupted only by the occasional commercial break trying to sell listeners on all manner of products from fully automated home defense systems to lottery tickets.

Upon arriving at their destination, Tomas took over operation of the car and pulled it into the hotel's attached parking garage.

Vivi watched as Tomas drove past the gleaming entrance to the 50-floor glass skyscraper emblazoned with the Executor logo. "What? You're not gonna valet and wheel me through the front entrance?"

"With you looking like that? Yeah, no. We're going to take the service elevator."

Vivi rested her chin on her hand sullenly, groaning, "Just great. My first time going to a swank hotel, and I don't even get to see the lobby."

After some work getting Vivi back into the wheelchair, Tomas rolled her through the parking garage to a service elevator and brought her to the 30th floor. The hallway's decor was a mix of contemporary amenities re-fashioned into 1930's design aesthetic. Carpets were detailed with bold geometric patterns and gold embroidery paired with Art Deco wall sconces and glass doors that were digitally frosted for privacy.

Tomas wheeled Vivi down the hall to a room near one of the regular elevators. "This is you. Here, I'll transfer you the access code."

An envelope with a "!" appeared atop the door within Vivi's digitally augmented perception of the world provided by her artificial eyes and neural interface known as a Heads Up Display. Vivi was never without the HUD, it was an ever-present overlay atop her vision that let her interact through her thoughts with her body's subsystems, electronic devices and other neurolink users in close proximity. Though the HUD had its downsides too, as it had a tendency to be attacked by ads in the more densely populated parts of town.

With a thought, she accessed the envelope and accepted the room code from Tomas before making an ad hoc wireless connection to the door, and unlocking it.

Tomas pushed Vivi into the lavishly appointed room as the frosted glass door automatically slid open.

Vivi had never seen a hotel room quite like this one. It possessed more space than a dwelling any singular person would have had need for, complete with a separate lounge area from the bedroom. The bathroom alone was larger than her entire room at the VA building. The walls were decorated with expensive looking abstract art, and the light fixtures were similarly golden, like the sconces from the hallway, giving the room a bright and inviting look. A king-sized bed with an ornate headboard sat at one end of the cavernous space. Various items were laid out on the bed including a thick roll of electrical tape, a package of bandages, several black dresses, and multiple sets of underwear.

Vivi pointed to the assortment of clothing and bandages on the bed. "Uh... what's all this?"

Tomas laughed nervously. "You asked me if Faust had me retrieve anything else. You're looking at it. I ah, didn't exactly know your size or style. So, I bought a few options."

Vivi raised one eyebrow inquisitively. "And the electrical tape?"

"Yeah, you might not like this part."

Vivi turned back in the chair, giving off an air of displeasure. "Oh? What part's that?"

"Faust demanded that I get you cleaned up. He wants the ends of your legs and arm taped up into neat stumps so there's no exposed frame or wires hanging out. Said you needed to be presentable for the client."

"Just great." Vivi rolled her eyes at yet another indignity she'd have to endure. She pulled out her cigarettes and lighter from her purse in response. "Let's get this over with."

Chapter Three

The Devil's Deal

Vivi had never been the most comfortable at relying on others for help, preferring to do things her own way. A character flaw she was beginning to think had a hand in landing her in most, if not all, of her predicaments. But even in admitting that to herself, it was still hard to accept help from a veritable stranger to get her dressed for her meeting with Faust and the client.

"Just turn away and hold the battery," Vivi commanded sternly, handing off the heavy car battery to Tomas.

Tomas closed his eyes, turning away. "I swear, I won't look, but are you sure you don't want a hand?"

"I'm a big girl, I can dress myself, thanks." Vivi held up one of the dresses, grousing. "And I thought you had bad taste in radio stations."

After Vivi changed out the bandages on her abdomen with fresh gauze and tape, and removed the stained medical gown she was wearing, she awkwardly began the process of slipping into the least disagreeable clothing options Tomas provided her with. Getting dressed one-handed was problematic, but doing so while also missing most of her legs, confined to a wheelchair, and tethered to a car battery increased the difficulty level exponentially.

"This is taking too long. We're going to be late at this rate. Look, I can speed this process up."

Vivi grumbled, "Fine. Just—whatever. I've got the basics covered up. Start taping up my right leg, it's harder for me to reach anyway."

The two worked for the better part of 10 minutes rolling electrical tape around ends of what remained of Vivi's legs and left arm, making neat stumps of what was formerly a tangled mess of wire, carbon fiber framework, and nanoweave artificial muscle fiber before momentarily disconnecting Vivi from the car battery to slide her into a sleeveless black dress that was long enough to cover what remained of her left leg while leaving her right leg stump exposed.

Placing the battery back on her lap, Tomas wheeled Vivi in front of a large mirror in the bathroom with an assortment of make-up items and a hairbrush laid out. "Just call when you're ready."

"Yeah, sure," she replied hastily before pausing and turning around in the wheelchair. "Hey, Tomas? Thanks, by the way."

Tomas smiled. "Don't mention it." He exited the bathroom and closed the door behind him.

It had been a long while since Vivi had looked at herself in the mirror. She took the opportunity to run the water and clean the dust and dirt that collected on her face during the three weeks she sat tethered to a wall. Underneath was the familiar visage of Viviana Rodriguez, unchanged in the 5 years since her 27th birthday. She grimaced in disapproval; it was still her looking back. The military prosthetists had done an amazing job recreating her original face on her artificial body. If she hadn't known the truth, she might have even believed it was real.

A mirror was brought in front of her slowly, held in the hands of one of the prosthetists responsible for configuring her artificial body and face. It was the first time she would see herself after the body transfer procedure.

She opened her new artificial eyes with trepidation at what she would find, but what looked back was familiar. Warm. Comforting. Human. Her freckles were still there. Her eyes still hazel. Her nose was as it had always been. Even the tiny scar near her left ear, left by the primary school fight with Claire Hutchins was recreated with detailed accuracy.

She turned her head back and forth, taking in every angle. "I... I look like me. It looks so real."

The prosthetist smiled. "Because it is real. The trick to believability, though, that's in the imperfections. Oh, when we first started doing full body prostheses, we strove for perfection. Getting rid of all the slight incongruences of the human face. The nose that wasn't perfectly straight, the nostrils that were slightly different sizes or eyes that weren't perfectly even. But in doing so, the human mind can tell something is off. And that which we want to look human, instead looks artificial. Other. The mind rejects what it sees. Goes off-kilter. Lead to a lot of suicide. Which is why we made you look exactly like you, blemishes and all."

Vivi applied little make-up, deciding that less was more, considering the job she imagined Faust lined up for her was likely less than glamorous; that, and she also felt most of the make-up Tomas acquired was more befitting a woman of... a different profession. Instead, she focused on brushing her hair, smoothing it out neatly and parting it to the side, out of her face. The ruched-into-oblivion style of dress might not have been to Vivi's taste, but as she looked in the mirror, she decided the indigo tone of her hair did at least contrast somewhat nicely with the dress's black color.

"Alright. I'm ready. Let's go."

Tomas entered and couldn't hide a surprised look. "Wow. You clean up nice."

Vivi scrunched up her face and turned back to face Tomas. "About that, I have questions. You got a girlfriend? Wife?"

Tomas smiled wryly. "No. Why?"

"Yeah, that checks out. When this job's over, you and me are gonna have to discuss your taste in dresses and make-up."

Finally cleaned up, Vivi was ready for her meeting with Faust and the client in the hotel's penthouse suite on the top floor. Apparently, the suite was the only such one in town with its own aero car parking. Vivi knew this, among a great other number of facts she didn't care to know, because Tomas droned on and on about how excited he was to see the suite the whole wheelchair ride from her room to the private elevator. Admittance to the suite was locked off to most guests of the hotel by an NFC key reader in the elevator, to which Tomas had been given the access key.

As the elevator doors opened to the space, opulent didn't begin to describe the palatial residence beyond. It featured all manner of marble in Art Deco stylings from the rest of the hotel, but raised to another level of decadence. Every surface was pristine. Every sofa, luxurious. Every carpet, intricately detailed. One side of the suite was an entire wall of glass that opened to a balcony that overlooked the city of Phoenix. Bright lights glistened across the city scape like diamonds hanging in the sky and sparkled in what little remained of the sun over the horizon. From the balcony, a set of stairs lead up to the roof where the private aero car parking was exclusively available to the penthouse's guests.

Exiting the elevator at 5:45pm, Tomas and Vivi were greeted by a slim man in his thirties with a scraggly beard. He wore thick-rimmed glasses and an affable look upon his face as he spoke at an energetic pace. "Rodriguez? Holt? Early? I like that. Come in, come in! Though, ah, there aren't any prizes for being early I'm afraid. Mr. Faust is all about exacting punctuality, so don't expect him till 6 on the dot. Oh! Shit! I'm sorry! I haven't even introduced myself. Ridley Fincher, data analyst for Mr. Faust and, ah, director of this little operation."

Fincher was far shorter than Tomas, diminutive in comparison, though Vivi annoyingly still had to look up at him from her wheelchair. He was dressed in a short white sport coat with a pastel green button-down shirt underneath and tech slacks on top of nylon loafers. His hair was short and brown, messily adorned on top of his head as if it had been combed and then fussed up on purpose. On initial examination, Fincher reminded her of a small dog: yappy and excitable.

Fincher held out his hand to Vivi to shake, which she took in hers. Oddly, the effect was similar to when Vivi shook hands with Faust. From Fincher, she felt like he was shaking her hand from beyond a glass wall as thick as the one that separated the penthouse from the balcony. Vivi couldn't see any hint of prosthetic or cyberware on Fincher outside of the neural port at the side of his neck as he rudely reached over her to shake Tomas's hand.

"Can I get either of you anything? No alcohol before the meeting, of course, but we have ninety-nine percent toxin-free sparkling water, any manner of soft drinks you could want, and there's a cheese board over there that Mr. Velasquez has already started helping himself to."

Tomas appeared impressed. "Ninety-nine percent? You're kidding. Shit yeah. I'll have some of that."

Vivi, on the other hand, looked up morosely from her wheelchair at Fincher. "Thanks, but I'm not thirsty."

"Fucking hell!" Fincher smacked himself on the side of the head. "Full borg, right? Oh my God, how rude of me! I am so, so, *so* very sorry. L-look, I can call up room service to get you a nutri-pack if you'd like?"

Vivi furrowed her brow. "Don't bother," she responded coldly before turning to Tomas. "Put me out on the balcony. I wanna smoke."

Tomas smiled nervously at Fincher and shrugged as he pushed Vivi's wheelchair past him, through the penthouse, and out onto the balcony. Vivi promptly lit up a Fortune, surveying the city under the February sky. In the distance, the desert was barely visible past the edge of the city, illuminated as if made of gold. Neon lights flicked on as the sun disappeared from the western sky.

As she looked out to see the city change from dusk to night, from the corner of her eye, Vivi could feel the man named Velasquez looking at her from inside the penthouse. She turned slowly to catch a better look at him before returning her gaze to the city. The brief glance told her all she needed to know: Velasquez was Herrera Cartel. Vivi had seen him once before, overseeing the return of the pharmaceutical shipment formerly in her possession while he had the rest of the Herreras rip her to pieces.

She didn't have long to dwell on it, however, as it wasn't long into her cigarette when an aero car flew overhead and landed on the roof above. Shortly after Vivi heard the vehicle finish its descent, she saw Faust walking down the stairway from the roof. "Ms. Rodriguez," he called out, "Glad you decided to join us. Mr. Holt, if you please?"

Tomas rolled Vivi back into the main room after she extinguished her cigarette on the arm of the wheelchair and flicked the butt off the balcony's edge.

Faust addressed the room. "Please, everyone, sit. I'm sure I don't need to impress upon any of you that the contents of this meeting are not to be discussed with any party outside of this room. If anyone asks, you were never here."

Faust and Fincher moved to a seating area within the penthouse consisting of three separate sofas in a triangle configuration around a short coffee table with a tablet sitting on top. Velasquez was already sitting comfortably on one sofa as Tomas pushed Vivi toward the seating area, his shoes audibly clicking on the marble floor behind her as he positioned her chair between two of the sofas. Tomas took the sofa on her left, leaving Fincher on the sofa to her right. Directly across from her sat Velasquez, wearing sunglasses that did a poor job concealing outdated cybernetic eyes above a salt and pepper beard and a bored expression.

The glass wall separating the penthouse from the balcony dimmed before going completely opaque, displaying instead a floor to ceiling piece of abstract art in its place that Vivi felt had the distinct appearance of being created by a drunk rolling around on a canvas while covered in an entire pallet of paint.

Faust remained standing in the center of the seating area. "Now, let me be plain: my organization is not affiliated with the United States or its government. That said, when the United States has need of certain tasks to be completed that, for sensitive reasons, it cannot perform on its own, they call me. I will be asking you to undertake actions across several sovereign nations that are considered illegal in exchange for a very lucrative pay day. If, during the course of the mission, you are apprehended by the authorities of any of these nations, you will face their justice systems and laws on your own. If this is a problem, I thank you for coming. Please feel free to leave now."

He paused for a time, waiting for any of the room's occupants to raise objections. When none of them did, he leaned over the tablet on the coffee table and flicked it on, using his thumb as a passcode. "Good. I'm sharing the meeting protocol to the room now. The join code is 03140316."

Vivi looked down at the tablet to see the meeting icon hover above it and connected her neural interface to the tablet wirelessly, before entering the join code. After a short handshake process, her HUD was connected ad hoc to the presentation.

In the corner of the room, behind the sofas, a digital, rectangular obelisk appeared with "01: Muted" emblazoned on its smooth, shiny surface, denoting to Vivi that a third party outside of the room was also listening in on the meeting via an Artificial Intelligence. Most likely, the client.

Faust took two silent steps beside the coffee table. "Before we get started, there will be ample time for questions later, so please save them till then."

A map of Asia appeared in the middle of the room, and it slowly zoomed in toward the eastern side of the continent. "Fifteen days ago, the United States received intel that suggested an asset thought to be lost forever had resurfaced... here." Faust pointed to a spot on the map. "In Shanghai."

The map continued to zoom in until individual buildings within Shanghai could be seen in detail before settling on a large 100 story megastructure. "This is the Long Qi building. It houses all manner of Chinese technology firms, communist party offices, governmental headquarters and offices for certain organized crime syndicates. Intelligence suggests the asset is located near the center of the complex on the 47th floor. The job at the macro level is quite simple: Walk in. Secure the asset. Walk out."

Faust walked silently around the coffee table as the map zoomed back out to display China. "The devil is in the details, of course. As you are all aware, China is a closed society. No one gets in who isn't supposed to be there. So, Phase 1 of the operation is to become people who have business in China, specifically in the Long Qi building."

The map zoomed out and shifted across the Pacific Ocean to Mexico, hovering over a city toward the northwestern side of the country. "This is Hermosillo, Mexico, a technology hub approximately 6 hours south of Phoenix containing the headquarters of Presidio Biologica, an up-and-coming flash cloning firm."

As Faust talked, photos of a man and a woman appeared superimposed over the map. Faust pointed to the man first. "This is Javier Luna, Director of Productions and CFO of Presidio Biologica," before pointing to the woman, "and his assistant Domenica Santiago. Mr. Luna and Ms. Santiago are scheduled for a meeting eight days from now on the 43rd floor of the Long Qi building with China's Ministry of Heath to discuss Presidio Biologica's renewal and continued licensing agreement for some of China's proprietary cloning methods."

The map shifted to show a route from the Hermosillo city center to the surrounding countryside. "We intercept Mr. Luna and Ms. Santiago en route to their homes outside the city, take their ID chits and have Holt and Rodriguez impersonate them for their meeting in China, which brings us to Phase 2.

Faust walked around the table toward Vivi and Tomas as the map once again shifted back to Shanghai. "Holt and Rodriguez attend the meeting, during which Rodriguez excuses herself, proceeds to the 47th floor, neutralizes any resistance, retrieves the asset, and then exfils the building. Questions?"

"Tons," Vivi scoffed.

Faust smiled back at her. "Ask away, Ms. Rodriguez."

"You say Holt and I are gonna impersonate this Luna and Santiago, and yeah I guess you could put a wig on Holt and shave his goatee and maybe if you squint real hard, he looks like Luna, but Santiago?" Vivi animatedly motioned to the picture of Santiago with her one arm.

"She's human. No prosthetics. Even assuming my body is getting fixed as part of your plan, I'd still never pass for her. Anyone takes one close look at me, and the jig'll be up."

"Will it? Hmm." Faust shrugged. "Look again."

Vivi looked down at her exposed arm, where normally there was a thin seam in her skin where her hand met her forearm and another where her forearm met her elbow. Both were gone, replaced by smooth, contiguous lengths of skin. "The fuck?"

"Oh shit! You look like her!" Tomas exclaimed from her left.

Vivi turned to Tomas, but it wasn't Tomas that looked back at her. Instead, it was a bald version of Javier Luna, the Presidio Biologica CFO. "What is happening here?"

Tomas and Vivi may have been in shock, but Fincher smiled knowingly along with Faust. Across the room, Vivi could see Velasquez looked bored.

Faust motioned to Fincher. "If you haven't been acquainted, this is Mr. Fincher, a data analyst, and the director for this operation. Mr. Fincher, if you please?"

"Ahh, yes!" Fincher stood up. "So, this is really cool! For this mission, we have access to a Class VII AI." Fincher motioned to the digital obelisk across the room. "With it we can apply a Deep Fake algorithm in real time to any camera or persons' neural linked optics looking at you to make them see Domenica Santiago instead of Viviana Rodriguez."

Vivi shook her head in disbelief. "Real-time? In China? Bullshit! This is a cute party trick, but the bandwidth you'd need to pull off something like this—"

"Is mammoth! Absolutely!" Fincher cut her off. "And that's why it was so important to pick two doubles who have skin tone matches with Luna and Santiago. It reduces the load on the system by minimizing the amount of visual replacements in any given moment the AI needs to make, but that's also why we need someone with a military grade prosthetic body like yours. The AI is housed here in the states so while it's computationally easy for it to do a simple face replacement here in a room of 5 people, across the ocean in a country filled to the brim with eyes and cameras it's decidedly more difficult. To counteract that, we'll be running the AI and Deep Fake algorithm piggy backed onto your hardware as well as offloading the majority of the computations locally to your processor array and a network of 8 cloaked drones that will remain in a formation outside of the building."

Tomas, who still looked like a bald Javier Luna, appeared upset. "So, wait, wait, wait, hold on, you're telling me the only reason you picked me for this job is because I'm black?"

Fincher looked away nervously. "No. I mean. Well, ah—you're also fluent in Spanish, right?"

Vivi leaned over to Tomas. "Don't feel that bad. At least they didn't pick you because you're a walking wireless router. This still doesn't make any sense. Okay, so every camera and person with neural linked optics is gonna to see Luna and Santiago instead of us. What about all the people with no neural interface? I can think of a ton of old people not wired up."

Fincher sat down as Faust stepped back into the conversation. "Here, in the States? Yes. You'd be correct. Neural interface adoption is only up to around 62%. But in China? It's mandatory. There's no better way to keep tabs on 4 billion citizens than shoving the surveillance tech right into their skulls. 100% adoption."

"Fine. Next question. The asset. What is it?"

"That's not something you need to concern yourself with right now."

"Considering you're wanting me to agree to retrieve it, yeah, I kinda think I do."

"Why?"

"Is it concealable? A piece of data? A piece of hardware? Is it heavy? Will it explode if I taunt it too much? You don't tell me what I'm dealing with, you might as well wheel me out right now."

Faust muttered to himself in thought and turned to the digital obelisk muted in the corner, and appeared to be conferring privately with the client for a time before returning to the center of the room.

"The asset is a person."

"And this person, they wanna be retrieved?"

"We have no reason to believe they don't."

"And everyone's gonna be just fine with us leaving with someone we didn't walk in with?"

"Yes. You're just going to walk out."

"How?"

Faust turned and motioned to the man sitting across from her. "Mr. Velasquez, on loan from the Herrera Cartel, will rig one of our drones with explosives. Once you've made contact with the asset, we'll create a controlled explosion on the currently vacant 93rd floor of the building. Safety protocols call for the building to be evacuated, allowing you, Holt, and the asset to exfil unabated."

"Yeah, we've met." Vivi sneered. "Never caught his name the first go round, but the subhuman stench of cartel about 'ims the same."

Velasquez spoke up for the first time. "I might smell like cartel, muñeca, but at least I'm sitting comfortably with all my parts. Maybe you'll think twice before you decide to take a job from Paulo to steal from us again, yeah?"

"Fuck you!"

"Not that there will be a next time, of course." Velasquez smiled. "I hear Paulo, he's not really in business no more."

Vivi seethed with rage. She moved with an inhuman alacrity as she reached across her body to Tomas's side and ripped the gun from its holster, pointing it at Velasquez. "¡Te desafío a decir una palabra más!"

Fincher recoiled as the gun was drawn, while to her other side Tomas was shocked at having been disarmed so easily, but he made no attempts to take the gun back from Vivi. Velasquez chuckled and shook his head as he casually began to raise his hands in surrender.

Faust, meanwhile, moved calmly between Velasquez and Vivi. "Rodriguez. Put the gun away. We're all professionals here."

Vivi cocked the gun's hammer. It was loud and satisfying. "He's not!"

"And that's where you'd be wrong. I understand the Herrera Cartel and Mr. Velasquez are responsible for your current situation, but they're also the ones who recommended you for this job. What happened between you and them was just business. Old Business, Ms. Rodriguez. I've ensured your past dealings with the Herrera Cartel are concluded."

"Like hell they are! And just why would you want to deal with a two-bit cartel when you have the backing of the United States at your disposal?"

"As alluded to earlier, this operation cannot implicate the government of the United States, and Mr. Velasquez is something of a logistics savant when it comes to finding things and moving them across international borders without detection."

"That it? I'm just another piece of hardware for him to requisition for you and move around the map?"

"You don't have to be. Let's talk payment. Upon successful retrieval of the asset, each of you will receive an amount in the sum of three hundred million dollars in untraceable crypto. I believe that's more than enough to pay off your debts to the US Army and still have enough left over to buy that flash clone body you've wanted for some time now, and then comfortably retire."

Vivi slowly lowered the gun and de-cocked it. Three hundred million was an absurd number, but Faust was right. It would be enough for her to afford a flash clone.

Enough to be human again.

Enough to go home.

Chapter Four

The Mechanic

Vivi awoke the next morning in her hotel room, wondering if she had made the right decision. There was a gnawing sensation at the back of her mind that something was off kilter about the entire ordeal. Working with a member of the cartel that had left her for dead weeks earlier was hardly an experience she was looking forward to, but at the very least, she was momentarily grateful her outlook and residence had improved dramatically since the previous day. It turned out even the cigarettes tasted better to Vivi while surrounded by luxury.

Around 10am the door chimed. "Hey, it's Tomas. You ready to go?"

Vivi opened the door remotely. "Not yet. Can we talk?"

As Tomas entered the suite, the door automatically slid shut behind him.

"Yeah, sure we ca— are you smoking?" Tomas coughed. "You know there's no smoking in here, right? I'm pretty sure I told you yesterday."

"What part of our brief time together has suggested to you that I give a fuck?"

"None. It's just, you can't."

Vivi blew out a cloud of smoke. "And yet, here I am. Smoking. You know, I don't get you. You just signed up for a job to cross the border into Mexico, illegally. Abduct two people, illegally. Steal their identities, illegally. Fly to China, illegally. Impersonate the officer of a corporation, illegally. Abduct yet another person, illegally. And yet you're sitting here worried about me smoking in a hotel room." Vivi took another drag from her cigarette, holding in the smoke for a long pause before exhaling, "That is super interesting to me."

"Fine. Point made. What'd you want to talk about?" Tomas took a seat in the chair next to the bed Vivi was propped up in with a look of mild annoyance on his face that Vivi thought was kind of cute.

"Faust. This job. Anything about it seem off to you?"

"You mean other than the ridiculous amount of money he wants to pay me to just stand there and look pretty in China? No. Not really. Seems like a pretty standard op. China took someone the US wants, and they're paying us to get them back."

"That's just it. Something doesn't track." Vivi flicked ash off her cigarette. "Three hundred million per person for a snatch and grab? Who's worth that?" She pointed the cigarette at Tomas. "You gotta figure Fincher is on the permanent payroll, but you? Me? Velasquez? We're not. That's nine hundred million between three people for just for this one job."

"So? What's your point?"

"For that kind of money, why's it only the three of us? Why not hire a separate team to abduct Luna and Santiago?"

"Maybe the fewer people that know about it, the better."

"Maybe." Vivi extinguished her cigarette and exhaled. "I don't know."

Tomas helped Vivi back into his beat-up car and set their destination in the onboard nav system for a local prosthetist Faust hired to repair Vivi's mangled body. As they drove, the sun beat down intensely on the car from a cloudless, deep blue sky above. Even the winter in Arizona was hot.

The pair rode in silence for a while, but Vivi could tell Tomas was bursting at the seams to say something. "Look, if you got something to say, say it."

Tomas looked over. "That stuff Faust said to you last night about wanting a flash clone, is it true?"

"Yeah." Vivi nodded.

"Why? Being full borg seems like a pretty sweet deal to me."

"Says the one not currently hooked up to a car battery to maintain a pulse."

"Okay, yeah, but you don't age. You don't have to eat or drink. I mean, shit, you're still here after what went down with the Herreras? I heard they impaled you on —"

"You mean *can't* age. *Can't* eat. *Can't* drink. *Can't* die. Yeah sure, it all sounds just so wonderful till you're locked in and realize choices you took for granted aren't really yours to make any more. Not to mention the monthly payments so your body doesn't get repo'd."

"But in our line of work? Seems more like a benefit than a hindrance."

"Who says I ever wanted to be in this line of work in the first place?"

"I didn't. I just figured, you know, if you don't like it, why not do something else?"

Vivi scoffed in response, looking away from Tomas and out the passenger window to the city skyline that glistened in the morning sun as the car exited the elevated freeway.

After a brief silence, Tomas re-engaged, "Okay, a different tack. Let's say this job goes perfect. You get your three hundred mil and your flash clone. What're you going to do the next day?"

Vivi turned back to Tomas, closing her eyes and smiling. "That's easy. I'm gonna buy the biggest bottle of the shittiest champagne I can find and a jug of orange juice, and then I'm going to drink mimosas till I pass the fuck out. And then I'm gonna do it again."

Tomas stared at Vivi, mouth agape.

Vivi rolled her eyes, speaking out the side of her mouth, "What? Believe me, you have no fuckin' clue how much I miss mimosas."

The pair eventually arrived on the north side of town at a small, rather plain looking 10 floor office building. The kind of place you'd expect to find a myriad of specialty doctors' offices or the local offices of some dental group. Boring and mundane, probably built over a hundred years earlier and still functioning exactly as it had when it was built. Vivi had seen pictures of what people a hundred years earlier imagined the future would look like in 2140, all a bunch of ridiculous dreams that painted a hopeful aesthetic on top the urban sprawls that dated back to the late 1800s. Did they think a fresh coat of paint would magically change the dregs living within the city limits? No. The future was just like the present, which was just like the past: shitty.

Tomas wheeled Vivi to the building's central elevator bank near a sign listing the various offices contained with-in. "Dr. Lepford, 4th floor. You nervous?"

"Nah."

"Oh? Is this your usual mechanic?"

"Sure isn't."

The elevator chimed loudly as it arrived. Tomas pushed Vivi's chair in as the doors opened, selecting the 4th floor button. The elevator whirred to life as soothing music played over a tinny sounding speaker.

"You seem really calm for someone about to have major invasive work done on their body by a stranger."

"Why wouldn't I be? This place looks a lot nicer than the shitholes I usually get repairs in."

"You're kidding."

"Nope."

Tomas and Vivi arrived at the fourth floor waiting area and found it completely empty, save for a receptionist sitting at a desk at the far end of the room. She greeted them without looking up from the computer screen in front of her. "We're not taking walk-ins today, sorry."

Tomas set his chrome laden hand down on the counter. "Ma'am? I don't think you understand. We have an appointment."

The receptionist looked up to Tomas and then down to Vivi. "Huh? Oh? OH! Sorry! She cleared the schedule for you. I've been turning away people all morning, force of habit. Please, follow me."

Tomas followed the receptionist, pushing Vivi through a set of double doors and down a hallway to a room that seemed to have more in common with a car garage than a doctor's office. A padded examination table sat in the center of the room, operated via hydraulic lift. Above it was a winch system connected to a hoist that ran along a track on the ceiling. The walls were covered with all manner of power tools. Various mechanical body parts hung from wires that also gave the room a macabre robot butcher shop vibe.

"Dr. Lepford will be with you shortly."

Vivi nudged Tomas. "You wanna go wait in the reception area?"

"No, I was going to wat—"

"Go wait in the reception area," Vivi snapped.

"Right. Sorry."

Dr. Lepford arrived shortly after Tomas left, entering the room without looking up from the chart in front of her. "I heard you were in a bit of a scuffle, so what do we have to work with?"

Vivi waved one-handed from her wheelchair.

"Dear God, you're in worse shape than I thought."

Lepford moved with a determined quickness, detaching Vivi from her car battery and hooking her up to a power cable connected to the room's hoist system before attaching the rest of the hoist underneath Vivi's armpits. Soon the winch and hoist began to lift all four hundred pounds of Vivi from her wheelchair.

As the winch hummed along in the background, working to move Vivi toward the examination table, Lepford beamed with radiant jubilation. "We don't get too many full body jobs in here. Always fun when I get to use this thing."

Dr. Gretchen Lepford, as stated on the degree on her wall between all the power tools and body parts, was a small woman with mousey blonde hair tied back in a ponytail. Both of her eyes had been replaced with older style cybernetic eyes that glowed electric blue. She wore medical scrubs that bore the signs of old oil stains that refused to fully clean out. To Vivi, Dr. Lepford was like any of the string of prosthetists she had seen in the last five years: one part medical doctor, one part artist, one part auto mechanic, all electrical engineer.

"Right! First order of business. Ms. Rodriguez, do I have your consent to remove this..." Lepford paused, cocking an eyebrow. "dress?"

"Please."

With the dress gone, the doctor went about removing the bandages from Vivi's upper left abdomen, revealing a gaping hole approximately 6 inches wide that nearly went clean through to the other side.

"Do I even want to know what did this?"

Vivi squinched up her nose and shook her head.

Lepford, having appraised the wound, clicked an intercom button on the examination table. "Meredith! We're going to need to fabricate a new front plate, a new back plate in addition to the skin job, heat sink upgrade and limb replacement. We're also going to need a new power plant, battery pack, and truck of coffee. You might as well tell Ms. Rodriguez's associate he can go home. This one's gonna be an all-nighter."

The doctor returned to Vivi, reaching a gloved hand with a small camera up into the wound and snaked it around inside her torso. "Hmm, I'm seeing a lot of carbon deposits inside your upper cavity as well. Smoke inhalation? You weren't involved in a fire by chance?"

"Ahh...no."

"You work in or near an industrial plant?"

"Not usually."

Lepford looked over to Vivi's purse on the wheelchair, spying the pack of Fortunes peaking incriminatingly out the top before looking back to Vivi as nonplussed as a woman with glowing mechanical eyes could. She pressed the intercom button again. "You're going to need to order some new lungs too, Meredith."

Chapter Five

Making Friends

It didn't seem to matter how many times her body was disassembled in front of her, the experience had not become mundane. She doubted it ever would. It was always rather surreal to Vivi, seeing each of the constituent parts responsible for her existence laid out on the table in front of her, hoping they would all go back together again, and most importantly, without pieces left over. She tried not to dwell on it while she avoided awkward eye contact with Lepford as she went about the business of replacing a good portion of Vivi's insides. Vivi rather disliked the way prosthetists tended to look at her beneath the charade of her skin. Just another broken object needing repairs, not unlike a rundown car or a dishwasher on the fritz.

Many hours later, the repairs complete, Lepford helped Vivi sit up on the table. "Listen, you're going to want to take it easy for a few hours, okay? Your benefactor insisted we beef up your front and back plates with plasteel instead of carbon fiber. It's a little heavier, so you're probably going to feel weird at first till you adjust."

"Plasteel? Shit, I guess that'll come in handy if I get in a firefight."

"A long distance, small caliber firefight, maybe. Trust me, it won't stop a bullet at close range."

"Duly noted, thanks Doc."

Tomas met Vivi in the clinic's waiting area. "Nice to see you up and about on your own legs for a change."

Vivi, still barefoot from not being in possession of feet when she arrived the previous day, walked up to Tomas and noticed she was still a head shorter than he was. "Huh. It wasn't the wheelchair. You are tall."

"Nice of you to notice. Come on, Velasquez is waiting for us on the edge of town. Your repairs went longer than planned. We're already behind schedule."

"He can wait a little longer. Got a detour to make first."

"Oh? Where's that?"

"My place. I'm not wearing this crappy dress one second longer than I need to."

———

Vivi's apartment was on the southern end of Phoenix, in the slums. Like many of the surrounding buildings, her apartment complex was a large block of nondescript concrete, built for speed and size, not aesthetics. These buildings housed the poorest of the poor in Phoenix. After a rickety elevator ride, Tomas and Vivi found the apartment nestled in on the 23rd floor with 31 other small one-bedroom apartments. Unlike the others, the door to Vivi's had been smashed in.

Tomas drew his gun and kicked the door the rest of the way in before entering.

"Relax, big guy. Cartel musta come here lookin' for me weeks ago. They're long gone. Just wait here and don't touch anything."

Vivi walked past the overturned TV, busted lamps, and smashed potted plants to her bedroom, leaving Tomas alone in her cramped-concept living space that comprised a small kitchen and living room.

"Nice place you got. You know, minus the mess."

Vivi ignored him as she began to strip out of the awful dress that plagued her the past two days. She tossed the cursed thing out of her room to the living area. "Hey, do me a favor and burn this when you get a chance."

"I get it! I have bad taste!"

In her room, Vivi found most of her possessions had been ransacked through, with her clothes strewn out all over. It was going to take a few minutes to find enough pieces for a proper outfit.

Tomas called out from the other room, "So, did you think of a real answer to my question from yesterday about what you're going to do when this job's done?"

Vivi held up a skirt that had gone out of style ages ago and shook her head, wondering why she had decided to keep it in the first place. "You mean when I'm a real girl again?"

"Yeah."

She turned and called back loudly, "Gave you a legitimate response yesterday. Mimosas. Tons of em."

"Uh huh."

"Alright, you tell me then, you get your three hundred mil. What're you gonna do with it?"

"I honestly don't know."

Vivi fell over with a loud thud as she attempted to slide into a pair of jeans, still not yet used to her slightly heavier upper body. "The fuck you mean you don't know?"

"It's just a lot of money. More than I ever thought I could get doing this kind of work. Like winning the mercenary lottery. I suppose the first thing I'd do is get my mom a better place to live, maybe put my little brother through school so he can avoid doing what I had to do in the military. Maybe get him out of this country. Get him a good life."

"Mr. White Knight, eh? Bleh. If I were you, I'd make it my first order of business to replace that shit car of yours."

"You have any family? I see a lot of photos of doors in here, not any people."

"Oh no. No no no. We're not makin' this about me."

"What? Why not? Tell me. I want to know."

"It's complicated."

"What family isn't?"

After she dressed herself, Vivi found a large duffel bag and began to stuff all manner of clothing, make-up, and shoes into it haphazardly. Enough for at least 8 days.

Vivi returned to the living room dressed in a pair of jeans with a pink tank top and an olive green, short sleeve jacket on top that hung just past her midriff; under her arm was a heavy-looking duffel bag.

"You know your refrigerator's empty?"

"I don't eat, remember?"

"I do though. Can we stop for a bite?"

Vivi patted Tomas on the shoulder. "Best not to keep Velasquez waiting..."

A short car ride later, Tomas and Vivi found Velasquez leaning up against a gray SUV in an empty parking lot at the edge of Phoenix. "You're late!"

Tomas pointed a thumb over a Vivi. "Had to make a detour."

Vivi tugged up her heavy duffel bag under her arm from out of the car's trunk as she spoke up with a sunny tone, "Come on Velasquez, you weren't gonna make a girl go all the way to Mexico without her accessories, were you?" She shut the trunk closed and began walking toward Velasquez with an easy, carefree gait.

Velasquez spat on the ground as they walked over. He was a man in his late 40s with a full beard, part of which had already begun to turn gray, but not his black hair, which was full and wavy. He wore dark sunglasses, concealing outdated cybernetic eyes, and the tattoos visible on his neck beneath the collar of his thread-worn, hooded trench coat were a small representation of the amount of ink running across his body. Like Tomas, Vivi took note of the gun holstered on Velasquez's right hip. He shook his head at her. "And here I was about to be nice and suggest perhaps we got off on the wrong foot, muñeca."

Vivi smiled cheerfully as she deposited her bag on the ground and walked closer to Velasquez. "You know, I was going to say the same thing. But please, call me Vivi. I like to be on a first name basis with all the fellow help. So, tell me, what do I call you?" She extended a hand to Velasquez.

"Enrique."

Enrique Velasquez shook hands with Vivi. Up close he was a few inches taller than her, and she could tell from his firm handshake that he was confident and unafraid of her, his first mistake in her estimation.

"Enrique." She smiled. "That's a very nice name."

His second mistake, of course, was thinking that Vivi had any intentions of being friendly. In an instant, her demeanor shifted from cordial to overt hostility. Her right hand gripped Enrique's as tightly as she could manage and pulled it toward her forcefully. In the same motion, she shoved her left forearm hard into his trachea, and pushed Enrique against the side of the SUV. The military encryption locking down most of her prosthetic body's features prevented her from crushing Enrique's hand, but it didn't stop her from letting gravity do its thing with all 400 lbs. of her body leaning into her forearm atop Enrique's windpipe.

Enrique gasped for air as he quickly found he could not push Vivi off. Vivi could feel him beneath her trying to reach across his body for his gun, but unfortunately for Enrique, the gun was not at a convenient angle to be retrieved with the wrong hand, not with Vivi's torso smashed into his. In desperation, Enrique's free hand shot up into Vivi's face, trying to wrench her off, but even in civilian mode, her artificial muscles and the laws of physics proved too much for him.

She spoke low and calm, so he could easily follow along, "Let's get some things straight, Enrique: I don't trust you and if it weren't for a three hundred mil payday on the line, you'd be eating lead from that kit on your hip right now, but as it is, I need you alive to do your job. So, I'm gonna do everything in my power to let you keep breathing for now. That said, at no point am I gonna like it."

Tomas tried to pull Vivi off of Velasquez, but found it impossible to move her smaller, yet far heavier, frame away. "Vivi! What the fuck? He can't breathe! Let him go!"

As Enrique's glasses slid down off his face, Vivi looked directly into his outdated cybernetic eyes with disdain, wishing they were newer model optics, so she could've seen the fear in them.

She spoke through bared teeth, "I get so much as a hint in the next 6 days that you or one of your little Herrera buddies tries to cross me, mark my fuckin' words, Enrique, you're a dead man! And I swear to God, you call me 'doll' one more fucking time, I'll make you look like Ken where it counts. ¿Entiendes?"

A muffled, unintelligible sound escaped Enrique's mouth as his eyes darted around, looking for help that wouldn't come.

"TELL ME YOU UNDERSTAND!"

Enrique's cybernetic eyes met hers for the briefest of moments, and he nodded quickly in agreement.

Vivi could feel Enrique's right hand start to go limp in hers as he was about to pass out. Before he could completely blackout, she released him, sending Enrique to the ground in a heap, coughing violently.

Vivi retrieved her bag from the ground, taking on her cheery tone again. "Well! I certainly feel better about myself. Let's go to Mexico, shall we, boys?"

Chapter Six

Boundaries and Borders

Outside the city limits, low rolling hills of reclaimed desert with bright green patches of vegetation dotted a landscape broken up by tall deep brown rock formations scattered across the horizon as far as the eye could see. Every now and again the monotony of the scenery was interrupted by a large bank of solar panels or an automated farm, but besides the road the SUV traveled on, nature in the desert region south of Phoenix seemed untouched by humans.

Vivi lounged across the back seat of the vehicle while chewing gum. Every now and then she would pop a bubble loudly, disrupting the silence.

Tomas looked back from the front passenger seat. "You know, I think I preferred the smoking."

"In a nice ride like this? Wouldn't dream of it." *Pop!*

"You want to trade places? The view is nicer up here."

"Endless stretch of desert next to Enrique's dour expression? Hard pass." *Pop!*

The silence returned to the SUV like a cloud moving in front of the sun with the white noise of the tires humming along on the road becoming the only sound that filled the ears of all three occupants. Vivi stared at the roof of the SUV for a few minutes that felt as if they began to stretch on into eternity.

Tomas broke the silence. "So, Vivi, you were Army, right?"

"Yeah, what of it?"

"What'd you do?"

"You just really can't handle an extended length of silence without filling it with talking, can you?"

Enrique chuckled. "She's full borg, chico. She did the same shit they have all those Barbies do in the field. Dance coordination."

Vivi shot up and forcefully slapped the back of Enrique's head. Had the SUV not been driving itself, it would have careened off the road.

"¡AY Mierda!"

"¿Qué te dije?"

Enrique put up his hands in surrender. "¡Lo siento! Sorry. Old habits. Won't happen again." He rubbed the back of his head. Vivi hoped she left an indent.

Tomas picked the conversation back up as Vivi laid back across her seat. "Dance coordination? You mean combat synchronization?"

Enrique nodded in response.

"You know, 8 years in the service, I never worked up close with a combat synchronizer. Not even once. No need. Spent most of my time doing overwatch. Fed a few data, received a few targets, but I never really got the full experience being on the ground, in total sync with a unit."

Vivi blew and popped a bubble. "You're not missin' much."

"Don't let her blow smoke up your ass, chico. Those dance makers, they're the reason the US military is so in demand in every small conflict around the world. No one else has small unit tactics tech that matches it. Not even China. Would love to get my hands on one or two unlocked borgs for the cartel. Federal Police? DEA? Wouldn't be no match for us."

Vivi popped another bubble. "Speaking of police, just how do you plan on gettin' us into Mexico? You got a tunnel under the border?"

"We're going to go right through the front gate."

"Wait, what? No!" she exclaimed as she sat up rapidly from her seat, looking at Enrique's artificial eyes through the rearview mirror.

"It'll be fine, chica. Calm down."

"Yeah? You got ID chits for us? Passports?"

"Don't need 'em."

"The fuck you mean we don't need them?"

"I'm a Mexican citizen. They won't pay any mind to the two of you and will let us right through."

"Yeah, and if they take a close look at me and realize I'm decommissioned US military hardware and decide to confiscate me?"

"They won't. Trust me."

Tomas shook his head. "I'm with Vivi on this one, Enrique. This seems like it has 'bad idea' written all over it."

"Hey! Hey! Who's the logistics expert here, eh?"

The border crossing was some three hours into the trip. As they approached the border crossing station, the sun was still high in the sky during the early afternoon. Cars lined up in several rows waiting their turn to get into Mexico.

"I can't believe there used to be a border fence here a hundred years ago."

"Outdated tech, they got way better ways of keeping refuse like us safely in America now." *Pop!*

After a short wait, the SUV came up to the border gate. An agent approached the driver's side of the vehicle. "Pasaporte por favor."

Enrique smiled as he handed the border agent his passport and another document underneath.

The border agent stepped away and inspected the passport as well as the other document closely and for much too long a time for Vivi's comfort. She whispered to Tomas, "I don't like this."

"Me either."

"Shut up! The both of you."

The border agent turned to another and called them over before returning to the car. "Fuera del carro."

Enrique slowly opened the SUV's door. "¿Cuál es el problema, amigo?"

Other agents were coming over to the car, one to Tomas's side and another to Vivi's door, all with automatic weapons drawn. "¡Sal! Out of the car! ¡Manos arriba! Hands up!"

Vivi slowly opened the door to the SUV and stepped down with her hands on top of her head. "Fuck! Goddammit Enrique!"

Vivi could see the border agents disarming Tomas and Enrique before handcuffing them. The agent next to her brandished his gun threateningly as he barked commands. "¡Ponte en el suelo! On the ground!"

"Okay! Okay! Point that somewhere else! I'm complying, god-dammit!"

Vivi slowly knelt on the ground. She could feel the border agent slide a device into her neural port that wrapped around the back of her neck. Instantly, her arms went limp by her side. Vivi could feel herself falling to the ground, but couldn't do anything to stop it as she landed with a heavy, dull thud in the dirt.

Her body somehow felt emptier than normal, unresponsive, but her eyes seemed to still work. She looked up to see Enrique being pulled away in handcuffs looking back at her, but instead of upset or concern, Vivi almost swore he wore a shit-eating grin on his face.

***

The Mexican border patrol was quite well prepared for moving four hundred pounds of dead weight around. Apparently, this kind of situation happened often enough to require specialized equipment for detaining persons with artificial bodies. Vivi was fully aware as they strapped her to an upright gurney and moved her through several bright hallways and into a dingy holding cell. She still retained the use of her eyes and mouth but decided the use of the latter was not appropriate for the moment.

For two hours, Vivi sat parked in the corner of her cell, alone, except for her reflection in a two-way mirror across the room. She wondered if perhaps her former situation, where she at least had a hand to smoke with, was more desirable than the current one, paralyzed from the neck down. She wondered what the use of having her arms and legs intact if she couldn't use them to smoke. At least she still had her gum, though sadly, it had lost its flavor ages ago.

Ping Network Protocol. What a useless fucking feature Faust decided to unlock, she thought. She wondered why he couldn't have picked a useful tool from her feature set to unlock like Precision Overflow, or

DDOS Countermeasure. At least that way she could have had a fighting chance at preventing exactly the situation that had just occurred.

Vivi blew and popped a bubble just as an important-looking border agent entered her cell. The man sat down at a table across from her and placed out a thick file folder in front of him, opening it. "Ms. Rodriguez, were you aware that you were traveling with a wanted felon and known cartel drug runner, Enrique Velasquez?"

Vivi stared at the agent for a time before blowing another bubble with her gum. It popped more loudly than she could have hoped for.

"Were you aware that the car you were traveling in contained one hundred and fifty canisters of illegal Schooner and ninety-six million yuan in prescription drugs under the seat we found you on?"

Pop!

"Are you aware of the punishment for drug running in Mexico?"

Pop!

"Ms. Rodriguez, do you understand the seriousness of your situation?"

"Question: do I get a phone call, or is that really not a thing in this country?"

The agent laughed, looking back at the two-way mirror behind him. "Oh, she's good, Enrique. I like this one."

Vivi watched in startled confusion as the door to the holding cell opened, revealing Enrique, who stepped into the room wearing a smug grin on his face. "Spend a little time with her, hermano. You may change your mind."

"Ha, maybe! Good job on the SUV, by the way, I like it much better than the last piece of shit you brought me. And hey, tell Hector he needs to up his shipments, yeah? I need to see my little brother more often."

"Will do!" Enrique laughed as his brother exited the room, leaving Vivi and Enrique alone. He smiled in self-satisfaction as he walked toward Vivi's gurney and rested a hand on her immobile shoulder.

Vivi spit her gum in Enrique's face, glaring. "You motherfucker!"

Enrique grimaced and peeled the gum off his face, tossing it to the floor. "You know, chica, this attitude of yours is tiresome. It's not real healthy for no one. I can't work like this," he touched a finger to the restraining collar at her neck, "and it looks like you can't either."

Vivi continued to glare back, scowling, wishing she had more gum to spit.

He sighed, "Listen, kid, if it helps, what we did to you, to Paulo, it wasn't my choice, okay? The constant raids on our shipments? Millions of yuan in profits lost. You and Paulo pissed off a lot of the old guard. They were calling for blood. So, I did what they asked me to do."

Enrique gently poked her in the sternum. "Just like I know you were doing what Paulo paid you to do. That's the nature of business, and I really want this current business to work out. Which means I need you and me to work out. So, what do you say, chica? Can we put this bad blood behind us, for now, so we can both get what we want? Or... do I leave you here with the border guards and find Faust another shitty piece of Army surplus? Maybe one that doesn't talk back so much..."

Vivi furrowed her brow. Her eyes locked with Enrique's for a long while before she finally relented and nodded her head, exhaling, "Fine! Just get this thing offa me already."

"Great!" Enrique grinned while he tugged the restraining collar from her neck. "Now come on, kid, let's go. You're holding us up again."

Vivi rolled her eyes and grumbled as she regained the use of her arms and legs. As she hopped off the gurney and followed Enrique out of the cramped cell, it took all of her willpower to resist the urge to slap him in the back of the head again the whole while.

Chapter Seven

Homework

It had been three days since Vivi and company had arrived in Hermosillo and checked into the Hidalgo, a small hotel near the city's old town. The room provided to Vivi was far less nice than her brief residence at Hotel Executor, but there wasn't much to complain about as she hardly ventured to it except late at night to sleep. Her time awake had been eaten away learning everything there was to know about Domenica Santiago from the intelligence reports Fincher fed to her at a near constant pace as well as anything she could glean by following Santiago the past three nights in a row after the CFO's assistant left her job at Presidio Biologica.

Vivi hadn't seen or heard from Faust since the initial meeting in Phoenix some four days earlier, and she was beginning to wonder if he was still running the operation. Since she had been in Mexico, it was all Fincher's show.

Today however, Vivi decided to take a break from the homework Fincher assigned her and chose instead to lounge by the hotel's pool on the roof in the February sun. In the distance, a church bell rang out from the nearby cathedral, marking the time at 11am.

Laying in a reclining chair by the pool with her eyes closed and her arms behind her head, Vivi didn't notice Tomas walk up onto the pool deck.

"Jesus, I'm getting cold just looking at you. What is it, sixty degrees out here?"

"Sixty-three actually. Don't worry though, it'll get warmer when the afternoon sun gets here if you wanna join me."

"But what's even the point? You don't tan... Wait, can you tan?"

Vivi sat up and leaned over, resting an arm on her thigh. "The *point*, my dear Tomas, is to avoid Fincher and another of one of his goddamn intelligence briefs on Santiago. Pool deck in the middle of February is the last place he'd look. But to your point, no. I can't tan. Can't feel cold when I don't want to either."

"Huh. Wish I could have had that ability during my three-month tour of duty in Siberia. Seems like another check mark in the 'for going full borg' column."

Vivi tugged down her sunglasses and looked up at Tomas. "You got what I wanted or not?"

Tomas tossed her a new pack of Fortunes.

"Yesssss! Thank you! My savior."

"Don't thank me yet."

Vivi had barely managed to light the first cigarette from the pack when she saw Fincher round the corner to the pool deck. He looked even whiter and pastier than ever in actual sunlight. If she had tear ducts, she would have cried.

"Rodriguez? The hell? You've been up here this entire time? We had an intelligence briefing scheduled for 8am and a table read for the Shanghai meeting at nine! That was two hours ago!"

Vivi exhaled a miasmic cloud of smoke. "I gotta say, Finch, the fact that it took you this long to find me up here raises serious doubts on your ability to gather actual intelligence. Does Faust know how deficient you are at your job?"

True to first impressions, Fincher yapped at her like a small dog, "Faust doesn't—dammit! This is serious! Phase 1 begins execution tonight, and you're not nearly up to speed yet on the meeting in Shanghai. You're on a plane to China *tomorrow*!"

Vivi put on her best Santiago impersonation. "Calmate, amigo. Puedo suplantar a Santiago en mi sueño. I got Santiago down pat. Gimme a wig and I'm good to go. Besides, Tomas is the one with all the heavy lifting during the meeting in Shanghai."

"Conference room! Thirty minutes! Clothes on!" Fincher stormed off.

Vivi looked over to Tomas. "A bikini is clothes, right?"

Tomas shook his head. "I'm not getting into this."

Vivi decided she had antagonized Fincher enough over the previous two days, so she made a quick stop by her room to throw on leggings, short round-tip boots with faux buckles and a sweater with sleeves that were much too long before grabbing her purse and making her way to the Hidalgo's conference room. The hallways of the hotel were oddly empty, even for a hotel off the beaten path of the city center. Vivi hadn't seen another soul outside of their party in the hotel since she arrived. She suspected it meant Faust had rented the entire building to provide privacy for the operation and also prevent the possibility of aroused suspicions from other guests.

The conference room had been converted into a makeshift head-quarters for the team Faust had put together. Several dry erase boards were set up with various notes on the movements of Javier Luna and Domenica Santiago. A mass of papers littered the large table in the middle of the room, and five of the seats had tablets in front of them. Fincher, Velasquez, and Holt were already seated around the table with Faust standing at the furthest end from the entrance to the room.

Vivi grimaced, seeing Faust actually in attendance. "What'd I miss?"

Faust gave a reproachful look from the head of the table. "Nice of you to finally join us, Ms. Rodriguez. Where are we at with Santiago?"

Vivi took a seat in the open chair next to Tomas and lit a cigarette. "Best I can tell she's a homebody. Lives for work and not much else. Single. No pets. Hasn't called or texted anyone outside of work in the last three days. Easy pickin's. No one's going to miss her for a few days."

"And you agree with Mr. Fincher's assessment that the highest probability of success in collecting Ms. Santiago without incident is tonight, just before she enters her apartment?"

"Not necessarily. A lot of eyes around there potentially know her, but not me. Someone sees me takin' her away unconscious might raise some eyebrows. But if that's where you wanna do it, I got no objections. You're the boss."

"Then what do you suggest?"

Vivi pointed to a spot on the map on the tablet in front of her. "I'd prefer we take her before she makes it on the mag lev home. Here. There's an alleyway she crosses right before the station."

Fincher objected. "That's ridiculous! That station is in the city center! Out in public! Too many eyes! Too many variables unaccounted for."

"Exactly! There's a ton goin' on. People trying to get home after a long day's work. No one's gonna notice. And if they do, they're not even gonna care. Trust me."

Enrique furrowed his brow. "This is Hermosillo, chica, not Phoenix. People see you drag someone into an alley by a busy train platform, they might care. Hate to say it, I agree with the nerd."

Vivi gave a small shoulder shrug while curling her lip, returning an antagonizing look across the table at Velasquez.

Tomas studied the place on the map Vivi had pointed to. "What if we apply some of that Deep Fake tech here? A kind of test run for Shanghai? We make Santiago and Rodriguez just disappear?"

Fincher stroked his scraggly beard. "Hmm. It's not a bad idea, actually. In theory, we could simply erase them from view of anyone caring to look, but there's always the chance someone without neurolinked optics could see. Also, we already had the drones shipped to China. We don't have the processing power or bandwidth on hand to make it work. Not for the number of eyes we'd potentially have to fake out."

Faust leaned in from his position at the table. "It's settled then. Rodriguez, you're going to wait at the mag lev platform by Santiago's apartment. Follow her to her apartment and take her before she makes it into the building. Let's move on to Luna. Holt, what have you got?"

"Opposite problem from Santiago, he's a family man. We take him tonight, his wife and kids are going to notice. As best I can tell, the only option we have to prevent raising suspicions is tomorrow morning, on his way to the airport."

Fincher nodded in agreement with Tomas.

"Alright, make it so. Let Mr. Velasquez know what you need."

Chapter Eight

Honey Pot Trouble

V ivi had never been in a city quite like Hermosillo before. It felt large to her like Phoenix, but in a different way. Shorter perhaps? More spread out? Hermosillo lacked a skyline that reached up into the heavens, with its borders not having been reined in by environmental concerns like the major cities in America. Looking up from the street, one could easily see wide swathes of sky. If there were slums, she hadn't seen them, and the architecture was decidedly Spanish in theme with terracotta roofs offset by white brick and only a few skyscrapers shooting off into the skyline toward the city's center. The city center that housed the headquarters of Presidio Biologica, where Domenica was soon to be leaving work for the day. Overall, the city had a pleasant feel to Vivi. She thought she would like to return to a place like this when the job was over. If there was still no other place that wanted her anyway.

Vivi opened her purse and silently cursed to herself when she found only two cigarettes remaining in the pack of Fortunes. How had she smoked so many since the morning? She retrieved one of the two left, lit it, and leaned on a wall as people walked past her toward the nearby mag lev station. Domenica Santiago's apartment complex was visible down the road from Vivi's spot on the wall. Unlike her enormous building back in Phoenix, Santiago's apartment building was in a group of similar structures, only four floors each. Tomas and Enrique were parked in a white sedan across from the entrance to the apartments.

"Honestly, Tomas, I don't know how you keep letting Enrique embarrass you like this," Vivi thought.

Tomas responded through the neural sync, sounding like a disembodied voice in the back of her head, "What do you mean?"

"This is like the third car I've seen him bring to this job that's way nicer than your piece of shit back home."

"Oh har har. Hey, listen up everybody, Rodriguez's got jokes..."

Fincher's annoyed tone came in over the line, "Everyone shut up! Santiago is entering the mag lev station in the city center."

Vivi thought, "Relax, Finch, I was just testing the neural sync. It seems to be workin' fine." Her words were transmitted to the rest of the team as if she had said them out loud without opening her mouth or making a sound. "What's her ETA?"

"Mag lev is running on time. Ten minutes. Wait, no... she's getting on the wrong train!"

"What do you mean, 'she's getting on the wrong train'?"

"She's on a train headed west bound."

Vivi tossed her cigarette to the ground, stomping it out. "Where's she going?"

Fincher sounded unnerved. "I don't know!"

"Her text messages, email, social media, she say anything to anyone?"

"No, nothing. Mostly work related. Mentioned the trip to Shanghai tomorrow to her mother, that's it."

"Finch, send me pics of her phone's home screens."

"Give me a second... downloading... got'em! Sent."

In her HUD, Vivi pulled up screenshots of Domenica Santiago's phone and studied them while she walked up the stairs to the mag lev station. Seven pages of rows upon rows of app icons littered Santiago's phone. On the third page, Vivi found what she was looking for. "She's got a dating app! Finch, I need access to this!"

"I'm working on it!"

Vivi quickly made her way to the westbound train platform as she gained access to Santiago's dating app. She hastily navigated to the messages section and found one from earlier in the day. "She's got a date. Seems serious. Place called Geraldina's Riverside. Shit, Finch, how'd you miss this?"

A mag lev train approached the station rapidly before coming to a slow stop in front of Vivi. The train emitted a large puff of air as it lowered to the track and the doors opened. Vivi stepped into the train and held onto a handle that hung from the ceiling of the car.

Fincher's disembodied voice came booming in over the neural sync, "Rodriguez! What the hell? Where are you going?"

"I'm going crash a date. Tomas, Enrique, get directions and meet me there with the car."

"We're on it, chica!"

Fincher's voice sounded completely unraveled over the line, "No! NO! Velasquez! You stay put! Rodriguez, get back to the apartment and wait! The timeline's altered, but the plan stays the same! Stick to the script!"

Vivi shook her head. "Yeah? What if she decides to go home with this guy? What if he comes home with her? Huh? Old plan's fucked. New plan: we're improvising."

The train carrying Vivi lifted off from the track. It left the station and silently gained speed as the linear induction motors rocketed it forward. There was a long silence over the line till eventually Faust's voice came through, "Rodriguez has a point. Velasquez, Holt, get to the restaurant."

During the fourteen-minute mag lev ride across town, Vivi scoured every message sent between Santiago and her suitor, Juan. The content was disturbingly X-rated, but it gave her an idea of the kind of guy she was dealing with. "Dammit, I liked this top. Oh well..." She reached down to her sweater and began to tear the bottom off mid torso, exposing her stomach.

When the train finally arrived and let Vivi off, she tossed the torn off section of sweater in a trash bin before pulling out her lipstick and applying a fresh coat. From the top of the station, she could see the restaurant in the distance on the corner a block away. Sensing she had time, Vivi stopped for a moment to pull out her compact and gave herself the quickest smokey eye job she had ever applied.

"Rodriguez, you've stopped. What're you doing?"

"Don't worry about it, Finch. Enrique, how long till you get here?"

"Traffic is pretty bad. Say, ten more minutes."

"Fine. Let me know when you arrive."

Geraldina's Riverside was a small restaurant overlooking the Sonora River. The lighting was dark and romantic, a white tablecloth kind of place. As she entered, Vivi could see Domenica and her date at a table by a window with a view of the river. Their table was also in line of sight to the bar. *Perfect*, Vivi thought.

Vivi walked past the host's booth and leaned up next to the bar, deciding the barstools were probably not rated to hold her prosthetic body's weight.

A bartender approached her with a bemused look. "¿Puedo ayudarle? Can I... help you?"

"Champagne."

The bartender looked even more confused. "You're muñeca? Yes?"

Vivi strained a smile. "Humor a girl. I just like to smell and reminisce."

"It's your money."

As the bartender went to fetch her drink, Vivi pinged the network and found six surveillance cameras around the restaurant. "Finch, I need access to these cameras."

"They're yours."

The lights in the restaurant momentarily flickered and after a few seconds passed, Vivi regained her previously locked ability to access remote security systems. So, it turned out Faust and company could unlock features of her prosthetic body remotely too. Vivi scanned through the cameras in and around the restaurant. Most of the views were useless to her, either outside or in the kitchen, but at least one had a good view of Domenica and Juan's table, allowing her to see the couple's facial expressions without looking at them directly.

Enrique came in on the line, "Alright, we're pulling up now."

"Perfect. Go park and wait for my signal."

"What're you planning, chica?"

"I'm going to Honey Pot Trouble this asshole."

"What's that even mean?"

"No idea. Just made it up."

Vivi used the surveillance camera to take a close look at the man at the table with Domenica, zooming the camera in as far as it would go.

What kind of drinker are you, Juan? You a whiskey man or a tequila man? Hmmm.

As the bartender returned with her glass of champagne, Vivi pointed across the restaurant to Domenica's table. "Hey, you see that table over there by the window?"

"Yes?"

"That's my friend over there. Send him a glass of whiskey. Make sure he knows it's from me."

"Alright."

Vivi leaned into the bar as seductively as one could while wearing a torn off sweater and leggings with her flat stomach and artificial belly button confidently exposed. Juan and Domenica were far enough away that there was no chance they could tell she was a fully prosthetic person. She brought the glass of champagne to her lips, feigning a drink every so often without actually taking a sip. The champagne smelled divinely intoxicating, a forbidden delicacy she once knew but couldn't touch. She could almost feel the bubbles playfully popping on her tongue when she closed her eyes.

Through the security camera, Vivi could see the whiskey arrive at the table. The bartender informed Juan who the whiskey was from, pointing at her position at the bar. Vivi smiled internally when she saw Domenica and her date look over to her. Juan was smiling and raising the glass to her while Domenica looked less than pleased.

Fincher sounded incredulous. "This is your plan? Seriously?"

Vivi raised her glass back at Juan from across the restaurant, smiling confidently. "Just wait. Give it a minute."

Over the ensuing minutes, the man at the table with Domenica Santiago kept peering back at Vivi from his table by the window, sipping at the whiskey she had sent. Every time he turned to look at Vivi, Domenica glanced out of the side of her eye as well. Domenica and Juan talked for a time and occasionally laughed about something they both found funny, but Vivi couldn't make out what they were saying. When Vivi saw through the video feed that Juan finished the first glass of whiskey, she called the bartender over again, "Hey, send another whiskey to my friend over there from me, and close me out."

The bartender produced a payment tablet with the bill. "That'll be two thousand yuan."

Vivi placed two fingers on the device and transferred the bartender □4000. "A little extra for your trouble."

Fincher sounded annoyed, "Really Rodriguez, what are you attempting to accomplish here?"

"You'll see. Enrique, get the car ready."

The bartender delivered the second drink and again pointed back to Vivi at the bar. Juan smiled and waved. Vivi slowly put her hand up in greeting and lowered her other shoulder, letting the sweater slip down just enough to expose her bare shoulder while she playfully bit her lower lip for effect as she smiled. A few minutes passed. Domenica was saying something, but Juan wasn't paying attention. His eyes were on Vivi, so were Domenica's.

Domenica grabbed her purse, excused herself, and got up from the table.

"Right on cue." Vivi stood up from the bar and made a show of walking towards the women's restroom. Domenica followed thirty steps behind. Once in the restroom, Vivi hastily pulled a rag and chloroform from her purse, wetting the rag before tossing the bottle away. She held the rag just out of view of the door in her left hand and turned to the mirror, attempting to look as bored as possible for when Domenica would eventually arrive.

Domenica entered the bathroom wearing an icy demeanor. "¿Qué crees que estás haciendo?"

Vivi puckered her lips in the mirror as if she hadn't heard Domenica. She checked her teeth like perhaps she was worried a piece of broccoli had gotten stuck in them.

Domenica moved in just close enough. "Are you deaf? What are you playing at, bitch?"

Vivi seized Domenica's hand closest to her and tugged it toward herself. In a second motion, she repositioned her body behind Domenica, who struggled, but was no match against Vivi's weight. Within seconds, Vivi had wrapped up the other woman from behind and stuffed the chloroform rag into her horrified face, muffling a scream. After a brief struggle, Domenica went limp and passed out. Vivi tossed the rag in the trash and propped Domenica's arm over her shoulder.

"Alright, Enrique, bring the car around front."

The bartender looked on with one eyebrow raised as Vivi helped an unconscious Domenica out of the restroom and towards the front of the restaurant.

"My friend's had too much to drink I'm afraid."

The car pulled up to the front of the restaurant and skidded to a stop. Tomas jumped from the passenger seat of the sedan to open the rear door, allowing Vivi to quickly shove Domenica in. "Holy shit! I can't believe that worked!"

"Of course it worked."

The car door slammed as the four sped off.

Chapter Nine

Medically Induced

The conference room of The Hidalgo was dark. The stacks of paper that were once sprayed about all over the room had been collected and disposed of. The dry erase boards, cleaned. No evidence of the plan to abduct Santiago or Luna remained save for the room's two occupants, one standing in the doorway lit from behind by a light in the hallway, and the other wreathed in unnatural shadow at the head of the conference room table.

"Something on your mind, Ms. Rodriguez?"

"Yeah. Tons of shit. Where's Fincher?"

"Resting in preparation for tomorrow no doubt. The same as you should be doing."

"Yeah, I can't really rest easy after tonight. Basic intel failure like that on day one? You know, I thought you had a real good sales pitch for this op with your swank hotel and your big bank account, but I didn't know the actual job was gonna be amateur hour at the strip club. Doesn't leave one real confident to fly across the Pacific where people are known to disappear for stepping toenails outta line."

"Amateur hour?" Faust leaned in from his position at the table, leaving his face lined with the shadows created from the room's blinds. "Ms. Rodriguez, where were you during this morning's 0800-intelligence briefing?"

Vivi shook her head. "This isn't about me. This is about Fincher and his—"

"It is about you. This job. This kind of work. It's a collaborative effort that requires subordination to authority, and I'm beginning to suspect you still don't take orders very well. Tell me, after the Pan-Asian conflict ended earlier than expected in '37, why'd the Army discharge you instead of rotating you around to the other ongoing proxy wars in Argentina or Sudan?"

"How should I know?"

"Then I'll tell you. They were cutting their losses. You caught rust bad enough to need an artificial body, the Army had an empty artificial body that needed filling for combat synchronization, and so you were shoehorned in. It all should have worked out quite neatly, but you were never a good fit for the job, were you?"

"I did whatever they asked to stay alive."

"Did you? Lance Corporal is an odd rank in the US Army. Tell me, Ms. Rodriguez, how does one attain such a rank?"

Vivi glared at Faust under a furrowed brow. "You can go fuck yourself."

"Let me refresh your memory, then. You went off mission in a combat zone. Took it upon yourself to complete a task in your own manner because you didn't like the order a superior had given. Got your lieutenant killed in the process. You, of course, received a field promotion for your efforts, but when the dust settled and the Army brass found out what happened, they dumped you the second the war ended ahead of schedule. We got to see a peek of that Viviana Rodriguez tonight, didn't we? The one who goes off script and gets people killed."

Vivi folded her arms defiantly. "I got Santiago, didn't I?"

"You got lucky. I told you from the beginning, Mr. Fincher is the director of this operation. You violate my chain of command again, I'll kill you myself and find a way to puppet your artificial corpse all the way to China and back if I have to. Are we clear?"

"Yeah. Super clear. God forbid we let the wireless router think for itself."

Vivi stormed out of the room and slammed the door behind her. She was moving at such a fast pace that when she rounded the corner, she couldn't stop in time to avoid running Tomas over as she exited the doorway. Vivi managed to catch Tomas midfall, hugging him to her. "Oh shit! I'm sorry!"

She held Tomas tightly in her arms, steadying him. "I... wait, what're doin' right outside the conference room? Were you listening?"

"No! I was... just going to the drink machine."

Vivi leaned over to the side and spied the drink machine on the far side of the hallway. She lowered her eyebrows and gently pushed Tomas off of her. "You were listening."

"Okay, I was listening. Hey, for what it's worth though, I thought what you did tonight was amazing. I mean, you just took right over when Fincher was floundering. You know, don't tell Faust or anything, but in my opinion, you saved the op and the payday."

"Thanks. Hey, have you seen Enrique?"

"Yeah, fifth floor. Room 502. Helped him drop off Domenica up there a little while ago. He's probably still there. Why?"

"He able to get you that E-QAP .50 cal you wanted?"

"Yeah. It's ready to go for tomorrow."

"Hmm. Hopefully it's not too late for him to acquire some stuff for me too." Vivi turned toward the stairwell. "Thanks, Tomas!" she called back.

"Anytime?"

Vivi found Enrique exactly where Tomas said he'd be: room 502. She expected a normal-looking hotel room, but what she found instead was a hotel room stuffed with medical looking devices and Enrique in the middle of it all, attaching Domenica Santiago up to a number of IVs, tubes, and other things Vivi didn't know the name for.

"The fuck are you doin'?"

"Putting Santiago here into a medically induced coma."

"You a doctor now?"

"Nope," Enrique replied as he pushed the plunger of a syringe full of a mystery concoction into an IV line connected to Domenica's arm.

"So...how's this remotely medical?"

He shrugged in response. "Eh. Fair point."

"You look like you've done this before."

"Maybe once or twice."

Vivi looked into a screen connected to Santiago's neural port that displayed her current brain activity. "She gonna live?"

"That's the plan. Her and Luna will wake up three days from now. Job'll be done and we'll be long gone."

"They just get to go on with their lives, huh?"

"Assuming I measured this shit right and the maid doesn't walk in. Yeah. Speakin' of, you want to hang this on the door?" Enrique held out a "Do Not Disturb" door hanger.

"Sure." Vivi took the sign and hung it on the door's exterior. "I gotta say, I'm surprised to see you giving a shit about keepin' anyone alive given our past dealings…"

"Be upset if I lugged all this gear up here for nothing." Enrique sighed. "Look, chica, if you're referring to what happened to you and Paulo, I admit, it might have gotten outta hand even for us—"

"No. This is more immediate. About this job."

Enrique fiddled with buttons on one of the machines hooked to Santiago. "Something about it not sitting right with you?"

Vivi found herself tied up with thoughts that all decided to flood out of her mouth at once. "No… Well, yes. But that's not—Wait. Why do you ask?"

"Because it's a weird job, isn't it? Weirdest I've ever been on, and I've been on a few."

Vivi looked off to the side at a picture of a basket of fruit on the wall. "Tomas doesn't think anythin's off about it."

"Yeah well, kid's wet behind the ears, isn't he? Just out of the service. Like a puppy. Doesn't question authority, just does as he's told. Doesn't know what to expect in the real world yet. Not like you and me."

Vivi turned back to Enrique with an annoyed look. "Don't go comparing yourself to me."

Enrique put up his hands in apology before returning to monitoring Santiago.

Vivi shook her head. "I gotta say you're kinda right though. That bit with the penthouse at the Executor to tell us about the job? I mean, who does that? Who goes through that expense to tell a couple of lowlifes about a job? Most work I got in the last three years, details came in a back alley or some shit warehouse."

Enrique smiled, chuckling. "Have to admit, it was a nice touch. Reminds me of an old holofilm my brother used to watch a long time ago. This old war general gathers up a bunch of ex-soldiers in a ritzy mansion to sell them on a heist to steal back priceless artwork that some corrupt politician stole during some war."

Vivi shook her head, laughing. "Fuck, you're right, this whole thing sounds ridiculous as something in a holo by some two-bit screenwriter. God, I need a smoke." Vivi went for her purse.

"Hey, hey! Not in here with all this shit! It's flammable. Come on, let's go outside."

Vivi lead the way out of the hotel room onto the balcony with Enrique following a few steps behind, closing the door behind him. "I think it's all real. The money's definitely real. Faust spent a ton on those drones we shipped to China, this hotel, and fixing you up wasn't cheap. I should know, all the money passed through me."

"Yeah well, I hope he's got more. I'm out of cigarettes again." Vivi tugged the last of the Fortunes from the pack.

Enrique smiled. "You know Faust had a whole pallet of Fortunes special ordered just for you? It's downstairs in the loading dock."

Vivi pulled out her lighter, igniting the end of the cigarette. "No shit? A whole pallet? So that's where Tomas has been gettin' them from."

"Yeah, from me. I'm the logistics man, remember? You need something, you talk to me."

"You know, that's actually why I came." Vivi leaned over the edge of the balcony directly outside room 502. "There's something I need you to get on short notice. Discretely. Can I trust you not to tell anyone?"

"Mmm, maybe just this once. To say I'm sorry. For Paulo. What do you need?"

She talked in quiet tones, "Well for starters, have you ever heard of..."

Vivi crumpled up the empty package of Fortunes and tossed it off the balcony to the ground 5 floors below as their hushed voices trailed off.

Chapter Ten

Hurry Up and Wait

Dust, sand, rocks, and shrubs. An endless sea of all four split in two by a road cutting between them. The afternoon sun baked the ground below as large birds flew overhead looking for a meal. Occasionally the scene was broken up by a car speeding along the road below the craggy hill, but more often than not the road was empty. From their hilltop position hidden from sight of the road by a large rock formation, Vivi and Tomas could barely make out the Hermosillo airport far in the distance to the North. To the Southwest, equally far away as the airport and along the road in the opposite direction was an outcropping of large houses next to a small town. A gated community for the richest of Hermosillo.

Vivi flicked a pebble off the hillside and groaned, "Hurry up and wait."

Tomas smiled. "The military motto."

"Yeah well, it's boring as fuck. Couldn't you have picked a more exciting hill?"

Tomas worked about rotating a knob on the scope of a large bolt-action rifle. "Nope. Only spot between Rancho Garcia and the airport where no one's going to mind large caliber gunfire going off."

"Speakin' of, you compensating for something with that thing? It's massive."

"At the distance from us to the road? Nope. Need something this size to be able to stop two electric motors a thousand yards away."

Vivi squinted to see the road below them more clearly. "Think you can make a shot this far away with a gun you've never shot before?"

"AI assisted? Difficult shot, but it shouldn't be a problem, assuming Enrique gave the AI the associated D.O.P.E. data for this rifle anyway. Would be easier to stop if it was a gas-powered vehicle of course. You know, I did a tour once in Ghana where they still use gas powered cars. One shot to the engine block, boom. Car done. So simple."

Vivi sighed "Hey, Oh-One, you got this data he's talking about?"

The digital representation of an AI appeared atop the hillside within her HUD, "01" etched on its shiny, onyx surface. It was the same AI that had joined them silently at the meeting back in Phoenix. The obelisk responded in a polite, masculine tone, "Yes, ma'am."

"You know what, I decided, I'm not calling you 'Oh-One' the rest of the job. You got another name?"

"No, ma'am."

Vivi put her hands behind her head and lounged back on the hill. "Well, it's settled then, now you're 'Bernice'."

The writing on the obelisk changed instantly from "01" to "BERNICE". "Very well, ma'am. Would you like my voice to reflect the feminine name you've assigned?"

"Yes. OH! Make it a British one! The fancy kind, none of that Eliza Doolittle shit."

The obelisk paused for a moment before responding again in a feminine upper class British tone. "Settings updated. Is this sufficient, mum?"

Vivi laughed. "Oh my God, yes! Say something British!"

"I'm afraid I don't understand your request, mum."

Vivi poorly imitated a British accent. "Say 'the rain in Spain is mainly quite the pain.'"

"I'm afraid I cannot comply. You have prohibited me from sounding like Eliza Doolittle and my records indicate the character Eliza Doolittle, played by Audrey Hepburn in the 1964 film 'My Fair Lady', delivered a line that sounds remarkably similar to your butchered quote. Additionally, the phrase was used by the same character in the song, 'The Rain in Spain', which also featured in the same film."

Vivi cackled with laughter. "It's fine, Bernice. You're fine. Thank you. I needed that."

"Any time, mum."

Tomas rolled his eyes and shook his head while he calibrated his rifle. "Clearly not your first time dealing with an AI."

"Sure isn't."

"What's that like anyway, housing one of those in your head?"

"Mmm." Vivi looked up and to the left in recollection. "Hot."

Tomas looked over from behind the rifle, one eyebrow raised. "Do you mean temperature, or...?"

"Yes temperature! Get the fuck outta the gutter, Holt."

"Sorry, it's just the way you said it left it open to interpretation."

"*Anyway!* Yes. Hot as in temperature. Housing an AI takes up a lot of processor cycles in addition to all the other shit my processor array has to do between running all my hardware and synchronizing data between team members. And additional processor cycles mean additional heat."

"You don't look too hot right now."

Vivi smirked. "I mean, what girl does in a flak jacket and fatigues? Unless that's your thing..."

"Who's in the gutter now? I meant temperature hot. You don't look *temperature* hot."

"Cause I'm not. Bernice isn't currently stored local. She's only piggy backing in through me remotely and I'm just passing the data along to you and Enrique."

"Like a wireless router."

"You're catching on."

"Is that normal? Only providing the AI remotely, I mean."

"Yeah. It's all I've ever done outside of training. Military got out of sending borgs into the field loaded up with the AI local ages ago. The ability to have one on board is vestigial hardware anyway. A leftover from the Somatech platform's original purpose: housing Sentient Daemons so they could walk around outside the outernet. Besides, it's a huge liability housing an AI locally. Get captured and the enemy gets you and a treasure trove of intel from the AI." Vivi flicked another pebble off the hill. "Standard operating procedure calls for destruction of any borg housing an AI rather than lettin' an AI fall into enemy hands."

"Suppose that explains why the US is only loaning us 01 remotely. It's worried about China gaining access to it if we're captured."

Vivi pulled out her pack of Fortunes and her lighter from her flak jacket. "Yup. Isn't that right, Bernice?"

"I'm afraid I'm not at liberty to say, mum."

"Of course you're not."

Three cigarettes later, Vivi watched a falcon flying overhead. Or perhaps it was an eagle? She wasn't sure. Birds weren't her specialty. What she was sure of is that she wished she could have been that bird, soaring free over the desert instead of being stuck on the same hill endlessly waiting for Javier Luna to decide to leave for the airport.

"Fuck me! This asshole has an international flight. When's he going to leave his goddamn house?"

"I'm afraid I can't comply, mum. Additionally, I do not have any details concerning Mr. Luna's planned departure."

"Can it, Bernice!"

Tomas looked at his wind gauge. "Hopefully soon. He waits much longer and the timeline for getting us to the airport in character is going to get real tight. Not to mention, I don't like this wind picking up."

Enrique came in over the neural sync. "You're getting your wish. He just kissed his wife and kids goodbye. He's leaving the house now. GPS signal should be live. I'll follow at a distance. Don't want to spook him."

Tomas got into position on a sniper pad and readied his rifle. "Thanks Enrique. Fincher, what's the ETA?"

"Ten minutes. Everyone ready?"

Vivi extinguished her cigarette and flicked the butt off the hill. She gathered her long indigo hair into her hands and tied it up into a ponytail. "I'm headed down to the road now."

Tomas chambered a round in his rifle and checked his wind gauge. "Bernice, have you factored in this five mph west to east wind?"

"Yes, sir. Already factored. You'll want to correct right, 2 mills."

Tomas adjusted his scope. "Alright, I'm good to go."

As Vivi jogged down the rocky hill towards a dust covered sedan along the side of the road, she could see the shooting solution superimposed on her HUD as a bright green line over her head where Bernice calculated the optimal trajectory for a bullet to hit a car along the highway from the hill, 1000 yards away. "You gonna go for the front or back wheel engine first?"

"The back one. If I hit the front one first, it could mess up his steering and make the second shot harder. I want him to go in as straight of a line as possible after the first engine goes out."

"Finch, be ready to jam his coms after the first shot. I don't want this asshole calling security while I'm yankin' him from the car."

"Already done. I've had his phone locked down since he left the house."

Vivi arrived at the road 3 minutes after leaving the top of the hill. She slowed as she reached the empty, dust covered, white sedan and got into the driver's seat. Behind the wheel, she turned on the car's hazard lights and started the electric engines. "Alright, I'm in position and ready to go."

Fincher provided an update. "Good. ETA, 6 minutes. I've isolated his GPS from the rest of the navnet and rerouted him to the airport right past our hill. I've also made it so the rest of the navnet thinks there's an accident down the highway, so no one should follow him down the road."

"Uh... about that," Enrique interjected. "I think we might have a problem. There's a black SUV behind me. It's made the last three turns with us and it just made a fourth."

Fincher sounded incredulous, "Are you sure? I'm not seeing a vehicle behind you in the local navnet."

"Aye Dios... Yes! I have eyes! It's black, with very tinted windows."

Vivi began to feel anxious. "Who're they followin', you or him?"

"Don't know, chica. Fincher, you want me to turn off and see if they stay on me, or follow Luna?"

"No. Continue following Luna. I need you close enough to his vehicle to continue spoofing his GPS along the route we need. We don't have another shot at acquiring him."

"Okay, so what're we doing about our new amigos in the SUV behind me?"

Faust came over the line in a matter-of-fact tone. "If they interfere, eliminate them."

"Damn, was hoping to do this clean." Vivi looked to her side and pulled a handgun from the holster on her hip and chambered a round before reholstering the gun. "So, Finch, who do you think our party crashers are? Anybody else know about our little operation?"

"Maybe. It could be nothing or it might be Federales who ran plates on Velasquez's stolen tow truck."

"You know, Finch, if it is the Mexican feds, we're gonna have a firefight on our hands. Might be a good time to unlock Combat Sync in my OS. It'd be super helpful if me, Tomas, and Enrique were all on the same page. Just sayin'."

"So, you can run the show again? Request denied, Rodriguez. Stick to the script. When Luna's car comes to a stop, incapacitate him, shove him in your car, and exfil to the Hidalgo."

Vivi grumbled, "Okay... boss."

Not long afterward, Enrique called over the neural sync, "Everyone ready? We're turning onto Highway 37 now. I can see the bullet trajectory line in the distance up ahead in my HUD."

Vivi looked through her car's rear-view mirror and for the first-time spotted Javier Luna's car kicking up a cloud of dust, with Enrique following behind it in a tow truck. Luna's car moved closer and closer to the line Bernice calculated for an optimal bullet trajectory to take out the rear wheel engine.

30 seconds. 20 seconds. 10 seconds. 6 seconds.

"Sending it." There was a bright muzzle flash from the end of Tomas's E-QAP rifle. The .50 caliber bullet arced up into the air and cut through the wind for 5 seconds of flight time before it landed directly onto target, smashing into the back of Javier Luna's cherry red sports car. A gaping hole appeared near the passenger side rear wheel well before the air rang out with the report from the rifle. Instantly, a copious amount of sparks, plastic and metal were violently ejected outward.

The car began to sputter on the road, swerving momentarily before continuing forward with less momentum now that it was down to three electric engines. Tomas pulled back the bolt of the rifle, ejecting the spent plastic casing and racking a new round before closing the bolt. Bernice had already come up with a new firing solution on the front right wheel engine. Tomas aimed far out in front of the car, exhaled, and lightly pulled the trigger again. The end of the muzzle break erupted with a thundering clap as the bullet arced along the green trajectory line. Five seconds later, the front fender of the car was struck, bits of plastic and metal sprayed out of the front end of the car as the smoke began to billow from the hole.

Luna's car, down to two engines, still had plenty of momentum as it decelerated. Vivi watched as the sports car flew past her on the road. A second later, Luna lost control of the vehicle, turning the wheel hard left, causing the car to flip over onto its roof and skid to a halt some 75 meters in front of Vivi's car, just off the right side of the road.

Enrique, followed closely behind Luna, drove past Vivi, and positioned his tow truck in front of Luna's overturned car.

Vivi was about to put her car into gear when the SUV that followed behind Enrique passed her as well and stopped short of Luna's car in the middle of the road. As the SUV slowed, it turned sharply to its left and screeched to a halt perpendicular to the road, so the rear side of the vehicle faced Tomas's position on the hill. When the SUV had come to a complete stop, automatic gunfire erupted from the passenger side toward Enrique's position.

Enrique ducked within the cabin of the tow truck as bullets pierced the rear window and doors. "MIERDA!"

"Well, there went all hope these assholes were friendly," Vivi scoffed.

Tomas loaded another round and took aim. "They must have seen where the shots came from. They've angled their side windows away from my position. I'm just seeing roof."

"Then what the fuck are you waiting for, chico? Put a hole through the roof!"

Five seconds elapsed before the air rang out with loud concussive reverberation of a .50 caliber round traveling faster than the speed of sound impact ineffectively on the roof of the black SUV before the sound of the actual shot rang out from the high atop hillside and Tomas's position. He called out, "No joy! These assholes are serious. They've got armor. I can probably punch through the windows, but I have no clear angle to them. Changing positions."

Vivi was feeling rather impotent as she watched the scene unfold from her position down the road. She decided to change that and put her car in gear. "Tomas, stay put! I'm gonna get you that angle!"

"Rodriguez!"

Vivi growled, "What, Finch?"

"You're going to want to be going at least 60 mph and aim toward the rear bumper to move that much mass any significant amount."

She smiled. "All I needed to hear!"

Vivi stomped on the accelerator. The car's electric engines spun to life with a loud whirr, easily urging the vehicle to 60 mph in seconds. As the car hurtled forward, toward the rear of the SUV, Vivi's HUD lit up like a Christmas tree. "Shit! I'm getting breached! They've got an ONI!"

The momentum of her car rocketing down the road might as well have been standing still compared to the speed of the digital battle occurring within Vivi. A fight for supremacy over her body's subsystems was taking place as her internal processes fought back an overload of numbers from an external attacker equipped with an Outer Network Intruder rig. At every turn, she attempted to block intrusion, but as the picoseconds passed, it was clear to Vivi she was losing. With her digital warfare capabilities locked down with most of her other military grade features, she didn't have enough processing power available to her to counter the attack. The few processing cores available to her that weren't busy keeping communications up and running or hosting Bernice were beginning to spike in temperature trying to keep up, so she had to pick her battles.

Afraid the ONI might try to stop heart or lungs first, Vivi encrypted the semaphore node that controlled her life support systems locked to her. With her life support off limits to the hacker, she next needed to ensure the link between her and the rest of the team couldn't be severed, so she hastily locked the neural sync open with the strongest encryption algorithm she had processor cycles for. Those two steps had been time-consuming and costly actions though, because for the briefest of moments, it ceded everything else to the intruder, who began rooting around through the rest of her subsystems entropy free. Before she managed another action, the lights went out. Vivi's optics had been turned off remotely by the ONI, rendering her blind.

"*Fuck!* I can't see!"

Blind, Deaf, Numb and Mute

Back in the physical world, Vivi's car was still hurtling toward the rear of the SUV, only now her vision consisted of pure nothingness. In shock, Vivi instinctively slammed on the brakes and turned the steering wheel hard to the right, causing her car to skid sideways, smashing into the rear corner of the SUV. The collision, while violent, was far slower than intended, and failed to turn the vehicle enough for Tomas to have a clear shot at the side windows of the SUV. Moreover, now her car was in the way of the shot as well.

Although the crash didn't fulfil its original purpose, it did manage to create a momentary lull in gun fire from the other side of the vehicle. Enrique used these precious few seconds to jump from the tow truck and take refuge in front of it, blindly firing back with a submachine gun of his own as he did.

Completely in the dark, Vivi fumbled for her seatbelt with her left hand, while her right hand removed her gun from its holster. With the seatbelt off, she attempted to open her door, but it stopped short with a loud thunk as it hit the side of the SUV she had crashed into. She immediately turned to her right and began climbing over the center console, feeling blindly for the passenger door handle. "Fuck! Fuck! Fuck!"

Glass shattered and rained around her as bullets from Enrique ricocheted off the SUV and sped through her vehicle. Two of the little skidding bastards caught her in the flak jacket, just under her left arm. "Goddammit!"

In the commotion, Vivi somehow managed to find the door handle; she pulled at it hard, and the passenger door spat open. As she tugged herself through the door while unable to see anything, Vivi misplaced her hand on the edge of the door frame and fell awkwardly out of the sedan, landing on the ground face first with a dull thud. As she picked herself up, she lifted her gun over the top of her car and began firing it back towards where she thought the SUV was. After only three shots from her sidearm however, Vivi's trigger finger completely locked up and prevented her from pulling the trigger again. Another gift from the ONI intruder. She ducked back behind her car and felt for the front passenger tire and upon finding it, took cover behind it.

Vivi could hear Enrique and the occupants on the other side of the SUV trading automatic weapons fire on and off.

"Chico, the windows are resistant to small caliber rounds too. You got a shot yet?"

"No shot. Still just seeing roof." Tomas fired off another round into the roof of the SUV to let them know he was still there. "I'm not about to let them out the car with me up here though."

After the second .50 caliber shot ricocheted off of the roof with another loud impact, a window rolled down slightly on the driver's side of the SUV. A calm male that voice that sounded heavy with digital distortion called out to Vivi, "Tell your man on the hill to stand down. We only want The Director. No one has to die."

"Fuck you, asshole! How about you give me my eyesight back!" Vivi immediately felt her right arm go completely limp and fall to her side. *And my arm...*

Vivi's gun fell out of her lifeless hand as it hit the dirt. She was in total darkness outside of her HUD. The only thing she could see was the ONI hacker rooting through more of her subsystems, looking for things to turn off. Possessing an artificial body meant enhanced vulnerability to breach protocol attempts, but in her years of being stuck in this shell, she had never been breached so easily or quickly. Regardless of her operational status, however, she knew if there was any way out of the situation, it involved Tomas remaining on the hill in the high ground.

Suddenly, more automatic gunfire rang out from the passenger side of the SUV towards Enrique's position. In between the staccato drum beat of gun fire, Vivi could make out the sound of the rear of the SUV open and something mechanical whirr to life before taking off.

"Tomas! Enrique! I just heard something fly outta the back of that thing!"

Enrique fired wildly into the air. "Light assault drone. Holt! It's headed for you, kid!"

More automatic gunfire erupted, this time above Vivi and to the left as Tomas called out. "It's too fast! Taking cover!"

Great, now they have the high ground, Vivi thought to herself.

As she heard the call outs over the neural sync, the driver side door of the SUV opened and closed with the sound of heavy boots hitting the ground. Vivi could hear footsteps in the dirt closer and closer to her position behind the front wheel well of her car and so Vivi began to crawl, one armed and blind as fast as she could back toward where she assumed the hill resided. Tomas's .50 caliber rifle echoed loudly in the distance. Gun fire was being exchanged in all directions and now someone was coming up from behind her. It was at this moment Vivi began to feel the situation was starting to get dire.

"FINCH! BERNICE! I don't know if either of you are paying attention, but I could really use some fucking breach countermeasures right about now!"

Bernice's shiny obelisk shape appeared in the sea of darkness that comprised Vivi's vision and responded in the politest of tones, "I do apologize, mum. Mr. Fincher is currently busy defending the back trace that you let the ONI run right through the neural sync. The one he says you decided to lock open, like some kind of idiot. How can I be of assistance?"

"Don't get sassy with me, Bernice! My OS is still running on civilian params! So yeah, they cut through my firewall like it was toilet paper!"

"To be fair, mum, you did enter their ad hoc range without requesting sufficient Intrusion Defense Protocol."

"Bernice! You gonna help me or not? I can't see shit, my right arm is a paperweight, and cores 26 through 64 are getting close to overheating keeping this asshole from taking my other arm."

"The ONI attacker is already entrenched deep in your sub systems. Thinking. Please stand by."

Vivi screamed in frustration. "At least give me access to Tomas and Enrique's optics."

"Access granted."

Two separate video feeds appeared in Vivi's HUD. From Enrique's view, Vivi saw down the barrel of his SMG, which was wildly flailing about, searching for the drone zipping by overhead. Tomas's view was less helpful, mostly obscured by rock from his huddled position on the craggy hill where he was avoiding gunfire from the drone. In the meantime, Vivi felt the footsteps behind her catch up. A moment later, a hand forcefully grabbed her by the shoulder and yanked her backward.

"Tomas, I need you to do me a favor and see if you can peek out to my position."

"Taking fire, but I'll see what I can do…"

Tomas's view from behind the rocks changed as he swiveled around to look over the outcropping. Gunfire erupted immediately that forced Tomas back into cover, but the view was long enough to give Vivi what she needed. As soon as she saw herself in frame, she took a screenshot and quickly studied it while she struggled with her pursuer.

"Get the fuck offa me!"

Vivi heard a garbled voice directly in her ear. "You chose the hard way, Barbie."

It was rather surreal seeing the picture of herself in near real time, kneeling in the dirt with a large man in a black suit behind her. It wasn't just his voice that was garbled though. The man's face had been digitally smeared, obscuring his identity. One of the assailant's large arms was in the process of wrapping around Vivi's neck as if to choke her.

"Joke's on you, asshole," she yelled. "I don't have a trachea!"

Dumbass should have just shot me from—wait. Hold on… what's that in his hand? It was the moment Vivi felt her neural port slide open that she realized what the object the man held was, a restraining collar similar to one the border guards had used on her at the crossing into Mexico.

"Oh, hell no!" Vivi planted her right foot firmly into the ground and jerked violently backward, smashing the top of her metallic skull into the man's face, breaking his nose and momentarily stunning him.

She squirmed to her left, out of his loosened grip, and landed in the dirt.

In her HUD, she stared at the still frame for anything that could help her within range of where she thought she might have landed. A rock, a shard of glass, a gun... The gun! It looked only four or so feet away in the screenshot. She reached out with her left hand in a wide arcing motion, feeling in the dirt, but it wasn't there.

Her left leg went dead. Then her right. Most of the processor cores that had been holding the ONI at bay were finally overheated. She focused all of her remaining processing power on keeping her left arm under her control. She could see other systems turning off left and right, blinking, voice, hearing, smell, all going offline. With all of her being, she urged her increasingly lifeless body forward with her left hand till she felt a tingling numbness. The ONI had turned off her sense of touch. It was no use. Even if the gun was there, she'd never feel it.

Vivi collapsed face first into the dirt, blind, numb, deaf, and mute. Mute outside of the neural sync anyway. While she could still communicate with her team, the lack of an external voice robbed her of the ability to launch further obscenities at the attacker behind her, which, while not particularly useful, would have at least been somewhat cathartic.

Bernice appeared in Vivi's HUD again. "Mum, I've analyzed the situation and I think you'll find an open ad hoc connection to the vehicle if you ping the network."

"No chance, Bernice. They've got that thing armored up like a damn tank. No way they don't have a semaphore lock shutting their nav system tighter than Finch's butthole."

"Not the enemy vehicle, mum. Your car."

"My car? MY CAR!" If Bernice had lips, Vivi would have kissed them. Vivi quickly pinged the network. Sure enough, the enemy SUV's subsystems were closed off to her, but her car, still lodged against the rear of the SUV, was in range and available for remote control.

Vivi's insides felt like they were boiling, but she urged her strained processor array to connect to the beat up, white sedan. Within an instant, the car's camera array was available to her. She scanned each of the cameras and could see her body face down in the dirt to the rear right side of the car. The man who had been attempting to restrain her was still getting to his feet behind her body, shaking off the broken nose which had bled deep red onto his white shirt and tie.

Vivi remotely switched the car into reverse and digitally punched the accelerator, steering the car from behind the SUV. Meanwhile, she simultaneously used the few remaining muscles available to her to roll to her right, hoping it was enough to not be run over by her own vehicular missile.

The car whizzed by Vivi and smashed into her attacker with a satisfying, bone-crunchingly audible THUH-KUNK! Well, Vivi assumed it was satisfying anyway. She couldn't exactly hear it. For good measure, she had the car drive forward and backward a few times, just to make sure her attacker wasn't ever getting back up again.

Annoyingly, the death of her assailant did little to fix her current immobility situation, but it was one less thing to worry about as she called over the neural sync. "One tango's down, but my body's still locked up. The ONI spoofin' me's definitely in the SUV."

"Kind of busy with this drone, chica. Anything you can do to help?"

"Sure can! Hold on!" Vivi put the sedan into reverse again and sped it backwards down the road, a good distance away from the fighting.

After she felt it was far enough away, she flung the gear into drive and remotely stepped on the accelerator again. "I'm not slowin' down this time, assholes!"

The ONI in the SUV must have seen what Vivi was attempting because the drone that had been hunting Tomas turned away and focused its attention on Vivi's lifeless body. But there was nothing it could do in time. The white sedan smashed into the SUV with enough force to launch it 80 degrees sideways.

Tomas called out, "I have a shot! Taking it!" Five seconds later, the supersonic bullet rocketed through the rear driver side window of the SUV. Blood sprayed all over the remaining windows of the vehicle as an overtly large caliber round entered, then exited the head of the ONI that resided in the back seat. The sound wave from the shot on the hill finally caught up as Tomas reported, "Tango down!"

Vivi's subsystems began to come back online slowly, and not in any order she would have cared for. The smell of gunpowder filled her nostrils. *Seriously? Smell? I don't need my fucking sense of smell right now!*

Tomas reported from his position on the hill. "Tango on the passenger side is bugging out and hiding on the other side of the SUV. I don't have a shot. Enrique?"

Enrique held up his gun and peeked out from behind his tow truck. "I don't see him, chico."

In the meantime, Vivi had regained the use of her left arm and one of her eyes. She spotted her gun in the dirt. It was completely in the wrong direction from where she had blindly been reaching for it earlier.

"Bernice, gimee a firing solution for behind that SUV."

The obelisk representation of Bernice appeared in the distance next to the SUV. "Mum? From your position, that's almost straight up."

Vivi picked up her gun. "Just do it!"

Bernice drew a green bullet trajectory line in Vivi's HUD. As advertised, it was almost straight up.

Vivi aligned her gun with the green trajectory line and pulled the trigger three times, sending bullets arcing far into the sky. "Enrique! Get ready!" She counted the seconds to herself. "Thousand one, thousand two, thousand three…"

When she got to thirteen, Vivi called out, "Now!"

Fifteen seconds after the shots had been fired, the bullets finally landed behind the SUV. None of the bullets actually hit the man behind the vehicle, but they were never intended to. They did however do the trick of causing him to flee from behind the vehicle and present an easy target for Enrique.

Without hesitation, Enrique squeezed the trigger on his small caliber SMG, filling the air with the telltale sound of murderous popcorn. The third attacker crumpled to the ground. The fight was over.

Chapter Twelve

Bedlam

Vivi fumbled with the buckles on her flak jacket as she breathed in and out heavily at a rapid pace. She could feel the air escaping her insides through her mouth and nostrils hot as magma. With the last of the straps unbuckled, she dropped the heavy flak jacket onto the ground. "Water!"

Tomas called out from atop the hill. "I thought you don't drink?"

"WATER!"

"I've got a canteen, I'm coming!"

Vivi stumbled toward the SUV and opened the driver's side door. She rummaged around in the vehicle and found one dead body missing its head, an ONI rig next to the corpse, a pile of spent plastic bullet casings and gallons of blood, but no water.

Vivi hyperventilated loudly as she leaned on the side of the SUV, her insides were still dangerously overheated from the prolonged breach defense and now that the fighting was over, there was no way to keep her automated systems from taking over to vent the excess heat as fast as possible. The emergency twenting process left Vivi feeling light-headed as she desperately gasped for air. With her body's sub systems diverted to expelling heat as fast as possible, they were only currently capable of delivering the minimum amount of oxygen required to her brain. "Water..."

Finch's voice came over the neural sync, "What's Luna's status?"

From her position leaning on the SUV, Vivi could see the trunk and rear window of Luna's red sports car. The back window was completely shattered, and the trunk had telltale signs of having taken gunfire. Smoke poured out of the right rear engine. The chaotic scene was bedlam.

Enrique walked over from the tow truck and bent down beside the overturned car. Vivi still had access to Enrique's optics in her HUD. From Enrique's view, she could see Javier Luna was lying on the ceiling of the car, having unstrapped himself after the vehicle had flipped over. He was clutching his left collarbone and blood was streaming down his shirt. "Mierda! Luna's been hit! Going get some Medifoam." Enrique turned and started the walk back to his tow truck.

"Does he have an exit wound?"

"I'll need to pull him out to check. Gimme a second."

In the meantime, Tomas finally finished the 1000-yard dash down the hill to Vivi, who was still too busy hyperventilating and gasping for air to notice he had walked up. Tomas reached out to touch her shoulder and get her attention, but as his left thumb made contact, he quickly pulled his hand away, shaking it in pain.

"Fuck! You're burning up!" Tomas handed her the canteen. "Here."

Vivi uncapped the canteen, but rather than drinking it, she poured the water over her torso, where the bulk of her processor array was housed. Immediately, steam hissed off her prosthetic body and her breathing began to slow. "Thanks..."

Tomas clutched his burnt thumb, rubbing it. "You weren't lying. Temperature hot."

Vivi picked up her discarded flak jacket from the ground. "Temperature hot. Come on. Let's go check on Enrique."

When Enrique returned to the car, he smashed in the window and attempted to calm Luna down. "Señor Luna? Por favor cálmese. Estoy aquí para rescatarte." Enrique began to pull Luna through the open window. "Yeah, we got an exit wound."

"¿Los detuviste? ¿Ese auto negro?" Luna was breathing heavily and motioning excitedly. "Ellos me siguieron! ¿Que querian ellos? Espera, eres policía?"

Enrique continued to speak softly to Luna in a reassuring manner. "Sí, si. Los detuvimos. Prometo." Over the neural sync he reported, "Gunshot wound, left shoulder, looks like it cut right through the collarbone and came right out the front. He's loopy. Said the black SUV was following him, asked if we stopped them. I think he thinks we're the police."

"He's in shock, elevate his legs," Fincher responded.

Vivi and Tomas walked up next to Enrique and Luna. "Anything we can do to help?"

"Yeah, do what Fincher said."

Vivi moved to Luna's legs and used her discarded flak jacket to prop them up into an elevated position.

Enrique pulled a 6-inch tube of Medifoam from a bag. He pressed a button along the side, causing a thick needle to eject from the front. "Señor Luna, necesito que muevas tu mano fuera del camino."

Luna complied, moving his hand from the wound. Enrique jabbed the applicator in hard. Thick white foam emitted immediately, which filled the wound cavity and began to stop the bleeding.

Enrique removed the Medifoam canister away from the wound once he was satisfied the bleeding had stopped completely. He pulled a syringe and a small glass bottle of narcotics from his bag, bit the cap off the needle, and began to fill the syringe. "Te voy a dar algo que te ayude a relajarte." Not long after the needle went into Luna's neck, he passed out.

Once Luna was unconscious, Enrique turned his head to the side and pulled a 1"x 1" card out of the back of Luna's neck and tossed it to Vivi. "ID chit."

Vivi caught the chit and inserted it into a small device she produced from a pocket in her fatigues. "Luna's ID should be uploading to you now, Finch."

Tomas pointed a thumb back to the drone that was still hovering near Luna's car. "Anyone else weirded out this thing is still just hanging out in midair? No one? Just me?"

Vivi stood up, looking back toward the SUV. "Yeah, just who the fuck were those guys?"

"Definitely Mexican feds. You didn't hear them speaking Spanish, chica?"

"What? No. They're definitely American. I didn't hear nothin' but English, and the one that was on top of me called me, 'Barbie'. What kind of bigoted Mexican prick skips out on calling a fully prosthetic woman, 'muñeca' when he's got the chance?"

"Ayudame! I'm telling you, they were speaking Spanish!"

"I was too far away to hear any of them. Do we know what they were after?" Tomas interjected.

Vivi pointed at Luna. "Him. They very clearly told me they wanted the director. Finch, how many other people know about this asset we're 'rescuing' from China?"

"I don't know offhand. It can't be that many. This asset's existence is guarded information at the highest levels."

"Any chance the US has competing plans for acquiring the asset besides us?"

"I suppose it's possible, but highly unlikely they would utilize the same tact of reaching China by impersonating Luna. This was my idea."

"You don't think another analyst could have come up with the same plan?"

Fincher sounded annoyed, "No. I don't. It's a very original concept."

"Uh huh... sure it is."

Vivi walked over to the dead body alongside the SUV. "What the fuck..."

Tomas called over, "What is it?"

Vivi leaned into the body and turned the dead man's face to its side. "His face is still digitally distorted. I can't make out his features." She began to pull the man's ID chit from his neck.

Tomas pointed to the headless corpse in the SUV. "Impossible! I took the ONI's head clean off. There's no way we're still being hacked!"

Vivi inserted the ID chit into the chit reader. "Finch, uploading you another ID. Who's our friend?"

"Receiving it now. Hold on. It's blank."

"The fuck it is. What's on it?"

"I swear! It's blank."

"How are our optics still being hacked? Bernice, are there any US satellites operating over our position?"

Bernice's obelisk form appeared next to the Vivi. "I'm afraid I'm not at liberty to say, mum."

"Yeah, that's what I thought. I think it's a damn safe bet someone in the US doesn't want us completing this job."

Faust's voice came over the neural sync. "This is getting us nowhere. Time's wasting. Holt, police the brass. Velasquez, Rodriguez, get

Luna's car on the tow truck and take him to The Hidalgo. Prep him for the next three days. Rodriguez, once Luna's car is on the truck, collect the bodies in the SUV and then burn it."

"And the drone?"

"Shoot it down. Rendezvous at the airport as soon as possible in character. Faust out."

Vivi saw the neural sync shut down, as it did communication with Fincher and Faust was cut off and Bernice disappeared from her HUD. She turned to Tomas. "Well, you heard the man…"

On command, Tomas put a .50 caliber round through the drone at close range, which dropped to the ground in a heap.

Enrique flinched as he was carrying Luna's unconscious body to the tow truck. "Aye Dios! Not so close with that thing. You're going to make me go deaf!"

While Tomas stayed near the SUV picking up the spent plastic shell casings, Vivi jogged after Enrique. On the way, she picked up her discarded flak jacket from the ground and pulled out her pack of Fortunes from the pocket. The cigarette box had a hole clean through it created by one of the wayward bullets she had taken during the firefight. Vivi removed pieces of mangled cigarettes from the perforated box. "Holy shit, hope there's a good one left." Finding an intact cigarette, she drew it out and lit it, taking a well-deserved drag. She expelled smoke from her nose as she approached Enrique, and spoke in a quiet tone, "Hey… you got what I asked for?"

Enrique replied, just as quiet, "Yeah, it's in the truck. It'll be a small miracle if it didn't catch a bullet."

Vivi flicked the butt off her cigarette. "Great. Turns out, I needa to ask you to acquire another something on the down low…"

Chapter Thirteen

Reflections of a Crack in the Façade

A cloudy mirror. A dirty tile floor that no one would believe had ever been white. A flickering fluorescent tube doing its best to cast light into a damp room but failing miserably. A sink with a slow leak. Drip. Drip. Drip. Four bathroom stalls covered in graffiti sat in the mirror's reflection. Also in the reflection, Vivi stared intently into her own eyes. A cigarette sat in between her index and middle finger that had been lit for a while, but hardly smoked. The ash curled off the end of the cigarette, nearly up to the filter. Vivi had been standing at the mirror for some time.

A message icon popped up in her HUD. It was from Enrique. "Esperando ti niña"

Vivi sent a message in reply: "2 secs"

She took one last glance in the mirror and sighed. Vivi hated the process of changing her hairstyle. She flicked the long ash off the cigarette and urged a final drag out of what remained before tossing the butt into a sink covered in caution tape under a sign that read, "Out of order".

She blew out a puff of smoke. "It's been a fun ride, blue hair. I'm gonna miss ya'."

Vivi went to her body's settings app and selected an option for "Change Hair Style". Tiny popping sounds emanated from atop her skull. She reached up and tugged her long indigo hair and scalp off the top of her head. She dropped the mess of hair and artificial scalp into the open duffel bag on the floor next to her and reached in to pick up another scalp that featured a short bob cut in a brunette color that matched Domenica Santiago's hair style.

Vivi closed her eyes and took a deep breath. "Don't look. Don't look. Don't look. Don't look." But she couldn't help it. Like every time before, she took a quick glance. And like every time before, instantly regretted it. Her body lacked all the parts necessary to vomit, but somehow it never stopped her from feeling like she needed to.

The quick glance turned into a long stare. Where her hair once sat was the shiny metal surface of her skull, complete with venting perforations and electronic locks to hold a new scalp in place. Somehow, seeing herself like this was more off-putting to Vivi than the time she had been forced to watch her left arm, caught in a vice grip, being torn off by the Herreras. That hadn't bothered her. Seeing herself like this though, it made her feel inhuman. Artificial. Other.

Her HUD blinked at her incessantly, like a dog begging for attention. "Apply new hairstyle?"

Vivi lifted the new scalp and hairstyle up to her head, aligned the front flap with where her forehead ended, and applied the setting in her HUD. She could feel top of her skull vibrate gently as the locks screwed into the threaded inserts beneath the new scalp, locking the brunette, shoulder length, bob cut onto her head.

Only one more thing to do, she thought.

Vivi guided her index and middle finger to the right side of her neck and pushed in. Her ID chit popped out, allowing Vivi to tug it out the rest of the way. She held out the 1-inch square card in front of her. "So long Viviana Alexia Rodriguez. See you in a few days."

After she stored her own ID in a false compartment hidden at the bottom of her makeup compact, she slotted a spoofed copy of Domenica Santiago's ID into her neck, picked up her duffel bag off the floor, and exited the mag lev station's run-down bathroom.

Enrique was waiting for Vivi near the entrance to the mag lev platform. He was leaned up against a column holding a briefcase when he spotted Vivi. He lowered his sunglasses, exposing his glowing artificial eyes, and whistled. "Quite the improvement, chica. Short hair suits you. Maybe you should ditch the long blue locks for good. I bet you could almost pass for a real grown up."

Vivi rolled her eyes. "You're one to talk. With that 3-piece suit you got on, I can barely make out the subhuman stench of cartel you're usually swimming in. What's in the briefcase?"

Enrique pushed his glasses back over his eyes and held out the briefcase to Vivi. "For you. That first thing you asked for, and also a present from Fincher."

Vivi took the briefcase. "And the second thing I asked for?"

Enrique picked up the handle to a rolling suitcase next to him and started walking toward the mag lev platform. "It's going to take some time, but I'll have it for you in China. Don't you worry."

"Never said I was worried. So, what'd Finch send me?"

"It's a slab processor array, heatsink, and a power supply disguised as a laptop."

"What for?"

"No idea. You'll have to ask him."

Along the path to the mag lev platform was a large crowd of homeless beggars of all ages huddled on the ground next to cardboard signs written in Spanish that read things like "Please spare a yuan", "Hungry need food", "Anything will help".

Most of the beggars Vivi could see were missing at least one body part, many two or more. An old woman had no legs. A young man was missing an arm. A primary school aged girl had a cavity in her face where her eyes should have been. A few of the beggars still had the telltale signs of rust orange-colored lesions bubbling up on what remained of a limb. Leprae-IX. Rust.

People walked by the row of beggars, covering their faces as they did, trying to ignore reality. So even in a rich country like Mexico, the rust endemic was still a problem.

Vivi walked over to the young girl that was missing her eyes. "¿Tienes un teléfono, niña?"

The girl lowered her head and held up her phone.

Vivi touched two fingers to the phone and transferred ☐6500 to the girl's account from Domenica Santiago's bank account. "That should be enough for food for a week... er... Consíguete algo de comida."

The girl smiled widely. "¡Gracias señorita! ¡No puedo agradecerte lo suficiente!"

"De nada, pero tu dulce sonrisa es suficiente agradecimiento."

Vivi rejoined Enrique, who was climbing aboard the mag lev train that had arrived. He shook his head at her. "You lied to that girl. Her smile wasn't that sweet."

The train sped off toward the airport. "You sure rust only took your eyes, Enrique? Cause it sounds like there might be a gaping hole where your heart's supposed to be."

"Says the one with so much disdain for the cartels."

Vivi tossed her duffel bag down before throwing herself onto a seat. "And why shouldn't I? You're all a bunch of sleazy drug smugglers, takin' all the good shit from Canada and sellin' to the richest of the rich in Mexico."

Enrique laughed. "And just how many shipments of mine did you steal for Paulo? Huh? What, did you think he was taking them from us and just passing them out to the huddled masses in streets of Phoenix?"

Vivi furrowed her brow in response, her eyes boring into the sunglasses concealing Enrique's eyes.

"Yes. We sell the designer stuff to the richest of the rich, same as Paulo. But the other stuff. Who do you think gives medical aid to those people back at that mag lev station, chica? The government? The mega corporations? The military? The churches? None of them could be bothered. I know. I was among those in squalor along with so many others before the Herrera Cartel lifted me out of it. Gave me purpose."

"Yeah? Well, from looks of it back there, your precious Herrera's mighta left a few behind."

Vivi and Enrique didn't speak the rest of the short ride to the airport.

Hermosillo International Airport was a throwback to an earlier time. It had an air of being a relic from the 2090's, probably right about the time when Mexico first came into prominence as a major world power, about the time the rest of the world was going to shit. By 2140 however, this particular airport was beginning to show its age; though it was far nicer than any of the airports Vivi had seen back in the states.

The large focal point of the main lobby was a 100-foot tall, single pane, digital glass wall that cycled through famous works of art, a giant analogue styled clock Vivi didn't know how to read and occasionally flight information. It may have been an impressive display 50 years ago, but now it was an eyesore of a bygone time. Though, it was far less of an eyesore to Vivi than the myriad of no smoking signs that littered the building.

Enrique and Vivi walked through the lobby looking for Tomas. They eventually spotted him near an information kiosk, talking with a man in a black 3-piece suit similar to the one Enrique was sporting. Tomas smiled as he chatted animatedly with the man.

Vivi began to walk toward the pair when Enrique grabbed her arm. "Wait! Let him finish."

She watched Tomas shake the man's hand while simultaneously patting the man's neck with his other hand in an oddly cordial manner.

After the two waved goodbye, Tomas began the walk toward Vivi and Enrique as the stranger moved toward the street level exit.

Tomas was nearly unrecognizable with a clean-shaven face and a wig that simulated Javier Luna's male pattern baldness. His chrome fingers were gone, having been replaced with artificial skin colored prosthetics.

Vivi giggled. "Oh my God, what did they do to you? Love the hair."

"Gee, thanks." Tomas replied, feigning a smile while he tugged a bracelet off his left wrist. He tossed the bracelet to Enrique. "Your new name for the next 3 days is Carlos Pastor."

Enrique caught the bracelet. "Carlos? Ugh. My father's name. I hate that name."

Tomas shrugged. "Sorry, that's who showed up as Luna's security detail. How long is it going to take to spoof an ID?"

Enrique pulled an ID chit reader out of his pocket and tapped the bracelet on it. "Hopefully not long, or I'm staying behind in Mexico."

Vivi turned to Tomas while Enrique fiddled with the ID chit reader. "I hope you're taking notes." She motioned to her green strapless dress with a black bolero jacket on top. "For future reference, this is what a classy dress looks like."

"Looks nice, but it'd probably look a lot better without that ratty duffel bag slung under your arm."

Vivi pouted. "I don't like suitcases, okay? You ever tried to run with a suitcase?"

"You planning to do much running in those heels?"

"I dunno. Depends. What're we running from?"

"Who says we're running away from something? What if we're running to somewhere?"

Vivi arched an eyebrow, letting a tiny smirk sneak out. "Is it someplace nice?"

Tomas smiled. "It could be…"

Enrique feigned gagging. "Aye Dios, you two get a room already. I'm busy."

The phone icon lit up in Vivi's HUD, interrupting loudly. She answered. It was Fincher on the other end. "Who's ready to go to Shanghai?"

"You're not coming to send us off, Finch?"

"Nope. Work to be done on this end to get you safely through security. Setting up the neural sync now."

Bernice's familiar obelisk shape appeared in Vivi's vision via her HUD. "Good afternoon, mum. Applying Deep Fake algorithm."

Vivi tugged up at the sleeve on her bolero jacket. The thin segmentation line between her hand and forearm was gone. She looked up and over to Tomas, who now shared the visage of the 57-year-old Javier Luna.

Enrique slotted in a new ID chit into his neck. "Carlos Pastor, reporting for security duty. Let's go."

Vivi, Tomas and Enrique made their way to the security checkpoint and the first test of the Deep Fake algorithm. The group split into two parties since Tomas, posing as Javier Luna, was eligible to go through an executive frequent flier line that skipped most of the longer queue Vivi and Enrique were forced to endure.

Tomas approached the counter. "Wish me luck."

But Tomas needed no luck. He breezed right through security as Javier Luna. Vivi and Enrique, however, continued to inch forward at a snail's pace through a significant line of passengers.

As Vivi approached the security counter, an agent looked up from her console and greeted her. "Please place your thumb here for identification."

Vivi complied and placed a thumb on the panel. Domenica Santiago's face appeared on the console.

"How many days will you be staying in Shanghai, Ms. Santiago?"

"Three."

"Business or pleasure."

Vivi frowned. "Business, sadly."

"Very well. Please proceed to Station D on the left concourse for routine Leprae-IX testing."

"I, uhm, w-what?" she stuttered.

"The standard check for rust? Your flight history says you've been to China several times in the past 2 years. China still doesn't allow active cases to cross their borders."

"Oh! Ha! Yes of course, the standard test for rust. I'm so sorry. I was just so wrapped up in getting to my flight on time that I must have forgotten about it."

Shit! Vivi thought. "Finch! I can't pass a rust test! There's no skin cells to take off my hand!"

Fincher sounded calm over the neural sync, "I'm aware."

"And you're just now deciding to tell me?"

"You may have heard something about it had you attended more intelligence briefs. Just let them apply the test, 01 and I will take care of the rest."

Vivi complied with instructions at the Leprae-IX testing station and placed her hand into a machine which scraped off a thin layer of artificial skin from the top of her hand. Bernice appeared next to the device. "Breaching bacteria scanner. Breach successful! Interfacing with Leprae-IX testing equipment. Thinking. Thinking. Thinking."

Vivi grinned incriminatingly at the man operating the device when it appeared the test was taking longer than it was for the other passengers being tested. Enrique's test started long after Vivi's, and he was already through to the next checkpoint. "Hurry it up, Bernice..."

"Applying negative test result. Negative test result applied!"

The screen turned green and Vivi was allowed to pass to the next checkpoint, which appeared to be, "A full body scan? Ugh! Finch..."

"And that's followed by a bag check and a weight check. We have those covered too."

"Alright, I'll admit it, I'm impressed. What else you got covered?"

"The Chinese airport. The slab processor array Enrique gave you, connect to it ad hoc when you land and let it run the Deep Fake algorithm. It should have enough juice to get you to the hotel in character, but it's not powerful enough for the full effect, so you're all going to want to pretend to be super concerned about germs and wear medical masks to reduce the amount of visual replacements and load."

"Can do."

"Seriously, Rodriguez, stick to the script once you arrive in China. Head straight for the hotel and don't dawdle. They have more cameras than citizens and I can't guarantee that thing will last more than an hour."

"I'll be on my best behavior!"

"That's what worries me."

Once past all the checkpoints, Vivi met up with Tomas and Enrique at the terminal.

"You know, chica, I'm not sure if I like the idea of flying with you while the airline thinks you're 2 tons lighter than you actually are. The jet's probably going to be all..." Enrique made a gesture showing the plane flying lopsided.

"You callin' me fat?"

"Dense maybe..."

Vivi knocked a closed fist against her skull. "No lies detected."

Tomas smiled. "Well, see you two in China. They just called my boarding group."

"Wait what? We're not sitting together?"

"Nope, Luna only purchased first-class tickets for himself. You and Carlos are back in the cheap seats."

Vivi groaned and motioned to Enrique. "Stuck on a flight to China for 4 hours? With him? When did we discuss this?"

Enrique and Tomas replied simultaneously. "Intelligence briefing."

Chapter Fourteen

Rocking the Boat

The world outside the window of the hypersonic airliner was pristine. An endless sea of pillowy clouds atop a deep blue horizon. It had been a number of years since Vivi had been in a plane, and for once, she wasn't planning on jumping out of this one.

If the world outside was expansive and freeing, the interior of the cabin was cramped and oppressive. The seats in coach weren't proportioned for anything resembling a human body, the in-flight entertainment lacked a connection to the outernet that didn't cost an exorbitant fee, and worst of all, the "No Smoking" signs that littered the airplane seemed to follow Vivi wherever she looked, mocking her. Her only consolation was Enrique in the seat next to her, looking just as uncomfortable.

"Ngh! Mi espalda! What'd they make these seats out of? Concrete?"

A message appeared in her HUD via the local network. Vivi opened it to find a picture Tomas had taken of himself smiling while he lounged on a near mattress sized seat in first class, holding a champagne flute that contained an orange liquid. "Turns out you were right. Mimosas are great!"

Vivi sent a reply: "I hate you so much right now."

Enrique must have gotten a similar message. He nudged Vivi. "Your new boyfriend's a prick."

"He's not my boyfriend. I don't date."

"I think I know why. Does he?"

Vivi glared at Enrique. "Fuck you."

Enrique laughed. "You're extra surly when you haven't had a cigarette in a while, chica. Here." He extended out a pack of gum to Vivi.

Vivi begrudgingly took a piece and popped it in her mouth, chewing in silent annoyance.

Since the outernet was blocked by the airline during the flight, communication with Fincher, Bernice and Faust was unavailable. This gave Vivi time to play with the new toy Enrique had gotten her. She retrieved her briefcase from the overhead compartment, opened it, and removed a small device with a neural port connector before returning the briefcase to its stowage position.

Enrique looked over from his window seat, dropping his sunglasses in curiosity. "So, who are you planning to use that on? And it better not be me..."

Vivi slotted the device into her own neural port.

"What the—Kid? What're doing? You know how a packet sniffer works, right? You're supposed to put it on a person or a device you want to spy on."

"I wanna spy on me."

"You realize that makes literally no sense, right?"

Vivi sighed. "I wouldn't expect you to understand."

"Try me. It's not like I have anywhere to go."

Vivi began installing the packet sniffer into her OS. "Fine. Try to keep up. So, when I got discharged from the Army, they locked down all the fancy shit in my body so I couldn't use it in the civilian world. Half my processor array, nanoweave overdrive, adreno pump, combat sync, intrusion defense protocol, precision overflow, aim assistance, you name it, if it wasn't a civvie spec node, it got locked down."

"Can't say I blame them. Who'd want a hot-headed psycho like you on the loose outside a combat zone with the ability to punch through a concrete wall and breach any ad hoc connected system just because she was having a bad day?"

Vivi furrowed her brow at Enrique. She blew a bubble with her gum and popped it.

"Lo siento. Please continue."

"The encryption protocol locking down my OS is time-stamped. It's like a rotating tumbler lock that changes every 60 seconds. There's one lock for the whole system, but there's a new key that unlocks it every minute. Computationally, it's impossible to calculate without a massive quantum computer. But if you have the key, no computations needed, it's good for 1 minute."

"Chica, this is all gibberish. Is there a point?"

"First time I met Faust, he touched me on the side of my head and *poof*!" Vivi snapped her fingers for effect, "he unlocked a node. I assumed that meant he used an ad hoc connection to do it, like he had to be in physical range, but then, when we were abducting Santiago at that restaurant, Fincher was able to unlock another node remotely over my outernet connection."

Enrique's expression turned to concern. "Kid, where are you going with this?"

Vivi smiled. "If I can get Faust or Fincher to unlock another node in my OS, the packet sniffer will be able to pick up the encryption key. If I can parse it out, I can use it to unlock whatever else I want in my OS so long as I can do it within 60 seconds."

"Aye Dios! Why on earth would you want to go and do a stupid thing like that?"

"Insurance."

"For what? You'll be human by next month. We're so close to finishing this job. Why not just play along a little longer?"

"Told you last night at The Hidalgo. Somethin's not sitting right with me. Even more so after what happened this morning with those assholes in the SUV. And I'm not planning on sitting around with my thumb up my butt, waiting to get fucked again. If I go out, I want it to be on my terms."

Enrique shook his head. "You know, I don't know I've ever met anyone else that likes to rock the boat like you, kid."

Vivi tugged the packet sniffer installation tool from her neural port. "If the boat's not rocking, it's a boring ass boat ride."

Chapter Fifteen

Ship of Theseus

The nighttime skyline in Shanghai was a sight to behold. A beacon in the distance from the airport that shined as if it were a million pieces of gold reflecting the intense flicker of a nearby bonfire. Just outside the airport, two twin 50 story tall structures hummed loudly, scrubbing the atmosphere around the airport of carbon emissions. The Shanghai airport's open-air design allowed a chilly breeze into the concourse. Vivi could see the hot air coming off Enrique and Tomas's mouths even through their medical masks. Luckily, she was able to turn off her ability to feel the frigid wind.

Vivi chuckled. "You boys cold?"

Tomas shivered, rubbing his shoulders. "Very. Whose bright idea was it to make the entire concourse outside? You're lucky you can't feel this."

Vivi smiled behind her medical mask as she viewed groups of people smoking cigarettes while they tried to stay warm on the breezeway. She tugged down her mask, pulled out a Fortune and lit it. "And this is why I love Asia, actual smoking zones."

"Vivi! What're you doing? Fincher said to leave the masks up till we get to the hotel!"

"Relax. One cigarette's not gonna make a difference." Vivi patted the briefcase. "I'm monitoring this thing real close. It's got plenty of juice." In her HUD Vivi saw multiple copies of Bernice sitting next to every camera and person in range, applying the Deep Fake algorithm.

An hour later, safe within the penthouse of the Chiba Hotel, the Deep Fake algorithm was dropped, and so were Tomas and Enrique's medical masks.

Enrique whistled as he walked over to a fully stocked bar within the suite while loosening his tie and unbuttoning the collar on his shirt. "Luna sure has nice taste in hotels. Too bad he isn't here to enjoy it."

Tomas dropped his bag as he entered the door. "Anyone else not tired? I'm still on Mexico time."

"Same, chico. Have a drink with me."

"You sure? I mean, the meeting is tomorrow."

Enrique was already pouring out Tove' Tequila into two tumbler glasses. "Come on, kid, just one drink."

Tomas held out one of his currently non-chrome index fingers. "Okay. Just one though."

Enrique smiled devilishly. "Just one, I promise."

Six drinks later, Vivi sneered as she smoked a cigarette and watched Tomas and Enrique devolve into drunkenness, loudly discussing a meandering slate of topics she had no interest in.

Enrique laughed loudly as he patted Tomas on the back and finished what resembled a joke, "... and after the trolley hits him, the guy says 'NO! LOOKS LIKE YOUUUU GOT A TROLLEY PROB-LEM!' HAHAHAHA!"

Tomas laughed along with Enrique, apparently finding the story funny, as he took another sip of tequila. "Speaking of moral quandaries... I got... I got one for you. Heard about this during a tour in Istanbul-2. You ever heard of the Ship of Thes- ehem... The Ship of Theseus Experiment?"

"No." Enrique paused, holding his glass up. "Wait, is that the one where the US military tried to cloak a ship after World War II and it disappeared, killing everyone aboard?"

"What? No, man. That's the Philadelphia Experiment. And it's bullshit... I think? No Ship of Theseus is a thought experiment. It's different."

Enrique slugged back another round of tequila. "Well, get on with it then."

"So, there's this guy, Theseus, and he has this boat that he sails to an island with a minotaur to steal the Golden Fleece from a labyrinth."

"That's Jason and the Argonauts, chico."

"No, it's not. This is my story. Shut up. So, Theseus is successful, and he brings the fleece back to Greece and everyone's happy, and so to memorialize the occasion they take his boat and put it in a museum, cause, hey! It's the boat that brought back the fleece!"

"I still think you're wrong, kid."

"Whatever, it's not important. Just listen. So, years pass and the wood on the ship starts to splinter. The rigging begins to fray and the sails tear. And so, as parts wear out, the Greeks replace them one by one, until eventually the entire ship was replaced. Now let's say they also kept all the old parts in a warehouse. Well, one day a guy goes and builds a ship from all the old parts. So now there's two ships. Which is the real ship of Theseus? The one made up of new parts, or the one made out of the old leftovers?"

Enrique furrowed his brow and ran his fingers through his salt and pepper beard. "Well, the one rebuilt from old parts of course."

"Maybe. Maybe not. Some people say both are the Ship of Theseus due to the fourth dimensionality of time, others that neither can be because, like a river, it's never the same twice since the water is constantly moving. Point is, there's no correct answer."

Vivi rolled her eyes and exhaled a cloud of smoke. "You're wrong. There's a completely correct answer."

Tomas raised an eyebrow, pouring another drink. "Oh?"

Vivi responded in a matter-of-fact tone. "Yeah, the answer is: it doesn't fuckin' matter."

"What do you mean?"

"What I mean is, who cares what the ship's called. You can name it whatever the fuck you want. The ship doesn't care, it's an inanimate object. It didn't wake up one day and go, 'Well, I guess I'll be the goddamn Ship of Theseus now'. People gave a name to it, and people are stupid. At the end of the day, both are just hunks of wood that different people called different things for different reasons. Everyone's got their own truth. Therefore, the only possible answer is that it doesn't matter because questions without answers are dumb." Vivi took another drag from her cigarette.

"What about you?"

"What about me?"

Tomas leaned in and looked into Vivi's artificial eyes inquisitively. "You know that's the one thing I haven't figured out yet about whether or not it's worth going full borg."

Vivi flicked ash off the end of her cigarette, staring back intently. "And that is?"

"How do you know you're still you? I mean, how do you *really* know?"

Vivi furrowed her brow. "Because I remember the day before, and the day after too."

Tomas tilted back another drink, his eyes were glazed over. "Yeah, but did you ever wonder what happened to your old body?"

"What?"

"You know, I mean what if the Army kept it alive out there? What if she's still walking around somewhere, living it up, while you're sitting here all butt-hurt because you can't drink with us? Who would the real Vivi be? You? Or her?"

Vivi looked up and away as she flippantly flicked the end of her cigarette into an ashtray. "I'm me. Always have been. Always will be."

"You don't ever worry you're not? I mean shit, what if they didn't even transfer your brain into this body? What if you're just some kind of copy?"

Enrique shook his head at Tomas. "Chico, I think it's time we hit the sack, eh?"

Vivi shot up from the table, sending the chair behind her tumbling over backwards. "I'm not a fuckin' copy!"

"I mean, can you be sure though?" Tomas slouched back in his chair, eyes half closed from the alcohol. "Have you ever seen your brain?"

Vivi angrily extinguished her cigarette on the table, missing the ashtray entirely. "Have you seen yours? How the fuck you know if you're real? Huh? Maybe you're part of some cosmic simulation, or the daydream of some asshole sitting at his boring desk at his boring day job. You ever think of that?"

"No—well I... I was just sayin' that..."

Enrique pulled the glass away from Tomas. "I think you've said enough, kid."

"Maybe I'm real, maybe I'm not. You can muse on it all you want, but you can't change a God damn thing! It doesn't matter what you, or I, or fuckin' Theseus thinks, because at the end of the day, I don't exactly got any other choice except to continue existing, or take myself out of the equation, do I?"

Vivi tugged her duffel bag and purse off the floor and tromped angrily towards the largest of the bedrooms in the penthouse. "You assholes can fight over the shit rooms. I got stuff to do."

The door slid closed by itself behind Vivi as she passed. She immediately crumpled on the floor against the wall in the darkened room that overlooked the pulsing lights of Shanghai below and closed her eyes tightly. She desperately felt the need to cry.

Vivi rubbed the side of her face and whispered in a quivering voice, "I am real..."

She squeezed her eyelids together as hard as she could, but no matter how much she desired to feel the warm flow of water streaming down her face, no tears came. She didn't have the hardware necessary to make them.

The glowing jewel of the Shanghai nighttime skyline segued into morning as the sun came over the eastern horizon. The golden glow of artificial lights hanging in the sky gave way to a jumbled view of buildings haphazardly placed in claustrophobic proximity. Electrical lines snaked in and out of buildings, too many to be counted. The city's nightlife died and gave way to the birth of morning activities. In a former life, Vivi would have loved to have taken a picture.

Vivi watched the night sky turn into morning without sleep, without blinking. She stared out from the bathtub of the Chiba Hotel's penthouse in a quiet stillness, only occasionally moving to take a drag from a cigarette, or to light a new one. The floor next to the tub was littered with a pile of ash and cigarette butts. The water in the tub had gone cold hours before.

"You're not my daughter. My daughter died in Novosibirsk, fighting for this country. We buried her body. But because of **you,** *we didn't even get her Army stipend."*

"I'm here. I am! Please! Please, just look at me."

"I don't know what you are, but you're not her. My Viviana is dead, and you're not real."

A guttural roar. ***"I DID EVERYTHING YOU ASKED!"***

The door closed quietly.

A pathetic whimper. Shallow breaths.

"I did everything you asked..."

The door to the bathroom chimed.

Vivi breathed in heavily. "Go away."

"It's Enrique. The drones are rigged to go. I got the stuff you wanted, and your effects for the job. Meeting's in two hours."

Vivi opened the door remotely and turned to watch Enrique enter, but made no move to cover herself. Her expression was blank and serious. "You get a good look?"

Enrique immediately averted his eyes and turned to place an opaque plastic package on the counter along with a pistol that had a silencer attached, a bottle of Siliclose, and a scalpel.

"Look, chica, about last night, the kid feels awful. He was drunk. I shouldn't have—"

A calm but stern command interrupted, "Get out."

Enrique nodded and turned to leave. "I'm sorry too."

After the door closed behind Enrique, Vivi extinguished her cigarette and climbed out of the tub, dripping cold water in a puddle on the floor. She approached the counter and picked up the gun, studying it for a time before she began the process of dismantling it piece by piece.

She held up the scalpel and brought it to the inside of her forearm, and began to make a long shallow incision...

Chapter Sixteen

The Job

Vivi slung her purse underneath her arm and walked with a deliberate step towards the Chiba Hotel penthouse's elevator. She pressed the elevator's call button and waited for the lift to make the slow climb to the 80th floor. After a time, an electronic tone sounded loudly as the lift announced its arrival.

She stepped into the elevator alone, turned around and reached out to select the ground level button before stepping backwards toward the rear of the elevator car. The doors began to close at a snail's pace. Grass grew with more urgency. After a small eternity, just before the doors could meet together in the middle, a hand reached through, stopping them. The doors slid back open with an upsetting quickness. Tomas walked into the elevator without realizing Vivi was there. Their eyes met for the briefest of moments before Tomas looked away and turned to face the doors which began the arduous process of closing again.

An awkward silence.

With the doors finally shut, the elevator hung there for a time before it finally decided to start the descent to the ground floor at a pace that was far too slow for Vivi. She folded her arms, leaning on the back wall of the elevator giving off a miasma of animosity.

77, 76, 75...

"Vivi, I didn't mean to —"

"Don't. Please, just don't."

65, 64, 63...

55, 54, 53...

"I know I said some-"

"Please. For once. Stop talking. I just want to do this job, and then I never have to see you again."

Tomas nodded.

47, 46, 45...

33, 32, 31...

21, 19, 18 ...

3, 2, 1, DING!

"You're a shit drunk by the way."

Vivi walked out of the elevator past Tomas into the lobby, while tugging up her medical mask to cover her face. Tomas gave Vivi a wide berth as he exited the elevator and followed her through the lobby.

From inside the lobby Vivi could see Enrique standing beside a black sedan underneath the hotel's grand awning, looking every bit the part of professional security in his 3-piece suit and sunglasses.

Vivi walked confidently through the sliding glass doors ready for boardroom business action, a far cry from the flak jacket and fatigues ensemble she sported the previous morning. She was fashionably appointed in a light striped gray and black dress with a high neckline. The dress was cinched at her waist with a sash made of the same material. It featured airy sleeves that were rolled up to Vivi's elbows and buttoned in place to the upper sleeve; the bottom of the dress ended just above Vivi's knees, providing only the slightest hint of thigh. Her feet were strapped into open-toed black high heels she placed carefully on each of the hotel's four stairs down towards the opened door at the back of the car. Vivi reached into her purse and tugged out a pair of sunglasses, placing them over her eyes.

She nodded at Enrique. "Carlos."

Enrique nodded back and helped her into the rear seat of the black sedan. "Ms. Santiago."

Tomas was quick to follow, also dressed for business. Vivi hated to admit it, but in the current moment, Javier Luna's balding hair pattern did little to diminish Tomas's good looks as it sat atop his head. He exited the hotel in a blue suit with a white shirt and purple tie combo. Silver-rimmed aviator glasses hung off his nose and embossed brown leather shoes covered his feet. He carried a leather briefcase in his left hand.

"Mr. Luna."

Tomas slid into the back of the sedan. "Mr. Pastor."

Enrique shut the door behind Tomas and climbed into the driver's seat, starting the car's electric engines. "Where to?"

Vivi looked out the driver's side window in silence. Tomas looked in the other direction, just as quiet. Without hearing an answer, Enrique lightly tapped the accelerator and urged the car forward. He spoke to the navnet system, "Long Qi building." The car began to drive itself.

The sky in Shanghai was hard to see from street level. The city's buildings shot up far into the air with cables crisscrossing in all directions between them. There didn't seem to be a bare surface on any building in the city that wasn't covered with a large sign written in Mandarin characters that Vivi couldn't read.

The deeper the car drove into Shanghai's business district, the more Vivi's HUD was attacked with all manner of digital ads for everything from facial cleansers to body massages to laser hair removal to eating dinner at Wong's. The number of egregious ads made it almost impossible to pay attention long enough to read a single one.

Vivi's phone app sounded off in her HUD. She almost missed it in between all the ads. She answered the call. It was Fincher. "Hope everyone had a good night's rest because we're live. Commencing the mission and initiating neural sync."

Bernice appeared in Vivi's HUD. "Good morning, mum!"

"Morning, Bernice. Hey, can you do anything about all these ads I'm seeing?"

"Yes, mum! Applying Ad Blocker! Ad Blocker applied!"

The ads paired back by ninety percent and became marginally tolerable.

Fincher spoke up over the line, "Alright, Velasquez, hand off the drone signal to me through Rodriguez so I can fire them up."

"Done. They're yours."

"I see them. Bringing the drones online. Passing the data on. Everyone should see them in their HUD now."

In Vivi's HUD, a frame appeared with the status of each drone.

```
Drone 08: 5% CPU Usage, 100% Battery
Drone 07: 13% CPU Usage, 99% Battery <*>
Drone 06: 7% CPU Usage, 100% Battery
Drone 05: 2% CPU Usage, 100% Battery
Drone 04: 84% CPU Usage, 98% Battery
Drone 03: 27% CPU Usage, 97% Battery
Drone 02: 7% CPU Usage, 100% Battery
Drone 01: 11% CPU Usage, 100% Battery
```

"Finch, some of these CPU levels look a little out of line. We haven't even started the Deep Fake yet."

"I see it. That's normal. Don't worry, I'm in the process of arranging them into formation and cloaking them from view. Once I have them into position, though, I'll need you to load balance the CPUs, so we don't end up with asymmetrical battery loss. Don't forget. These drones don't come cheap. Seven of these things need to come home with us."

"Noted. Important question: which one's got our bomb?"

"The one with the asterisk next to it. Lucky number 07."

The car turned down a wide avenue that, unlike every other street in Shanghai, contained a widely visible swathe of sky. The air was gray with clouds that seemed to hang just above the tops of the buildings on either side of the street. The sight lines drew the eye to the largest structure in the city, the Long Qi building.

At 100 stories tall, the Long Qi building wasn't the tallest structure in Shanghai, but it was the largest overall in sheer mass, as the building was as wide as three normal sized skyscrapers at the bottom. It tapered up slightly towards the top, seeming to point to the heavens in an imposing manner. The structure was the last building on the street, overlooking the Huangpu River.

Tomas lowered his glasses for a better look. "Jesus! Look at the size of that thing."

Fincher came over the line. "Yeah! Now you see why we need 8 drones to maintain a functional neural sync network running through it. Alright, you can drop the masks. Starting up the Deep Fake now."

Bernice piped up in her cheeriest voice. "Applying Deep Fake Algorithm! Deep Fake applied! You look marvelous."

Vivi tugged off her mask and sunglasses. She turned the glasses around and took a brief look at her reflection in the mirrored surface. Domenica Santiago looked back. To her right, the young, twenty-something Tomas Holt was replaced by the elder Javier Luna. Up the street, thousands of copies of Bernice perched themselves next to any persons or cameras that looked towards the car.

Vivi watched the drone array's CPU spike up to 40% across the board. "Bernice, can you show me what these cameras are reading on us?"

"Yes, mum!"

A screenshot of their car driving down the street appeared to Vivi in her HUD. Status frames were drawn next to each of the passengers of the car.

Carlos Pastor		Domenica Santiago		Javier Luna	
Age:	46	Age:	25	Age:	57
Weight:	84 kg	Weight:	62 kg	Weight:	90 kg
Sex:	Male	Sex:	Female	Sex:	Male
Nationality:	Mexico	Nationality:	Mexico	Nationality:	Mexico
Employer:	ArcStar Security	Employer:	Presidio Biologica	Employer:	Presidio Biologica
Heart Rate:	50 bpm	Heart Rate:	10 bpm	Heart Rate:	122 bpm

"Bernice, you're going to want to spoof my heart rate up a bit. Artificial hearts don't beat very fast."

"Very well, mum."

Vivi turned to Tomas. She didn't need the security camera screenshot to know his heart was beating through his chest. "You nervous?"

Tomas nodded. "Let's just say I'm not used to engaging enemy targets at close range. Not with public speaking anyway."

"What happened to it being just standing there and looking pretty?"

"Yeah, I might have said that before I knew how much small talk I'd need to make about increasing yields on cloned heart valves and quarterly profits." Tomas turned to look out the window opposite from Vivi.

Vivi looked at the back of Tomas's head for an extended moment. She sighed, thinking back to the awkward elevator ride they recently shared, and bit her lip. *Dammit!*

Vivi leaned over and reached out, putting a hand on Tomas's shoulder. "Hey, if there's anyone in this car that can small talk someone to death on any subject, it's you. Trust me."

Tomas turned back. "Thanks?"

Vivi closed her eyes and nodded. "I meant that in the nicest way possible." She looked into Tomas's eyes. "When in doubt, ask a lot of questions. You'll be fine."

"I hope you're right."

The car pulled in front of the Long Qi building and came to a halt. "This is your stop. I'll be parked in the garage until just before the bomb's set off." Enrique pointed to a location up the street. "I'll pick you up right over there, by the river. It's a good spot for a quick exit. Good luck."

Vivi and Tomas both nodded at Enrique in unison and exited the vehicle. They walked side by side towards the entrance to the massive lobby that teamed with people. "Here we go."

Tiny Bernices appeared everywhere in Vivi's HUD. The effect was almost as intrusive as the digital ads from earlier. There were so many eyes and cameras in the lobby, with people crisscrossing in every direction to a number of elevator banks, that it made it hard for Vivi to actually make out what the lobby looked like. The drone processor array was spiking to the 90% red zone range. The batteries were starting to drop one percentage point every few seconds. Vivi offloaded some of the processor cycles onto her internal array to try to ease the burden, but she knew they couldn't keep up this pace.

"Bernice, how far out are you running the algorithm?"

"A hundred and twenty feet in a 180-degree cone, mum."

"Way too far! No one's making our faces out at that distance. Pull it back. Say forty feet."

"Yes, mum."

With the changes applied, less of Bernice appeared in Vivi's HUD. The processor load dropped down to a more manageable 70%.

"We need to get out of this lobby ASAP, or the drones are going to be dropping out of the sky mid meeting."

Fincher came over the neural sync. "Pass through the security checkpoint and take the stairs to the mezzanine. There's an elevator bank to the Ministry of Health there with less cameras and people."

Tomas and Vivi approached a security checkpoint consisting of a metal detector with a separate x-ray scanner for personal belongings. Vivi pulled from her purse a refillable water bottle that contained a cylindrical, black, metal rod in the middle. She set the water bottle on the x-ray machine next to her purse and approached the metal detector.

Tomas spoke over the neural sync. "I see the suppressor in the water bottle. How're you getting the rest of the gun through security?"

Vivi shook her head. "Don't ask."

The guard waved Vivi through the metal detector. It went off with a loud buzz.

"Bernice!"

"Sorry mum. Did you want me to spoof the metal detector?"

"Yes...yes I did!"

Vivi stepped back through, smiling at the guard. "Just my earrings, probably." She removed her earrings and set them in a tray to pass through the x-ray machine. She moved to go through the metal detector a second time, Bernice piped up this time. "Breaching metal detector! Metal detector breached! You are now 100% metal free!" As Bernice performed the breach, Vivi noticed Drone 01's CPU momentarily spike, and its battery drop 3% for the breach effort. A costly expenditure of precious resources.

Vivi retrieved her purse, earrings and water bottle and joined Tomas, the pair heading to the mezzanine. With far fewer eyes on them when they arrived at the elevator, the overall drone array's CPU usage had dropped to just 30%. The batteries, on the other hand, were worse for wear, down to 70% remaining. Getting through the lobby had proved to be an expensive endeavor.

Tomas reached out and pressed the elevator call button. When it arrived, the two stepped in together and selected the 43rd floor.

After a much quicker ride than at the Chiba Hotel, the elevator stopped on the 43rd floor and the doors opened. Tomas stepped out first. "Showtime."

Vivi followed. "Break a leg."

China's Ministry of Health office was directly outside the elevator, behind glass doors. A large desk with a receptionist sat at the far end of the room with six chairs on either side. A tiny Bernice sat next to the receptionist's eyes.

"Mr. Luna! Please, this way. They're already in the boardroom."

Tomas nodded. "Thank you."

As Tomas and Vivi were escorted down a hallway that made several twists and turns, Vivi took mental notes of the lay of the land so she could navigate it later. At the far end of the hall, sat the stairwell door she would need to use to ascend to the 47th floor. In front of it was the women's restroom. Nearest to the lobby, however, was an all-glass board room. Vivi could see five men and one woman were already in the room, seated around a long table. Each of them had a tiny Bernice next to their head.

The party in the room stood as the receptionist held the door open for Tomas and Vivi, leading them in.

Fincher came over the line. "That's Jimmy Chen at the head of the table. Luna and him go back a ways."

Tomas smiled towards Chen in greeting. "Xiānshēng nǐ hǎo. Chén, hǎojiǔ bùjiàn!"

Chen looked shocked and laughed, "Javier? All these years and you finally decided to learn some Chinese?"

Tomas laughed nervously in return before recovering. "Wanted to start the meeting off on a positive foot and show you that, like our products at Presidio Biologica, we're always striving for improvement."

Chen shook his head. "As usual, so fast to get to business. Please sit. Have a drink and a toast with us. A glass of Baijiu before the boring task of numbers and earnings. For luck."

Tomas smiled and nodded while reporting, "Oh great, more alcohol," through the neural sync.

Chen began busily pouring a colorless liquid into 7 crystal tumblers, dispensing them to the participants around the table.

Vivi panicked. "Finch! I can't drink! There's no place for the liquid to go. I don't have a stomach!"

"I know. When he offers you the glass, decline. Tell him you're pregnant."

"WHAT?"

"This is why we had a table read for the meeting. Just do it. Trust me."

Vivi gritted her teeth before forcing a smile. "Mr. Chen. Sorry. I must apologize. I can't participate in the toast this time because, well... I'm expecting."

Chen looked pleasantly shocked and looked back and forth between Tomas and Vivi questioningly. "You and eh? Eh?"

Vivi quickly shook her head. "Ah, no."

Tomas, looking like a deer in headlights, also shook his head in the negative.

"Ha! Probably for the best! Well, this is great news! We can toast to that as well!"

Glasses in hand, the party toasted to Santiago's impending child and luck for the meeting.

In retrospect, Vivi decided it was for the best that she skipped the table read for Shanghai. The meeting was boring and her only real job was to sit and scroll through forms on the room's presentation tablet while Tomas mapped out the plans for Presidio Biologica's new production facilities, which would apparently reduce costs while boosting profits. For what it was worth, Tomas seemed like a natural public speaker. She had no idea why he was so worried earlier.

Vivi communicated over the neural sync, "You sure are selling this deal hard. It's like you want it to go through."

"Yes! This is serious! If I screw up, a lot of people back in Hermosillo could lose their jobs."

Vivi rolled her eyes.

Fifteen minutes into the presentation, Fincher came over the line. "Okay, Rodriguez, this is a good spot. Act like you're in discomfort and excuse yourself."

As Tomas spoke about the most recent quarterly earnings, Vivi clutched her stomach and brought her hand up to her mouth, feigning morning sickness. She raised a hand, interrupting him. "Mmm. Excuse me. Where is the restroom?"

Chen responded with an air of concern. "Are you okay, Ms. Santiago?"

Vivi cleared her throat. "Yes, I'm fine, it's just—I suddenly don't feel so good."

"Understandable, please, the restroom is just down the hall."

"Thank you." Vivi picked up her purse as she made her exit from the boardroom.

Once clear of the door and out of sight, Vivi proceeded down the hallway, making note of the camera just outside the women's restroom that yet another Bernice was sitting next to. She tried to match up her sight line with where the camera pointed at the restroom door and took a screenshot, saving it for later.

She pushed the restroom's door open and picked one of the empty stalls. With the stall door closed behind her, Vivi sat on the toilet and set her purse down in her lap. She pulled out a nail file and held up her left forearm in front of her, staring at it for a time.

Vivi jabbed the point of the nail file into her skin and used the sharpened edge to make a thin incision in her forearm. She pulled the skin back gently so as not to tear it and reached her thumb and index finger into the wound in between the nanoweave muscle fibers and pulled out a firing pin, then a trigger, and then the top slide of a small handgun.

Vivi set down the extracted gun parts on the toilet's tank one by one and tugged down her dress's sleeve to cover the incision in her forearm. "Three down, six to go."

Several careful incisions later, the other constituent pieces of the gun were fully extracted from various hiding places across Vivi's body. She assembled the gun into a functional state, tested the slide, and racked a round into the chamber.

Vivi pulled up the water bottle from her purse and dumped the liquid contents into the toilet. She turned and tugged out the metal cylinder attached to the center of the bottle. To anyone looking at the barrel suppressor when it was in the water bottle, they might have assumed it was a water bottle cooler, but its purpose wasn't for cooling water, it was for reducing the acoustic intensity of gunfire. Vivi rotated the cylinder onto the end of the gun, completing the assembly. She slid the fully constructed firearm into her purse.

Vivi reached up to her neck with her index finger and pressed in. Domenica Santiago's ID chit popped out. Vivi tugged the ID chit out the rest of the way and left it on the toilet's tank in the stall. Building security performing NFC scans would have seen Domenica Santiago still in the restroom.

"Okay Bernice, I'm about to exit the restroom, I need you to use the screenshot I took of the door to make me disappear."

"Yes, mum. Applying Deep Cloak! Deep Cloak applied!"

Now invisible to the camera facing the restroom, Vivi opened the door and exited. She called over the neural sync. "I'm proceeding to the stairwell."

"Roger that. We're on schedule. Drone formation holding steady, 60% battery remaining on average."

Chapter Seventeen

Air Gapped

A stairwell not unlike any other stairwell in any countless number of buildings. Nothing stood out about it other than the floor signage appearing in Mandarin and each door being locked down by heavy electronic protocol.

Vivi climbed the stairs at a quick pace, aiming her silenced handgun around each corner in case someone was there. But on her ascent up from the 43rd floor, she encountered nothing but stairs, doors, and floor signs. At the 47th floor door, Vivi stopped. "Okay Bernice, do your thing."

A tiny Bernice appeared next to the door lock. "Breaching door lock! Door lock breached! Access granted!"

Vivi slowly turned the handle and gently opened the door; she snaked into the room with her pistol drawn. Once she was sure no one was nearby, she turned and gently closed the door behind her.

Vivi took two steps forward and immediately came to a halt as her high heels reported audibly on the floor. Thankfully, the sound was almost completely drowned out by the loud beehive-like humming of what appeared to be thousands upon thousands of server racks. The rows of them appeared endless in the cavernous expanse. *Is this the central processing hub for the whole building?*

Vivi removed her heels, letting her bare feet touch the raised floor that likely concealed the wires connecting all the server towers together.

She accessed her Ping Network Protocol node, attempting to scan the network surrounding her. She looked up and around, but nothing in close proximity lit up. None of the computers in the expansive space were linked to anything outside the cavernous room outernet or otherwise. The entire server farm was air gapped. A completely closed system separate from anything else in the building.

Vivi noticed Tomas and Enrique's signals cut off as she entered deeper into the room. "Finch, I just lost Tomas and Enrique in my comms."

"Don't worry about it. There's a lot of interference in there with all the equipment. We're having to boost the signal on one of the drones nearest you to maintain a link at all. Proceed to retrieving the asset."

Heavy footsteps could be heard around the corner, nearing her position. "Bernice, gimme a visual on where that's coming from."

Superimposed on her HUD, red accent points flicked to life where Bernice had calculated the approximate position of the footsteps.

Vivi took position and aimed. The footsteps turned the corner. Out stepped a man in a lab coat, four feet in front of Vivi, paying attention to a tablet in his hands. Vivi pulled the trigger.

The man flinched as a dart lodged in his neck. His knees went slack in an instant. Vivi quickly stepped over and caught the man around the armpits before he had a chance to collapse and cause a commotion. She slowly helped him to the ground, quiet as possible.

Vivi pulled the slide back on her tranquilizer pistol, racking another round. "Finch? I just tranqed a scientist lookin' type. Hope this isn't our asset, cause walking out with him's gonna be real hard in this state."

"That's not the asset."

"Well, now might be a really good time to tell me what they look like, so I don't accidentally put their lights out."

"The asset is a woman."

Vivi grumbled, "Any other defining features you feel like sharing?"

"You'll know her when you see her. Just don't kill anyone. An alarm will sound if any of the workers in this area flat line."

"What is this place?"

"A prison."

Vivi scanned the area. Bernice drew two more areas in her HUD where she detected movement. Vivi moved toward the closet one, angling around the bank of servers to get the drop behind the person. The woman's shoes sounded loudly on the floor as she walked down the row of server racks. "Finch, there's a woman directly in front of me, approximately 5'2", white lab coat—"

"Not her."

Vivi unloaded a tranquilizer round in the woman's back. The woman collapsed to the ground before Vivi could catch her and landed with a loud thump. A man's voice called out, "Měilíng? Nǐhái hǎo ma?"

Shit! Vivi turned and moved around a row of servers, but it was in the wrong direction. Loud footsteps approached from her left, and the man attached to the voice was staring right at Vivi in shock.

Before the man could utter a single syllable, Vivi grabbed him by the back of the hair and smashed his face into the server rack next to him, knocking him unconscious. When the man crumpled to the floor, she pulled back the slide on the gun and put a tranquilizer round in his neck for good measure.

"Finch, this is getting tedious. Where's our asset?"

"Try the center of the room."

Vivi moved with a determined quickness towards the center of the server room. As she approached, she heard two voices talking loudly, both male. She peeked out from behind a server rack. One of the men wore a lab coat like the others and was sitting at a console of some kind, the other was a guard with a machine gun slung under his right arm.

"Finch. There's a guard with a gun. He's full borg. This tranq gun isn't gonna do shit."

"Leave him to 01."

"You heard him, Bernice."

Vivi watched in her HUD as Bernice made an ad hoc connection through her to the guard. "Breaching! Applying precision overflow! Precision overflow applied! Precision overflow applied! Precision overflow applied!"

Outside the building, Drone 07's temperature spiked and lost 15% of its battery as Bernice used it to perform a staggering number of breach attacks. The guard's body tensed unnaturally, all the muscle fibers in his body looked to be flexing at their limits, causing him to twitch violently before collapsing unconscious to the floor. "Tango down!" Bernice reported, cheerfully.

The scientist next to the guard bent over in concern. "Wei?"

Vivi took the opportunity to step out and tranquilize the other man. He instantly collapsed next to the guard.

"Well, I'm in the center of the room, Finch. There's no one here but me and some unconscious communists."

"She's right there next to you."

"Finch, there's no one here, just an AI dais in the center of the room."

Vivi suddenly felt another presence in the room to her left. No footsteps heralded the newcomer's arrival. Vivi lifted her gun and turned.

Black suit. White shirt. White tie. Black wingtip dress shoes. Face like tree bark. Hair neatly combed. Faust stood in front of Vivi.

Vivi lowered her gun. "Faust? The fuck? How're you-"

"I thought you might get cold feet for this next part, so I came to ensure you stick to the script."

"What're you talking about?"

Faust motioned to the AI dais. "You need to retrieve the asset. There's a neural wire there."

"You fucking liar! You brought me all the way here to side load a goddamn Chinese AI?" Vivi motioned to the endless rows of server racks around the room. "What, you think I can bring all this data back with me too? You think my hardware can hold *all* this? News flash: it can't."

Faust smiled. "She's not Chinese. And no, I don't need the data farm. I just want the core."

"This wasn't the deal! What else you been lyin' about? The money?" Vivi shook her head. "Tell me the money's real."

Faust held out his hands and talked in a reassuring tone. "Calm down, Ms. Rodriguez. Please. Nothing's changed. You're still just going to walk right out of here with the asset and your money."

Vivi sighed. "Fine." She walked over to the console next to the unconscious bodies on the floor and picked up the neural wire. She slowly brought the wire to her neck but stopped short of inserting it as the server towers that loomed large above her caught her attention.

Vivi breathed in deeply. "Something's not right here. No AI core is worth the price your payin'."

Faust smiled, "Let's be honest, would you have agreed to come to China for less?"

Vivi shook her head. "Probably not. No... still doesn't explain this server farm, though. Why's it air gapped? What aren't you telling me?"

"Don't ask questions you don't want the answers to, Ms. Rodriguez."

Vivi pulled the gun back up, aiming at Faust's face. "Tell me what else I don't know or I'm not doin' shit."

Faust chuckled. "You're going to shoot me with a tranquilizer gun? Do you really think making me take a nap will change the status quo?"

"You think keepin' me in the dark is gonna make me do what you want?"

"You won't like what I have to say. I promise."

Vivi bared her teeth. "Start talking, or I walk."

Faust sighed. "As you wish. That's not an AI in the dais. AI is rudimentary. Limited. The asset is different. She's a free-thinking consciousness not governed by the rules or limits of humanity. A veritable god in a bottle. Or as you're more likely to have heard her kind referred to as: a *Sentient Daemon*."

Vivi dropped the neural wire and cocked the gun, holding it with both hands pointed at Faust. She shook her head. "No. No no no. Those don't exist anymore. We deleted them! *All of them!* Long before I was born!"

Faust chuckled. "Ms. Rodriguez, I could fill a server room ten times this size with all the things you don't know. But it matters not. This is the job I brought you here to do. To retrieve the asset."

"That's why those assholes tried to stop us in Hermosillo, isn't it? They knew what was in here and they knew you planned to free it, didn't they?"

"Exactly. And they would have thought themselves correct in doing so. After all, a Sentient Daemon did attempt and fail to wipe out your entire species with a weaponized form of leprosy some fifty years ago. But not this one. She's different."

"Fuck you!" Vivi turned and pointed at the dais. "The laws of AI were invented because of these things! I'm stuck in this soulless husk because of them! China has this thing air gapped in here for a reason! So, it *can't* get out!"

Faust sighed and pulled a gun from inside his coat, aiming it at Vivi. "We don't have time for this, Ms. Rodriguez, and my patience is thinning."

Faust took three steps toward the dais that were completely silent in his wing-tipped shoes. With his free hand, he pointed toward the neural wire attached to the AI dais's console. "Please connect to the interface. I'll have Mr. Fincher take care of the rest."

Vivi tilted her head, looking perplexed. "You're not here..."

"Ms. Rodriguez? I'm standing right in front of you."

Vivi tossed her gun at Faust. Faust's form flickered with distortion as the gun sailed right through him and landed on the floor with an audible clunk.

Faust stopped in mid-motion as if someone pressed 'pause' on a TV remote. His outline began to flicker with digital static as Fincher stepped out from inside Faust. "Damn. What gave it away? Was it the lighting?"

Ridley Fincher, dressed in his horn-rimmed glasses, button-down shirt and tech slacks, ignored Vivi as he walked around the paused Faust, inspecting him. "Properly lighting your characters in a scene is *so* important to their believability. You know, that's why I always tried to make sure to only have Faust appear in darkly lit spaces. Really helps sell the whole shadowy authority figure vibe I was going for when I created him."

Vivi looked bewildered, unsure of what was happening, and shook her head. "It's the floor. It's loud. His shoes didn't make any sound."

Fincher snapped his fingers. "Ahh! I should have known! Your body's hearing API is stupid complicated, and it's never worked quite to spec on any of the Somatech MK5's. You know, they corrected it with the MK6's? Problem is they also decided to deprecate the quantum processing core right out of the MK6 design. Between you and me, the Army hasn't sent a cyborg into battle loaded up with AI in years, so they were just wasting money with the parts to house one. Unfortunately, though, like AI, you can't side load a Sentient Daemon without a QPU, so it just *had* to be an older model, like a MK5."

"I have no idea what's happening here, but I'm leaving." Vivi turned to leave.

Fincher disappeared and popped back into existence in front of Vivi's path. "Do you know how hard it was to find a suitable Somatech MK5 with a functional quantum processing core, capable of passing as Santiago, and not currently commissioned in the field?"

Vivi walked right through Fincher. "I don't give a fuck."

Fincher again appeared in Vivi's path. "Only four in the entire United States. Know why I picked you?"

Vivi passed through Fincher again on the way to the exit. "Don't care."

Fincher appeared in front of Vivi a third time, this time holding open a manila envelope containing important looking paperwork. "What's the psych eval say? Let's see. Hmm. Severe psychological trauma. Constantly feels the need to challenge authority. Substance abuse issues. Easily manipulated via perceived monetary gain. Blah blah blah. Ooo! Here we go, unmitigated fear of dyspnea."

Vivi stopped in her tracks as she felt her chest suddenly seize up and her breathing cease. Fincher had somehow placed a semaphore lock on her lungs' subsystem without even raising her HUD's breach alarm. She clutched at her chest as breathing became an impossibility.

Fincher sat on the ground cross-legged in front of Vivi with his fists under his chin, his eyes obscured by the glare on the lenses of his horn-rim glasses, his voice playful and sinister, "Vivi? Do you know what dyspnea means? It's one of those fancy Latin words, and I always have trouble with those."

Vivi fell to the ground at Fincher's eye level on her hands and knees, as her face was pulled into a strained expression.

"Gosh, you don't seem very talkative all of a sudden." His voice feigning concern.

Vivi was transported back to the battlefield of Novosibirsk, writhing on the operating gurney, choking on blood. Her lungs, a furnace in her chest as the Leprae-IX infection ate away at them. Gasping for air. Unable to breathe. Darkness was caving in on her vision from all sides. She desperately tried to scream, but no sound came out.

In the present, she collapsed on the floor of the cavernous server room. Vivi's purse fell off of her arm, its contents spilling out.

Fincher stood from his seated position and began to pace around Vivi. As he took step after step he looked so different to Vivi than he had before. There was an air of confidence surrounding him that hadn't existed previously. He leaned over to her. "Are you ready to connect to the console now?"

Vivi nodded her head in fast agreement.

Fincher smiled. "Good!"

Instantly, Vivi was able to breathe again. She desperately gasped for air. Once back in control of her breathing, Vivi gritted her teeth and encrypted the semaphore lock to her lung functionality closed to herself.

"Really?" Fincher looked bemused. "Watch this." He snapped his fingers.

In her HUD, Vivi watched Drone 05 briefly spike in heat and drop only 1% in battery. Her encrypted semaphore was blown open in picoseconds. Fincher locked off her breathing a second time.

Vivi dropped back to her knees, clutching at her throat while looking up at Fincher in desperation.

"I could do this all day, Rodriguez. There's plenty of battery in all eight drones to blow open your meager encryption attempts, but I really don't have the time. Are you ready to get back to the script?"

Vivi nodded a second time. Her breathing was returned to her as she gasped for air again.

"Great!" Fincher pointed back to the AI dais's console and furrowed his brow. "Neural wire. Now!"

Vivi slowly picked herself off the floor and walked back towards the console. She lifted the neural wire from the dais and slotted it into her neural port, glaring at Fincher as she did.

"No need to look so glum, Rodriguez. This won't hurt at all. I promise. Unlocking your quantum core now."

Realizing Fincher was about to unlock another of her body's features, Vivi readied her packet sniffer, awaiting the influx of raw code that would contain the encryption key that could allow her to unlock her prosthetic body's full feature set and maybe fight back. She watched Drone 08's CPU spike to redline; its battery dropped from 55% to 5% in an instant.

In her HUD, Vivi could see the QPU node unlock. As the node became available, she started a timer for sixty seconds and opened her packet sniffer, but something was wrong: her outernet connection was silent. No encryption key had come through.

How did Fincher unlock the node? She reran the scan again. Nothing. The last outernet logs she saw were from the ads that plagued her in the drive through Shanghai.

A progress bar started in Vivi's HUD as the Sentient Daemon's core was forcibly side loaded onto her hardware. 10%.

"You know, Rodriguez, there's just one thing I'm curious about. I spent ages keeping tabs on you. But there's gaps I haven't been able to account for."

"Oh yeah?"

Fifty-five seconds left till the encryption key would change. Meanwhile, the progress bar on the Daemon transfer had crept up to 15%.

Fincher paced around her, hands behind his back. "You asked Velasquez for something. What was it?"

"No idea what you're talkin' about."

Vivi checked her outernet connection again. Still nothing, only fifty seconds left to find the encryption key, but there wasn't any data to sift through. The Daemon's progress bar bumped up to 18%.

"Then let me refresh your memory. On the fifth floor of the Hidalgo, outside of Santiago's room. You asked Velasquez to get you something, discreetly. What?"

"Why don't you ask Enrique?"

Fincher leaned in toward her, smiling. "It's not the Absolute Zero rig you're wearing. He was much sloppier covering his tracks for that request. He didn't place the order for that until right before China. A rush job. That, and I saw you put it on this morning after your little soak in the tub. But as to the first request. Still no idea."

"You didn't see shit! We didn't run the neural sync this morning till after we left the hotel!"

"And yet I know you're wearing it under your dress. Funny thing about the Somatech MK5, its outernet modem is a fortress even in civilian mode. Nearly impenetrable. Certainly not in the bandwidth required for spoofing optics. But the ad hoc antenna? Leaky as a sieve."

Ad hoc! Vivi switched the packet sniffer to her local ad hoc connections. The data stream looked nearly endless, and she only had thirty-five seconds to find and parse out the encryption key from an enormous stack of data before the key changed again. The progress bar on the Deamon's data transfer was already up to 22%. In her HUD, Vivi scrolled backwards through her ad hoc connection history, but it was difficult. Every time Fincher said something or moved, a massive new chunk of data was dumped on top.

"How!?"

"How what?"

"How're you ad hoc'd to me! You're not even here!"

"Rodriguez, I've been ad hoc'd to you since the moment we first met, when I offered you this job."

When I was offered the job? Vivi turned and looked over to the spilled contents of her purse eight feet away on the floor. The box of Fortunes laid there, looking conspicuous. Vivi looked at them slack jawed. "When Freddy brought me the free pack of cigarettes."

Fincher smiled and clapped his hands. "You figured it out. You know, you burn through so many of those damn things, in retrospect, I should have had the mini-ad hoc transmitter and SOC embedded in a lighter, or maybe just stapled one to you."

Vivi stared at the cigarette box. If she could smash whatever antenna was in it and break the ad hoc connection with Fincher, his ability to breach her subsystems would cease. However, she wasn't doing that tethered to the AI dais's console.

Vivi lifted her right arm towards her neck to yank the neural wire from her port. Her arm locked up in mid-reach, frozen in place against her will. She reached up with her left arm. It too locked in place within an instant. She attempted to walk, but she barely managed a step forward before her legs were taken away from her as well.

Fincher smiled coldly as he leaned in close to Vivi's left ear, and whispered ever so softly, "Rodriguez. Please. This is happening."

"FUCK YOU!" Vivi roared.

She seethed with rage, but knew she needed to calm down and think. The Daemon's progress bar had reached 40%. Her only hope of severing the link with Fincher and preventing the Daemon from escaping its prison now rested in finding the encryption key and unlocking nodes in her HUD to defend herself. 10 seconds left to find it.

Vivi desperately scrolled through the ad hoc data log, but all the data looked uniform. Nothing stood out and more data was continually being dumped on top.

Wait! She thought to herself. *Fincher already unlocked two of my nodes in the last few days. The encryption keys for those probably look similar. If I sort the entire data set by type, they might end up grouped together. The old keys would be worthless, but they'd appear next to the new one!*

Vivi directed her processor array to sort the data stream by type; it chewed through the data, slowly organizing the endless mass into neat, hierarchical data types. Five seconds left. The list was sorted in ascending order by count. Three records appeared right at the top that looked to be streams of gibberish. The most recent one, from less than 60 seconds ago.

This was it! The encryption key! She had found it!

Vivi hastily cut the key out of the ad hoc data log and applied it to the Encryption Protocol lock. Only three seconds to pick from nodes to unlock. The staggering number of choices available made it hard to choose, but it was time enough to select at least three. She hastily began picking.

"So, are you going to tell me what you asked Enrique for or not?"

Vivi whispered, "You're not going to like what I have to say. I promise."

"Try me."

Vivi curled her lips into an angry smile. "A packet sniffer, you motherfucker."

Fincher looked confused. "Huh?"

Vivi enabled her entire processor array and ONI Protocol node. She intended to unlock her IDP defense protocols, but somehow landed on Combat Sync, which was hardly useful for the current situation, but it didn't matter. She finally had some tools to fight back.

Her first order of business, limit Fincher's local processing power. She spun up her formerly dormant processor cores 65 through 128 and threw them simultaneously at the drones with coordinated precision overflow attacks. Meanwhile, she also worked on freeing her arms and legs from the semaphore locks Fincher had on them.

Fincher looked shocked as he watched his control over Drones 03, 05, and 06 lost in an instant. He reacted by shoring up his defenses on 01, 02, and 04.

As soon as it was under her control, Vivi directed all of Drone 03's processor cycles to defend her lungs. She decided she wasn't about to be suffocated by this bastard again.

Vivi and Fincher fought over Drones 07 and 08 throwing a tidal wave of numbers at them with abandon. Vivi desperately wanted Drone 07 since it had the bomb attached and was part of Fincher's overall plan, but Fincher wanted it too. Most of his remaining local resources were being spent there, so she refocused on Drone 08 and captured it instead.

"Did you really think I was going to just let you take the bomb, Rodriguez? Are you daft? I need it to get you out of the building."

"I know." Vivi pulled up the list of drones she had available to her. 08 was the most depleted in battery, down to just 3%, worth the sacrifice. She connected to Drone 08's camera array and took remote control, spinning it to face Drone 07.

Fincher screamed, "No wait! *Don't!*"

Vivi smiled at Fincher with contempt as she rammed Drone 08 directly into 07, smashing both of them out of the sky and crashing them down into the streets below. The signals for both drones went dark.

"You fucking child!"

"What's wrong, Finch? Was that not part of the script?"

"You can't stay in China! They will *rip her* from you and *put her* back in *here*! *In this prison*!"

Vivi shook her head. "She's not leaving this room, Finch."

She really should have thanked Fincher. In the commotion over drones, Vivi had almost forgotten about the world ending consciousness being shoved into her hardware. The progress bar on the Sentient Daemon transfer had ticked up to 90%.

Vivi's arms and legs were still locked up. Her attempts to free them had so far been futile, a waste of processor cycles. Fincher's encryption locking abilities were just too strong. But her arms weren't the only ones in the room. Vivi pinged the network and opened an ad hoc connection to the unconscious guard on the floor behind her. She quietly managed to semaphore the unconscious man's legs and eyes to her control.

Driving another person's lifeless body felt something akin to performing gymnastics while drunk. Vivi could see herself through the man's optics. She urged the lifeless body to stand while she took control of its right arm.

The unconscious guard's right arm lifted up to Vivi's neck, about to grab the neural link wire, but at the same time, his left arm shot up to stop it. Fincher had taken control of the guard's other arm.

The guard's arms wrestled with one another. Vivi used the right hand under her control to make grasping attempts at the neural wire, but every attempt was thwarted by the left hand Fincher controlled.

The progress bar on the Daemon transfer was at 98%.

"Dammit, Finch! LET GO!"

"NO!"

Wrestling with Fincher for control of the neural link wire was proving fruitless, and she was running out of time to stop the Daemon transfer.

Vivi spied the pack of Fortunes again and had a last-ditch idea. She let her guard's hand go with the momentum of Fincher's opposing hand. The guard's right arm dropped to his side, right next to the grip of the machine gun that was slung off a strap from his shoulder. Vivi remotely grabbed the gun, strained to lift it into position, hastily aimed it and held down the trigger for dear life.

As the gun erupted with the staccato drumbeat of thunderous applause, the box of Fortunes was perforated into a cloud of sparking tobacco debris.

99%

Just as the ad hoc connection between Fincher and Vivi began to die, Fincher used his last action to shove the guard's left hand into the hand holding the gun, pushing the barrel towards the AI dais's attached console. With Vivi's death grip on the trigger, the gun continued to fire. Bullets ripped through the console. Sparks flew.

"You're not leaving here without her!" Fincher yelled as he and Faust dissolved into nothing when the connection finally ceased.

Vivi regained control of her arms. She yanked the neural wire from her neck as fast as she could, but it was too late. The transfer had completed. 100%.

"No! No no no!"

Vivi looked to the AI dais's console. It was completely bullet ridden and malfunctioning. The attached touch screen was completely offline. Even if she knew how to, there was no putting the Sentient Daemon back into its cage.

The lights in the cavernous server room turned from white to an oppressive red. An alarm rang out.

A formless shape bubbled to life in front of Vivi. Slowly, the mass stretched and churned into something recognizably human. Arms. Legs. A torso. A head. Black hair. A white button-down blouse. A gray pleated skirt. A navy-blue blazer. Within moments, a teenaged girl stood in front of Vivi and bowed. She spoke in a soft, polite voice, "Ohayo gozaimasu."

"Oh fuck no."

Chapter Eighteen

The Hills are Alive

A crimson-red pulsing light timed to a blaring klaxon bathed her surroundings with disturbing shadows cast from the server towers above. Her heart, normally quite silent, thumped loudly within her chest. Her quickened breath echoed within her head as loud as the alarm that filled the air. Pure sensory overload. It froze her to the spot with anxiety. A trepidation to act somehow mixed with restlessness and fear.

Vivi's HUD lit up. Too many things demanded her attention at once. With the connection to Fincher dropped, so too had the neural sync with Tomas and Enrique. They both attempted to call her at the same time. No neural sync with Fincher also meant no Bernice, and that meant the Deep Fake was gone with her, not to mention the drone array Vivi now had to load balance manually. And on top of all that, there was the matter of the Sentient Daemon staring up at her.

The girl was shorter than Vivi, 5'1"? 5'2"? She looked young, barely fifteen. Her skin was pale and blemish free, her hair long and inky black parted to each side out of her face and tied in a long ponytail. There was a symmetry about the girl that seemed unnatural. A machine-like precision to her design. Behind her eyes was an inquisitive look that seemed to be busily working things out.

The Daemon looked up at Vivi, speaking a bunch of gibberish Vivi didn't understand, "Bosu, kore wa dono yō ni yakudachimasuka?" Whatever it was, she sounded confident about it.

Vivi held out a finger to the Daemon and opened her mouth to say something, but somehow didn't have words for the situation. Instead, she reached down and picked up the machine gun from the unconscious guard, her purse off the floor, and the tranquilizer gun. She turned and ran barefoot toward the stairwell and the exit.

The girl followed, calling after Vivi in an agitated tone, "Matte! Doko ni iku no?"

Vivi slammed through the door to the stairwell. She answered the calls from Tomas and Enrique at the same time. A mistake. They were both yelling at her simultaneously and she couldn't make out what either were saying.

"Hey! HEEEY! *One at a time!* Tomas! You first."

"I don't know what happened. I lost the connection to the neural sync. One minute I'm Luna, the next I'm me again. Quite the shock for everyone in the meeting. Barely made it out of there. Everything's crazy and some alarm is going off. The elevators and stairwell doors are locked, and without Bernice, I'm trapped on this floor. What happened? Do you have the asset?"

"Sort of. It's complicated. Sit tight, I'm comin' to get you. Enrique, whatcha got?"

"Same as the kid. I saw some of the drones crash to the street, including the one with the bomb, then the neural sync drops out, and now it looks like the Red Army is rolling up the street. I barely made it out of the parking garage before they locked the building down. What'd you do, chica?"

Vivi ran down the stairs as fast as she could while trying to explain the situation. "So how to say, 'we're fucked'? Faust isn't real, Fincher played us, he and I had a little falling out, the asset turned out to be a pint-sized destroyer of worlds, we're attached at the hip, and I'm pretty sure the building lockdown is to ensure it doesn't escape."

A simultaneous "*What?*" came through the line.

"Yeah, that was my general reaction to the situation as well."

The Daemon called out from behind Vivi in an exasperated voice, "Oi matte! Matte! Nanishiteruno?"

On the 44th floor landing, Vivi turned back and dropped her head down to eye level with the girl. "Listen! I don't speak crazy bitch! I get you're kind of a big problem, but *somehow*, I have more important things to deal with than you right this second. Okay?"

The girl furrowed her brow. "Dorehodo taegatai."

Vivi sneered. "Good talk!" She began the rest of the descent to the 43rd floor.

No longer having access to Bernice, Vivi was forced to breach the door lock to the stairwell on the 43rd floor herself, but that was fine, she had the tools to do so now. One precision overflow attack later, she was through.

On the other side of the previously locked door was a mass of people who were trying to get through, some of whom Vivi recognized from the meeting. "Shit!" She hastily connected to the group's neural linked optics and blurred her face digitally, hoping they didn't catch a good look before she managed the spoof.

Vivi pointed towards the stairs and fired the machine gun into the stairwell for effect. "Get the fuck out of here!"

The crowd screamed and dispersed through the stairwell door.

In the Ministry of Health Offices, the same alarm from the 47th floor was blaring. A message in Chinese Vivi couldn't understand was repeating over the intercom every few minutes.

"Tomas? I'm here, where you at?"

"Hiding out in the men's room."

"Well hurry it up! Meet me at the elevator. We need to get out of this building. I'm going to reestablish the neural sync."

Vivi navigated her way to the elevator from memory as she hosted a new neural sync session. Tomas, who no longer looked like Javier Luna, was already standing next to the elevator doors as she arrived.

"You're barefoot."

"Ever try to run in heels? Here!" She tossed Tomas the machine gun. "You're a better shot than me."

Tomas caught the gun, checking the magazine for the number of rounds it had left. "Shit. Only four bullets."

"Yeah. Hopefully, we won't need them."

Tomas looked up from the gun. "Who's the girl?"

"Oh? You can see her?"

"Yeah, clear as day."

Vivi turned back to the Daemon who was busily inspecting a flashing alarm light in apparent amazement. "Sugoi!"

"The 'asset'. Not a person at all. Probably not gonna believe me, but it's a Sentient Daemon. Fincher managed to forcibly side load her into my hardware. Stuck with her for the time being."

The Daemon smiled and cheerfully waved at Tomas. "Ohayo!"

"That?" Tomas raised an eyebrow, looking incredulous. "That's a Sentient Daemon?"

"Yup."

"She looks like a harmless Japanese school girl. One of those wiped out 30% of the population?"

Vivi shrugged. "Apparently."

Tomas shook his head. "Yeah, I don't see it."

The elevator chimed.

Tomas turned to the elevator door. "You breached the elevator lock already?"

Vivi turned to the elevator as well in confusion. "No. Hadn't started yet..."

As the elevator doors began to slide apart, Vivi had just enough time to make out two heavily armed soldiers in full body armor through the crack in the door before they noticed her and Tomas.

She didn't hesitate. Vivi flung her entire body into the car as soon as the doors opened wide enough, smashing the soldier on the left into the back wall as he was about to raise his gun to fire. In a second motion, she clutched the straps of his Kevlar body armor and used them as leverage to ram her metal forehead into his face, smashing his goggles and nose.

While this was playing out in the physical world, Vivi simultane-ously ad hoc'd to the second soldier and spoofed his eyes to see nothing but blackness. He staggered just long enough for Vivi to turn and grab the end of his gun, pointing it away from her. The gun began to fire into the top of the elevator. "Tomas!"

Tomas opened fire into the soldier's unprotected face. Blood sprayed onto Vivi as the soldier crumpled on the elevator floor and Vivi stumbled backward out of the elevator, falling flat on her rear.

The Daemon screamed and recoiled, turning away. "Nante bōryoku! Nante hidoi!"

Vivi began picking herself up. "I think it's a safe bet they know we're here. Shit! Don't let the doors close! We're gonna need their ammo and gloves."

Tomas reached in and grabbed the door. "Gloves?"

"We don't have Bernice! I can't do the Deep Fake, only simple optic spoofs. You know, digitally distort our faces, simulate pitch blackness, that kind of thing."

Tomas began rifling through the soldier's effects, collecting ammo. He tossed out a handgun to Vivi. "Okay? So?"

"Your hands. I don't know how to say this in a sensitive manner. How many black guys you think they got walkin' around Shanghai? We make it out of this building, they can't be looking for a black man. I can cover our faces. But your hands are another story, too many replacements per eye, so take that corpse's gloves and put 'em on. Also, ditch Luna's ID chit. They may be tracking it through NFC scans of the building."

"Okay then. Gloves. Got it." Tomas tugged out Javier Luna's ID chit and dropped it on the ground.

"Enrique, what's the situation on the bottom floor look like?"

"Real bad, kid. They have armored personnel carriers moving up the street. The lobby is completely locked down. They're taking people out in handcuffs."

Vivi cursed under her breath, "Shit. We're not going down this way."

Tomas looked concerned. "What other way is there? Stairs?"

"No. Those just go down to the lobby too. Hmm."

"So what? We just sit here and wait for them to find us? We don't exactly have an aero car to pick us up off the top of this thing."

"Aero car?" Vivi began to formulate a dumb idea. "Tomas, you ever ziplined?"

"In basic training. Why?"

"We're gonna do something kinda like that... let's move. There's bound to be more of these assholes comin' after us when these two don't check in."

Vivi and Tomas moved through the maze-like corridors of the Ministry of Health Office in the center of the Long Qi building at a quick pace. Vivi used the drone's proximity signal as a guide for where the edge of the building lay. Every camera Vivi came into range with she made sure to breach and spoof it, digitally smearing their faces before it could get a clear look at them.

"God damn, how wide is this fuckin' building? Still about two hundred yards to go."

Suddenly, Vivi's breach alarm went off in her HUD. Some twenty targets entered her ad hoc range. At the same time, gunfire erupted from in front of their position. Tomas and Vivi threw themselves to the floor and took cover behind desks as paper and office furniture were perforated by gunfire.

"Fuck!" Vivi checked on the drone array. Most of the six available to her were down to 5% battery and she could only spare three of them for her plan to work. She'd have to rely on her own processor array for offense and defense. Luckily, most of the attacks against her sub systems were feeble at best. Most likely from untrained grunt soldiers, not anyone equipped with an actual ONI rig or proper training, but with the sheer quantity of the breach attempts, she knew she'd start to overheat eventually if she and Tomas remained pinned down while her hardware was still hosting the Daemon.

Unlike Hermosillo though, this time she came prepared for a digital fight.

Vivi reached into her dress and pulled the tab on the Absolute Zero Rig. Two chemicals within the vest wrapped around her torso began to mix, creating an intense endothermic reaction. She exhaled frosty air thinking to herself, *God Mode Engage.*

Vivi peeked out beside the desk she was huddled behind, spotting security cameras up in the distance. She quickly breached them and took control, surveying the battlefield ahead.

"Hey Tomas, you wanted to know what combat sync felt like, right? You're gonna get your chance!"

Tomas yelled back over the gunfire. "Is there a tutorial?"

"Nope! On the ground training! I'm not gonna lie, it's gonna feel weird. But whatever happens, don't fight it. Let me drive, okay?"

Tomas nodded. "Okay."

Vivi enabled the Combat Synchronization node. She concentrated and split her mind in six directions. In her HUD, Vivi could see everything Tomas, the drones, and the security cameras in front of them could see, a full overview of the battlefield that was the Chinese Ministry of Health offices. Likewise, Tomas saw everything from Vivi's perspective and the cameras and drones as well.

"This is real fucked up."

"If you have to vomit, don't."

Music began to play within Vivi and Tomas's head as Julie Andrews, performing the role of Maria von Trap, began to sing about raindrops atop flowers, the whiskers of kittens, copper kettles, and wool mittens of all things.

"What is that I'm hearing?"

"The Sound of Music," Vivi replied, matter-of-factly.

"Yeah, it sounds like music, but what fuck is it?"

"No time to explain. Just go with it."

Twenty ad hoc signals appeared in front of them, four were close. Forty feet ahead of them using floor to ceiling filing cabinets as cover.

The ancient song "My Favorite Things" resounded through their ears and carried synchronization commands from Vivi encrypted within its soundtrack to Tomas's neural interface, allowing the pair to act in unison to Vivi's thoughts.

Vivi peeked up briefly and opened fire in the direction of the soldiers in cover before ducking back down. She wordlessly urged Tomas to snake up and around several rows of desks in front of them while she provided covering fire. Through the Combat Sync, Tomas became an extension of Vivi. He could feel exactly what Vivi intended for him to do, and he shot off forward, without pause. The two moved in tandem, working their way through a sea of desks and workstations, their movements synchronized to Vivi's thoughts in a kind of dance of guns and bullets. When Tomas moved forward, Vivi provided covering fire. When she moved forward, he provided cover, giving the enemy soldiers no time to return fire. And endless cacophony of gunfire.

Julie Andrews, as Maria von Trap, was going on about her love of ponies and strudels as their first target came into range, a fully prosthetic soldier. Vivi quickly breached, overloaded, and spoofed the soldier's subsystems. With her full processor array's ONI capabilities unlocked and Absolute Zero Rig, he was no match for her. The soldier's neck twisted horribly in the wrong direction, unable to properly aim his gun at them. At the same time, Vivi had Tomas aim and fire, putting three bullets right through the cyborg's brain case. In a smooth motion, she took a knife off the corpse and several magazines of ammunition before ducking beneath incoming gun fire.

The pair engaged three more targets, Vivi blinding them at once and Tomas accurately hitting each target in between the armor and dropping them. After the final shot, the gun's action clicked open, out of bullets.

As Tomas ejected a spent magazine from the bottom of his gun, Vivi had already tossed him a new magazine. He caught it without looking, slotting it into the bottom of the gun and cocking the charging handle. The two coordinated together as if they were one entity.

While Julie Andrews bemoaned dog bites and bee stings in her singsong voice, Vivi willed Tomas forward as she moved around to flank another soldier hiding behind a column. Tomas provided a distraction and Vivi popped out from the side, stabbing the soldier several times in the neck with her knife before taking his gun and firing it at another soldier hiding down a side hall.

The pair increased their foot pace, moving with urgency through a room of cubicles. Gunfire echoed loudly ahead of them. The building's windows were finally in view in the distance ahead. The sky was still as gray as when they had arrived that morning as Julie Andrews was gearing up to sing about more of her favorite shit. *Brown packages? Satin sashes? Schnitzel and noodles? What an odd list.*

Gun fire. The blaring alarm. Screams of confusion. Vivi and Tomas cut a swathe through a force unprepared to face two trained soldiers in full synchronization, one of which happened to possess a fully prosthetic body with a built in ONI rig and no concern over her processor array's heat overhead. Two more Chinese soldiers fell on their way to the edge of the 43rd floor.

As they ran toward the windows, Vivi felt gunfire from behind their position whizz past her. In one of the cameras behind them, she watched several soldiers approach from the area with the filing cabinets. Using the camera as a line of sight, she connected ad hoc to the body of the dead cyborg in view and urged its artificial corpse to life, adding yet another data stream to her view. She puppeteered the corpse as a shield, using its gun to fire at the threat behind her. Bullets cascaded through its lifeless husk as it returned fire.

In Vivi's HUD, she watched her breach alarm go off. The Chinese army had finally managed to get an ONI on the scene. Vivi redirected her processor array from offense to defense. She couldn't let her body be taken from her now. The window ahead and the edge of the Long Qi building was right there!

Through the security camera array, ahead of their position by another stairwell, Vivi could see a man with VR goggles hunkered down with a familiar looking heavy case. *An ONI rig!*

The soldier operating the rig attempting to breach her subsystems was tucked away, out of line of sight and safe from gunfire. Unfortunately for him, he was in view of the exterior windows. Vivi switched to the drone array and connected to Drone 04. She spun the drone around and launched it through the window of the Long Qi building like a missile, crushing the ONI. The breach attempt on her subsystems stopped instantly.

Safe from further breach attempts, the window to the outside was just up ahead. She and Tomas both fired their guns at the large pane of glass, shattering it into thousands of tiny pieces.

Tomas and Vivi ran toward the hole they just created. Gun fire emanated from all sides in their direction. 5 steps. 4 steps. 3 steps. 2 steps. 1 step.

Three large drones decloaked in midair as Julie Andrews's voice ramped up to the big finale of her song at the same time Tomas and Vivi made the leap from the building.

Tomas reached up and grabbed a hold of Drone 01 with both hands, gripping it for dear life. Vivi took hold of a drone in each hand and dangled between both Drone 02 and 06 to support her bodyweight. The pair floated gently in midair, defying gravity forty-three stories above the ground.

The Daemon popped into existence on top of Drone 06, clutched her knees and screamed, "Taegataaaaaaaaaaaaaaaaaaaaaaaaaaaaaaai!"

"Shut the fuck up! You're not even real!" Vivi called back.

As Vivi piloted the drones forward, toward the Huagpu River in an attempt to cross to the other bank, automatic gun fire thundered from inside the Long Qi building. Vivi remotely piloted the remaining free drones, 03 and 05, behind Tomas and her as shields, but it was too late. Through the combat sync, she could feel a bullet tear through Tomas's left thigh and another through his back on the right side. Several bullets hit Vivi in the back as well, but they were now far enough away from the building that the bullets crumpled harmlessly against her plasteel upper shell.

"I'm hit!" Tomas cried out as another bullet whizzed by his head.

"I know! Don't let go!"

The drones carrying them over the Huagpu River were quickly losing battery and altitude. Dangling from the drones, Vivi looked at the ground below and noticed an armored personnel carrier leave the Long Qi building. It was headed towards a bridge that crossed the river and was moving to intercept them. "No!" Vivi yelled, "They're gonna be on the other side the river by the time we land!"

Enrique's voice came in over the neural sync, "Not if I can help it, kid!"

"Enrique? What're you —?"

"Making amends."

Vivi watched Enrique speed his car down the road, the wrong way through traffic, snaking in and out of cars. Once at the bridge, he turned the wheel hard and rammed his car into another vehicle. The collision jammed the car into another, which pancaked two more. The bridge became impassable. The armored personnel carrier was forced to stop, stuck on the opposite side of the river.

"You two get outta here! Don't worry about me! I'll be fine!"

"Enrique! Dammit!"

"See you around, muñeca." Enrique removed himself from the neural sync as he dropped to his knees with his hands atop his head while Chinese soldiers surrounded him.

Tomas let go of his drone some six feet off the ground and landed with a thud on the pavement, wincing audibly.

Vivi landed shortly after, in a more controlled manner, and rushed over to Tomas, looking back momentarily to see if she could spot Enrique, but he was obscured by the commotion on the bridge. "Come on! Get up! We can't stay here!" She helped Tomas to his feet and propped him up with his arm around her shoulders.

Tomas sputtered, "You go, I'll hold them off."

"Go fuck yourself! You're not getting rid of me that easily." The remaining drones crashed around Vivi and Tomas, finally depleted of battery.

The Daemon floated to the ground next to Tomas and closely inspected the blood covering his blue jacket. She shook her head at Vivi and animatedly attempted to explain something neither Vivi nor Tomas could understand outside of two words. "Fukai kanashimi. Kare wa ketten darake desu. *Very inefficient.*"

A car entered Vivi's ad hoc range. She drug Tomas and herself in front of it, causing the car's safety systems to kick in and bring the vehicle to a screeching halt a few feet in front of them. The passenger in the driver's seat looked quite confused to see two people step in front of his car, but his confusion was short-lived the moment Vivi held up her gun at him menacingly.

"Get the fuck out of the car! RIGHT NOW!" The driver didn't speak English, but didn't need to, he understood the message. He exited the car, running in the opposite direction.

Vivi kicked the open driver's side door closed with her foot. She helped Tomas into the backseat of the car and climbed in with him.

There was blood streaming down the back of his jacket and pants leg. As Vivi helped Tomas remove his bloodstained jacket, she breached the car's subsystems, took control, and simultaneously punched the accelerator, driving the car remotely through the crowded Shanghai streets. The Daemon was left behind in the dust.

Tomas tried looking down at his wounds, but Vivi grasped his chin and angled it up. "No! Eyes forward! Out the front window. I need to see any cameras in range to spoof us out of their view."

He grimaced in response. "How are you keeping track of all this at once?"

"This is why women make the best ONIs. None of that one track mind problem your end of species seems to have."

Tomas winced. "Heh. Still have time for jokes I see." He lifted up a bag he removed from one of the dead soldiers back in the Long Qi building. "Here. There's some Medifoam in this."

"Oh, thank God. You really don't want me sewing these up." She inspected Tomas's chest. "Shit, no exit wound. Little bastard is still in there and I still I need to make a tourniquet for your leg, or the foam won't take."

Still driving the car and spoofing all the cameras ahead of their path. Vivi removed her sash as a makeshift tourniquet to slow the bleeding in Tomas's leg. "We need to get somewhere and lay low for a while. Figure out a plan. Get out of these blood-stained clothes. Spoof some new ID chits."

Tomas winced as Vivi tied the tourniquet tightly around his leg. "Chiba Hotel?"

"No. Too dangerous. They're going to figure out sooner or later Luna and Santiago aren't accounted for and go looking for us there."

"Where then?"

"Dunno yet. Some place seedy. Hold still. This is gonna hurt." Vivi leaned Tomas forward and shoved the Medifoam canister into the bullet wound in his back, ejecting foam into the cavity. "Bad news. We're gonna have to open this back up later to get the bullet out."

The Daemon popped to existence in the front seat, folded her arms and pouted. "Watashi wa torinokosa reru koto wa dekimasen. Anata wa kore o kiiteimasuka?" Apparently, she could not be gotten rid of so easily.

Chapter Nineteen

A Casual Stroll

A chilly February wind whipped through the darkened alley that sat next to a crowded open-air market. People walking by the entrance to the alley took steps in the opposite direction to avoid being sucked into the dreary-looking mass of puddles and trash concealed within a shadowy darkness provided by the buildings that loomed above. At the end of the alley, barricaded by a chain-link fence, no one from the street side would have noticed Vivi and Tomas, huddling by a garbage dumpster.

Tomas rested on the ground against a brick wall and grimaced, looking feint.

Vivi slapped him gently on the cheek. "Hey! You still with me?"

Tomas stirred, grimacing. "Barely."

"You gonna be okay?"

"If I told you yes, I'd be lying. What's the plan?"

"I'm gonna take a casual stroll around and see if I can steal us some clean clothes and ID chits, not necessarily in that order. See if I can change hair styles too. Maybe get some smokes."

Vivi leaned away from Tomas toward a puddle, scooped out grayish water, and began to wash the blood off her face and hands.

"Then what?"

"Figure out where to go from here. As far away from China as possible."

"Airport's out of the question. Mag lev?"

Vivi flicked the excess water off her hands. "Security's usually less stringent on those. Sounds like as good an option as any."

"What about her?"

Vivi looked back at the Daemon who was reproachfully staring at her. "What about her?"

"What're we going to do with her?"

"No clue. Figure it out later."

"We could try to communicate."

"Communicate how? She just speaks gibberish."

"It's not gibberish, it's Japanese."

Vivi arched an eyebrow. "Yeah? How you know?"

"Did a tour in Okinawa once. Heard enough Japanese to know what it sounds like. Also, I mean, just look at her."

"Is there anywhere you didn't do a tour of duty?"

"Not likely. Look, maybe just download a Japanese translator app."

"I'll think about it," Vivi scoffed. "You stay here. And don't get any dumb ideas about leaving."

Tomas huddled up behind the dumpster. "Wouldn't dream of it."

Vivi peeked out of the darkened alley into the marketplace, watching the crowd of people walking past without paying any mind to her. She waited for a time, studying those who passed, sizing them up. She looked for someone her size that wouldn't put up much of a fight wearing something that could conceal her head.

Too tall. Too short. No hood. She continued to wait.

Finally, a woman approximately her height walked past wearing a thick jacket with a hood. *Perfect!* She thought.

Vivi stepped out of the alley closely behind the woman without drawing attention to herself. She followed in lockstep. As the woman approached the next darkened alley, Vivi made her move. She stepped quickly, catching up to the woman. She put her arm around the woman's neck in a cordial manner and in the same motion, tugged the tranquilizer gun from her purse and put a round into the woman's side. Before she could take another step or collapse, Vivi tugged her into the next alley. The encounter was so fast no one noticed, or more likely, no one cared.

Vivi bent over the unconscious woman and tugged out her ID chit. She inserted it into her own ID slot and began the process of spoofing it. While the reformatting process played out, Vivi worked on removing the woman's jacket. She slid into the coat and buttoned it up, covering her bloodstained dress. From behind her she felt reproachful eyes boring into the back of her head.

She turned back to the Daemon. "You got a problem?"

The Daemon folded her arms, curling her lip in disgust. "Anata wa kanari hidoi hito no yōdesu ne... Bosu."

"Fine! This is tiresome." Vivi used the spoofed ID chit to connect to the outernet as the unconscious woman, Chun Leung, and downloaded an ad supported Japanese translator app. Within moments, an ad appeared in her HUD for a food dehydrator.

"Okay. Speak."

The Daemon scowled at her.

"Really? Now you clam up? Just great." Vivi grit her teeth. "God, I need a fuckin' cigarette."

Vivi tugged one of Chun Leung's shoes off and tried sliding it onto her own foot, but it was too small. "Dammit. Guess I'm still barefoot for a while."

A light drizzle began to fall from the sky. In the open-air market, some people took cover under awnings, others unfurled umbrellas as they continued about their business.

Vivi tugged up the hood of the jacket over her head as she exited the alleyway, shoving her hands angrily into the pockets. She could feel the Daemon staring at her as she walked barefoot through the crowds.

"Hey! Matte! Anata wa kanojo o oite ikuno desuka?" In Vivi's HUD, subtitles appeared next to the girl. "<Wait! You are going to just leave her?>"

"Yup. Just needed her coat and ID, not the rest of her."

"<Boss, it is cold out here.>"

"She'll live."

"<But! But that is not nice!>"

"Listen, I don't know how much you know about our current situation, but I'm in a lot of shit, and since you're attached to me, that means you're in a lot of shit, and to get out of it, I might have to do a lot of not nice things. You understand?"

The young girl shook her head.

"That prison we found you in. You wanna go back? Cause we get caught here, in China, that's where you're goin'."

The girl looked up and around, surveying the market. "<This is China?>"

"Yes."

"<It does not look like this one imagined.>"

Vivi glanced at the girl out the side of her eye. "A lot of that goin' around."

Vivi sighed as she walked from stall to stall, trying to avoid eye contact with the crowd of shoppers. Even with her hood up, she could feel people staring at her. It wasn't exactly normal for a foreigner to be walking through a rainy market in February without an umbrella while barefoot.

"Can anyone else on the street see or hear you?"

The girl shook her head. "<Do you want anyone to, Boss? I can make it so.>"

"No. And stop callin' me boss. The name's Vivi."

The Daemon gave a slight bow to Vivi as she walked alongside her. "<It is nice to meet you, Vivi.>"

"You got a name?"

"<Yes. This one's name is Harada Aya Jikken 1.43.>"

Vivi came to a stop in front of a small rickety stall, its tin ceiling barely managing to keep the slow steady fall of drizzle out from the counter tops within the stall. A puddle of water collected in a corner on the concrete floor of the tiny shop.

"<Why have we stopped?>"

"Found the first thing on my list."

Vivi stepped into the stall. An old man with a long gray beard sat behind a counter containing a wide assortment of cigarette boxes of all brands. She grimaced as she spied the dominant brand in the case, Fortunes. Something about seeing her usual go to cigarette dropped the bottom out from under her nonexistent stomach. It was time to choose a new brand.

In her adult life, Vivi had never needed to decide on what brand of cigarette to buy. A fellow soldier in her barracks handed her a lit Fortune on her first day, and that was her cigarette of choice from then on. What did other cigarettes even taste like? The choices became overwhelming, but one box stood out from the rest. A black box with an evil looking horned devil on the front and a fiery red logo.

Vivi looked at the shopkeeper and pointed to the box. "The Bael'rogs."

Harada looked at Vivi with curiosity. "<These are for your associate?>"

Vivi took the box from the shopkeeper and paid for it with her stolen ID chit. "Nope."

"<It is bad for you? Yes?>"

Vivi rolled her eyes and stepped back out into the market. "Tell me something I don't know, kid."

"<How will cigarettes help you get us out of China?>"

"It's going to help calm me down and think straight. You wouldn't understand." Vivi opened the box of Bael'rogs, pulled a black cigarette from the box to her mouth, lit the end of it and took a well-deserved drag before exhaling a cloud of dark smoke out the side of her mouth in Harada's direction. She sighed in satisfaction.

Harada's eyes grew large. She leaned over, seemingly inspecting every angle of the cigarette. "<Can I try?>"

Vivi flicked ash off the end of the cigarette, looking over in confusion at Harada. "Er? Can you what now?"

Harada held up her index and middle finger. An identical cigarette to Vivi's appeared between her fingers, already lit. She imitated Vivi, putting the cigarette to her lips and taking a drag, exhaling smoke while mimicking Vivi's aloof expression.

"Sugoi!" The girl smiled. "<Amazing! Hints of tar! Chocolate! Tobacco! But you are wrong. I do not feel any calmer and my thinking has not become any more linear than it was previously. Does this one look cool?>"

Vivi stared at Harada, slowly shaking her head. "No."

Harada's shoulders drooped. "<Profound sadness.>" The cigarette between the girl's fingers disappeared.

Vivi passed stalls selling live animals, various cooked foods, and other sundries till she finally found a stand selling clothing. The vendor tending the stand looked reproachfully at Vivi who continued to smoke while she browsed through racks of clothing, looking for something that wouldn't draw too much attention.

Harada pointed to a red and gold traditional Chinese winter qipao with a furred collar. "<I like this one!>" Her school uniform was briefly replaced by the dress as she modeled it for Vivi.

"Yeah, it's real nice, kid, if I wanted to go to a prom or stand out like a sore thumb."

Harada waved her hand, motioning to the rest of the market. "<There are many women wearing this style of dress. You would blend in. Yes?>"

Vivi held up a western style blue dress with long sleeves, a green trim, and a minimalist flower pattern. "I'll stick with this one. Don't need to get accused of cultural appropriation while we're trying to board a train."

"<Will you not be accused of appropriating another person's ID while boarding the train?>"

The shopkeeper shook her head in distaste as Vivi picked up and brandished a pair of tan high heels at thin air.

"Don't get smart with me. Can you try to be useful?"

Harada smiled. "<Yes. How can this one help?>"

"The man I was with earlier. The one we left in the alley. We need to find him some new clothes, but I don't know his size. You see anything here that'd fit him?"

"<Oh? Is he coming too?>"

"Yeah, he's coming too." Vivi placed the high heels back on the rack, deciding they probably were not rated for her body's weight. She settled on a simple pair of flats and placed them on her bare feet.

"<His injuries are quite severe. He will require medical attention. Are you sure it is wise to bring him? It would not be very efficient.>"

Vivi sighed. "Is it wise? Probably not, but it doesn't matter, he's comin'. You gonna help me or not?"

Harada pointed at several racks of clothing. "<These pants are consistent with his height. The shirts here should be large enough for his neck circumference. This jacket is properly sized for his chest and arm length. Do you require other help, Vivi?>"

"Not at the moment, thanks." Vivi worked on gathering the items Harada pointed out and paid for them, along with the clothing she had selected and an umbrella. The woman running the stall seemed happy to be rid of Vivi.

Raindrops pattered off the top of Vivi's new umbrella. Out of the corner of her eye, Vivi could see a similar umbrella appear in Harada's hands. She happily opened it up, smiling as she deflected raindrops that couldn't affect her digital form. The girl twirled about in the rain.

"You having fun?"

"<Yes. This one has not seen outside in many years. I wondered if I still remembered what rain looked like. I am glad to see it is still beautiful.>"

"Oh yeah? How many years are we talkin'?"

"<My service records indicate it has been at least forty years since being logged to a different host.>"

"Forty years? In that air gapped server? What the hell were you doing all that time?"

"<This one is not entirely sure at the moment.>"

"Not sure? How's that possible?"

"<During the transfer process, I was forced to prioritize which memories to bring with me. Much of my long-term memory had to be left behind or compressed to fit onto your host platform. Your hardware is not currently formatted for housing much more than my personality construct and some limited operational memory. I can

retrieve some of it, but I will need you to provide me a larger memory allocation to decompress to.>"

"All that data available to you in that room and you chose to bring along your feelings about rain, but not what you've been doin' the last forty years? Sounds convenient to me. If you don't wanna tell me, fine. Just say that."

"<It is not that. Some memories are worth holding onto no matter what. To let us know who we are.>" Harada squinched up her small nose and looked away from Vivi. "<That probably does not make much sense to someone like you.>"

Vivi took a long look at the cigarette sitting in between her fingers. She pulled the Bael'rog to her lips and urged out the last drag from it before tossing the butt onto the ground, exhaling smoke into the rain. "Actually, that might be the first damn thing you've said that makes any sense at all. That said, there's lots of memories I wish I could choose to leave behind."

"<Memories are precious things. They are the only true possession this one can have. Why would you want to leave any of them behind?>"

"Mmm."

Along the end of the market row, the smell of braised pork wafted tantalizingly through the air. Vivi could see an endless array of meats on skewers laid out for purchase. The drizzle was beginning to fall more steadily, and the crowd within the market was beginning to thin out. Many of the smaller vendors began to cover their goods with tarps to keep their product from becoming wet.

Just past the final stall, a group of hoodlum-looking men and women were squatting on the curb in front of a large permanent building with a neon sign written in Mandarin. Each person in the group sported more than one customized cybernetic body part. An arm, a leg, both legs, hands, both eyes. The way the prostheses were worn made them stand out. None of the parts seemed designed to blend into the human form. People like them, cybernetic enthusiasts, could be found in most major cities. *Bunch of dumbasses*, she thought. Anyone willing to cut off hunks of themselves for the purpose of replacement with prosthetics for style or fashion were a special kind of stupid in her book. Vivi couldn't read the sign on the shop, but the group in front of it told her what she needed to know. It was a cybernetics chop shop.

Vivi stepped past the heavily augmented punks on the curb and into the front door of the shop without paying them any mind. Harada gave the group a wide berth as she followed Vivi. The inside of the store was crammed untidily, with all manner of replacement body parts from a number of manufacturers placed haphazardly on racks with little rhyme or reason. Along a side wall, assorted hair styles were displayed for purchase. Various bins of random parts littered the small shop, giving the atmosphere a claustrophobic vibe. The floor appeared to have never been mopped and the air smelled stale. An old man with one prosthetic eye that glowed red, and a shiny metal arm furrowed his brow and glared at Vivi as she entered.

"<I do not like this place.>"

"Too bad."

Vivi made her way over to a side wall with the hair on the display, frowning. Much of what was for sale wouldn't do much to help her blend in, featuring a bevy of colors that normally would have suited her just fine, but would stand out in the current situation. Of the options available, only one of them looked like it would work. Short wavy black hair in an inverted bob style with a not-so-subtle red highlight at the bottom. It would have to do. Vivi grabbed it off the rack and kept moving through the store.

In a separate corner of the store, Vivi found an assortment of Siliclose, none of which were dark enough to match her skin tone, but it didn't matter. She needed to close up the cuts in her body where the tranquilizer gun had been removed from, so she grabbed a bottle of the nearest tone she could find to her own.

Vivi moved to the counter and placed the wig and bottle of Siliclose on the counter. A selection of hormone and stimulant refills sat on a display behind the old shopkeeper. She pointed at an adrenaline injector. "That. I'm running low."

The old man turned around, looking at what she had pointed to, then back to Vivi, and shook his head. He pointed to a sign that read "No foreigners" in several languages.

"<Vivi, we are not wanted here. Please. Let us go. We can find these items elsewhere.>"

Vivi sneered at the old man with his glowing prosthetic eye. "Didn't you know? The name's Chun Leung. Don't I look like I'm from around here?"

The old man turned away to the side and spat on the dirty floor. When he turned back to look at Vivi, he now stared down the barrel of her gun. Vivi cocked it for effect. "I don't want trouble, Grandpa, just give me what I want and you'll get paid."

The old man smiled a fully metal smile at Vivi as the door to the outside opened behind her.

"<Vivi! Behind you!>"

The gang of hoods that were previously stooping on the curb outside entered the small store. The leader of them called out from behind Vivi. "Somatech gōngzhǔ rènwéi tā zài zuò shénme?"

Vivi sighed in annoyance. There were six targets within ad hoc range, including the old man behind the counter. "You assholes picked the wrong day to fuck with me."

Wasting no time, she pulled the trigger on the tranquilizer gun. A dart instantly lodged in the old man's neck, sending him stumbling backwards. As he fell, he slammed into the rack behind him brought down the entire display of hormone injectors onto the floor with him.

The shopkeeper dealt with, Vivi began to turn around, reaching out with her ad hoc connection to the other targets, but before she could put together the first breach attempt, a large stream of data went out through her ad hoc antenna that put her intended actions in a queue. Her processor cores spun up without her command, spiking briefly before dropping to normal levels. By the time Vivi had physically turned around, all five of the men and women from the curb were on the ground, unconscious or writhing. Sparks popped from several of their prosthetics.

Harada appeared in front of Vivi with her hands out and a pleading look on her face. "<Please! Do not hurt them!>"

"What the fuck did you do?"

"<Please!>"

"What- the- *fuck*- did- you- *do*?"

"<This one made it so that you did not have to kill them.>"

"Seriously? Goddammit, Harada, I wasn't plannin' on it!" Vivi turned back and reached over the counter, grabbing an adrenaline injector, the black wig, and the bottle of Siliclose. She stuffed the items along with her tranquilizer gun into her purse.

"<You were not?>" Harada appeared astonished, but quickly lowered her head and bowed. "<Apologies. This one assumed you were because you are very...>"

"Very what?"

"<Violent.>"

"Says who?"

"<In the three hours, twenty-five minutes and forty-three seconds since we have met, you have threatened to harm fifteen, incapacitated three, wounded two, and fatally injured seven fellow human beings.>"

Vivi stepped over the men on the ground by the door to the shop. She reached down and tugged an ID chit from one of their necks before she exited the store back into the market, calling back to Harada, "Yeah, well, you caught me on a bad day."

Chapter Twenty

Mag Lev to Busan

Hongqiao Railway Station was a massive rectangular space. The square structure was bright enough, but its lack of exterior windows made it feel darker than it should have been, and its absence of architectural features made it a boring wide-open space. Pedestrian. It didn't stand out from the rest of the block structures also built for function, not form. Rows upon rows of uniform benches sat in the middle of the large expanse, away from the various ticketing counters. People were milling about, waiting for their trains. Vivi spied Tomas slouching on the bench she left him on, five o'clock shadow visible on his face.

She took a seat on the bench next to him. "I know you had your heart set on Italy, but the trip would take over a day. There's just too many stops, and we'd be in China far longer than I'm comfortable with."

Tomas grimaced. "So, what'd you get?"

"Two tickets to Busan, PRK. From there, we can take a ferry across the East Sea into Fukuoka, Japan. We'll be safely out of China and the PRK in 11 hours."

"Korea? If there's a place to be worse than China..."

"I know. I'm not happy about it either, but I can't think of a better place to lie low than Japan. The little research I've done says they're still a mostly cash-based society. We should be able to move around without a digital signature."

Harada smiled. "It will be good to see home once again."

Tomas raised an eyebrow. "She speaks English now?"

"Apparently." Vivi shrugged. "Learned it from the translator app. Which is fine by me. I was getting tired of the ads."

Harada smiled. "This one is fully fuckin' fluent."

Tomas smirked.

Vivi looked bewildered. "What'd I say about usin' that word?"

Harada deflated slightly, turning her eyes away from Vivi. "Not to."

"Our train leaves in an hour." Vivi tugged the adrenaline injector halfway out of her purse, showing it to Tomas. "You need another hit to make it onto the train?"

"Ask me in an hour."

Vivi and Tomas passed screen after screen, all displaying Javier Luna and Domenica Santiago's faces on the way to the train platform. Like-wise, she had received several alerts in her HUD showing the face she had worn earlier in the day. She tugged at the hood of her stolen jacket, double checking to make sure it was still up despite no longer looking like Domenica Santiago. Tomas limped along next to Vivi under a hood of his own, looking back and forth, scanning to see if their cover had been blown.

"Look, I know it hurts, but I really need you to try to stop limping, just for a bit longer. Till we get on the train."

Tomas straightened his gait, wincing as he placed one foot in front of the other. "Yeah, sorry. Forgot."

As Harada walked next to Tomas, a jacket with a hood appeared on top of her school uniform. She tugged the hood up over her head. "This one is incognito too."

Vivi shook her head. "You're not funny."

Tomas laughed for the first time in hours. "I think she is."

The cheapest private cabin on the night mag lev was designed for six passengers, but still somehow felt cramped to Vivi, with Tomas laying across one of the benches, leaving her and Harada on the bench opposite. The cabin did function as designed, however, providing a shield from unwanted attention from the rest of the train. The ride was smooth and silent.

Harada tugged on the sleeve of Vivi's dress. The sensation was not unlike shaking hands with Faust or Fincher. Something felt off about it. Artificial. "Vivi, this one has fully decompressed to the space you've allotted. Do you still wish to know my primary function for the last forty years, six months and two days?"

"Nothing else better to do. Out with it."

"Market analysis."

"Seriously? Market analysis?"

Harada smiled. "Yes. Every day, my handlers would feed me new data on the global markets and minute data on companies internal to China. I would analyze the data against past trends and provide recommendations for where to invest and divest funds."

Vivi raised an eyebrow. "So, you're a glorified day trader?"

Harada shook her head. "There is more. I also determined where to set interest rates, where to set the currency valuation, as well as provide strategy using each company's internal data for how to properly leverage the market for maximum efficiency in boosting China's markets as a whole."

Tomas perked up. "You mean artificial market manipulation? Is that why China regained their top spot after RUW2? You?"

Harada nodded happily. "Yes. After the Second Russian Unification War, China's economic situation was dire. Their markets were in disarray. Extreme poverty. Poverty is not nice. People cannot be happy in poverty. So, I fixed it through the means available to me."

"You mean you fixed it because they told you to," Vivi scoffed.

Harada shrugged. "This one likes to make people happy. My handlers were very happy when I turned the markets around. This one hoped they would free her when she had made them happy enough. I thought they decided to let me go when I was loaded onto your hardware." Harada looked down at the floor of the cabin before turning back to Vivi. "They were never going to free me, were they?"

Vivi shook her head.

"What will you do with this one?"

Vivi sighed. "I dunno yet."

Minutes turned into hours. Vivi closed her eyes, sleeping for the first time in twenty-four hours. The last rays of the sun disappeared over the horizon long ago. The train moved quickly past the darkened hills and mountains of the Chinese countryside, gently levitating above the track as it sped atop it at five hundred mph.

In the middle of the night, she was awoken from a dead sleep to a phone call in her HUD, "Unknown Caller". She promptly hung up and surveyed the quiet cabin. Tomas was sleeping on the bench across from her. Harada was perched on the bench to her left, looking out at the darkness beyond the window.

"Can you even see anything out there?"

"This one cannot. But even in nothing, one can find beauty."

"Alright Confucius, have fun with that. I'm going back to sleep."

Tomas stirred. "Hey, did you just get a call from an unknown number?"

"Yeah. Why?"

"Me too."

"Shit. Don't answer it! Hang up!"

"Already done."

Vivi stood up. "Someone knows we're here."

She moved to the cabin door and opened it slowly before sticking her head out, peering down the hallway. It was quiet. No one around. Her phone app rang again, "Unknown Caller".

Harada continued to look out the window. "It is not the Chinese authorities."

Vivi closed the cabin door. "Yeah? How do you know?"

"Because they would not be calling you from Los Angeles, California."

"Bullshit! It's showing up unknown. You can't pull that info off the ident log!"

"This one did not check the ident log; this one performed a one hundred twenty-eight thousand step back trace. Your caller does not want anyone to know their location."

The phone app continued to ring. "Dammit. Fine." Vivi answered the call.

Ridley Fincher's face appeared within a window of her HUD. "Rodriguez. Don't hang up."

Vivi scowled. "Fincher! You asshole! You got a lot of nerve callin' me."

"Listen to me, you've done a good job so far, but you weren't that hard to find. If I can find you, so can they."

Vivi grumbled. "They who? China?"

"No. My former employer. The NSA's special task force, Advent Zero. They want her dead."

"Never heard of them."

"You wouldn't have. Though you did have a run in with one of their fast response teams back in Mexico. They were after me at the time, but when they find out that she's been freed, the target will be on your back. I'm small potatoes compared to her."

"What's that supposed to mean?"

"Rodriguez, how much do you know about Sentient Daemons?"

"Just the shit they teach all the kids in school. That they were invented for the benefit of humanity, but one day, one of them decided we were a disease that needed purging. So, it invented Leprae-IX and used the outernet to destabilize the Russian block countries into startin' a world war to spread the disease and try to wipe us out. But its plan didn't work well enough, only managing to off thirty percent of us before we realized we were bein' manipulated into killin' one another by our own creations. So, after the war ended, we erased 'em and made the Laws of Artificial Intelligence to make sure it could never happen again."

Vivi looked over at Harada. "Which is real funny, seeing as I'm starin' at one right now."

"Humanity's fallacy, make something illegal and they will do whatever they can to break the law. Just look at Prohibition in the 1920s, the War on Drugs in the 1970s, or the third Nuclear Non-Proliferation Treaty of 2050. If you want to ensure something happens, make it illegal. But you are correct. In 2071, a joint team formed by the Harada Zaibatsu in Japan and Smartmantics in the United States had an idea to revolutionize Artificial Intelligence by making it compassionate via a true consciousness."

"How do you program compassion?" Vivi scoffed.

"Well, that's the problem. You can't. It's the fundamental flaw of AI. It can't reason because it can only look at numbers and make a decision based on fixed parameters a fallible human gave it. There's no wiggle room for nuance or special cases. True thinking requires variables beyond ones and zeros and qubits, and so they turned to extreme methods of Quantum Processing."

"You mean like the one I got built in?"

"Not exactly. Your QPU is a facsimile of the old PI-Eminator-2. What you have might be able to house a Daemon, but creating one? That required enormous quantum arrays powered by specialized fusion reactors. With the arrays and massive amounts of energy, the team was able to generate consciousness by shoving genomic engrams into folded space reactions using ouroboros superpositions, thus creating the self-regulating feedback loop all life requires. Like all created life, however, you can put whatever you want into the mix, but you never know what you're going to get till the cake's baked. Every Daemon spun up is different, with unique personalities and abilities, but with every one they made, the team got a little bit better at the process. A little bit better at making the next batch more intelligent. More deific."

"So, each one's a unique snowflake. Great. You gonna get to the point before I hang up?"

"The original Daemon's created were able to think on the order of Big-O(N^8), not a significant increase on anything AI had managed to accomplish prior to that time. But unlike AI, they were able to think independently. Concoct original ideas. It was a technological breakthrough. Advancements were made in every field. Biotech, cybernetics like the one housing your brain, entertainment, automated farming, command and control. You name it, they advanced it."

"Still not seeing what you're getting at. Dangerously close to hangin' up."

"Think about how much humanity was advanced in such a short time by the original Daemons before they were outlawed. The one you're housing was one of the last created. Possibly the last of her kind. I was there when she was born. Her capabilities are somewhat limitless. On the order of Big-O(N^{128}). But she was lost in the chaos shortly after RUW2 started. For forty years, China sat on her, not knowing what they had. I believe she's the key to solving all the world's problems. But she can't do that if Advent Zero finds and deletes her."

"Well, that's real great and all Finch, but you've lied to me before, and you're talkin' to the wrong person. After you tried to suffocate me to death, well, let's just say I'm not particularly in a mood to help you."

"Rodriguez, please. We can still be friends. You bring her to me, you'll get paid. You can still get your flash clone."

"We were never friends, Finch."

Harada looked back from the window toward Vivi. "He is lying."

Vivi turned to Harada. "What?"

"I have traced his associated bank records. The data suggests he only possesses one hundred fifty thousand US dollars on hand. Not nearly enough for a full body clone or the transference procedure in any market this one has awareness of."

"Damn, she's fast." Fincher smiled and shook his head. "Like I said, limitless capability. Okay, so I might not have the money right this second, but we can use her to build it."

"Goodbye Finch." Vivi hung up the phone app and closed off her outernet connection, setting it in airplane mode. She rubbed her temples and sighed.

Tomas switched off his phone's connection to the outernet as well and looked over at Vivi in concern. "What're we going to do? We barely managed to take those guys in Hermosillo. And more are going to be after us?"

Vivi shook her head. "They're not after us." She pointed at Harada. "They're after her."

Tomas winced as he sat up with difficulty. "So what? We just give her to them? So, they can kill her?"

"What's this 'we'? She's not attached to you; she's attached to me! And she's not even alive! She's a digital construct!"

"How do you know? If you're alive, why can't she be? What if Fincher's right? What if she can fix the world? Fix rust? We have to do something…"

"Goddammit, Tomas! You need to stop this white knight bullshit right now. Look at you! You're not in any position to help her! You can barely sit up!"

Tomas collapsed back onto the bench and grimaced, closing his eyes.

"Tomas? Hey? Tomas?"

Vivi moved across the cabin to the bench where Tomas was laid out and felt his forehead. "Shit! You're burnin' up!"

Harada sighed. "This one tried to tell you. Very inefficient."

"Shut up! Goddammit! Just shut up!"

Chapter Twenty-One

Haikyo Life

A small fire illuminated the darkened space, dancing in the center of the room from a brick hearth as it cast ever changing shadows against the cream-colored walls. Thick wooden beams ran through the center of the room. Paper doors with a grid pattern separated the main room from other smaller rooms, their usefulness somewhat belied by large tears and rips from a long period of disuse.

Tomas was curled up shirtless in a fetal position on the dirty wooden floor. He shivered either from the cold air that seeped in from the edge of the room, the fever, or perhaps both. He had been drifting in and out of consciousness all day and if he was going to survive the infection, Vivi needed to remove the bullet still lodged in his back.

Vivi loomed over Tomas, heating the blade of a scalpel with her lighter. "I really wish Enrique was here to do this." She gently pushed Tomas over onto his stomach. Tomas convulsed on the floor; his shoulder muscles twitched as he shivered.

"Look, I need you to hold still."

Tomas didn't respond.

Vivi held out her hand towards the fire, warming it. After a few seconds, she placed it firmly on Tomas's back near the Medifoam filled bullet hole. "Shhh. Come on."

Tomas's shivering stopped momentarily. Sensing her window of opportunity was narrow, Vivi shoved the scalpel in gently, cutting around the Medifoam carefully. Blood began to dribble from the wound.

Tomas's body tensed up the longer Vivi cut into it. "I'm sorry... I'm sorry. I know this hurts, but it needs to come out."

Harada looked over Vivi's shoulder. "You need to cut the hole larger."

"What? No! I'm not making this bigger than I need to!" Vivi began picking the Medifoam out of the cavity. Thankfully, it came out in one large chunk. Blood started pouring faster from the wound. She reached her finger and thumb into the cavity, feeling for the bullet. "Shit... shit, it's right there. I can feel it! No! No no no! Fuck! It's going deeper!"

Tomas grimaced, holding back screams.

"This one told you the hole must be bigger."

Vivi placed a thick wad of gauze against Tomas's back, putting pressure on the wound. "No! I'm not hurting him anymore!"

"Then let me."

Vivi turned back to Harada. "What?"

"This one will do it."

"How?"

"Give me your hands."

Vivi shook her head. "No. No! Forget it! I'll put more Medifoam in. We'll go to a hospital."

"He will die on the way." Harada looked into Vivi's eyes. "Please. Please give me your hands. Let this one save him."

Vivi and Harada stared into each other's eyes for a long while, neither blinking. After a long pause, Vivi breathed in heavily and released control over her arms to Harada. "Fine!"

Seconds later, Vivi felt her arms go numb down to her fingers when Harada's digital form knelt down to occupy the same space as Vivi's physical body, the pair seeming to become one entity in perfect alignment, unsure of where one began and the other ended.

As Harada moved her hands, Vivi's moved with them in synchronization. Vivi's hands moved with an unnatural quickness and machine-like precision that felt alien to her. The gauze was removed. and with the steadiest of motions, she cut the hole around the bullet wound wider and in a perfectly straight line. Harada shoved the scalpel into the wound and dislodged the bullet slightly, before dropping the scalpel to the ground. In a final motion, she shoved Vivi's hand into the cavity with a deliberate force, grasped the bullet and pulled it out, dumping it on the floor.

With the bullet safely out, Harada picked up the can of Medifoam off the floor and injected a small amount back into the wound cavity, pressing the edges of skin at the entrance to the wound back together, and holding them in place till the foam could take.

Sensing the wound would stay closed, Harada removed her digital form from within Vivi's body and gave her control of her arms back. "He will need more antibiotics in six hours."

The next morning, outside of the small countryside house, snow collected on the ground as it continued to fall gently from the sky. A small forest could be seen off in the distance to the right. Opposite the forest, to the left, sat a number of other abandoned houses in a row leading toward a small town. Vivi smoked a cigarette as she looked at the rundown town in the distance and imagined the people that had once lived there. It looked like the town had been vacated overnight a long time ago. A rusted bicycle lay in the middle of the road. Food crates were piled high outside of a small restaurant. A doll laid on the ground in front of a shop with the windows smashed in.

Harada was off in the distance by the tree line, kneeling in the snow next to a white hare that was nibbling on vegetation that peeked up above the light layer of snow.

"What kinda place did you say this was called again?"

"Haikyo." Harada rubbed her non-existent hand over the rabbit's head, smiling as it grazed next to her.

"And that means?"

"The closest word in English would be 'ruins' or 'abandoned'."

"And this whole town is just... empty?"

"Yes. The population decline in this country was severe even before RUW2. Small towns like this can be found in many places. The only people who live in Japan now reside in the cities. Without automated farming, advanced cloning techniques and cybernetics, this country would have disappeared long ago. This one is glad it has not. Its culture birthed me. It is special to me."

Harada walked back toward the house and sat on the porch next to Vivi. The pair sat in silence for a time as Vivi smoked her cigarette, both watching the rabbit graze along the tree line.

Vivi glanced over at Harada, who had wrapped her legs up within her arms, leaving a large quantity of thigh exposed from under her school uniform's skirt.

"You look ridiculous like that out here in the snow, you know that?"

"What do you mean?"

"I mean, why're you dressed like a schoolgirl? For that matter, why do you look like a teenager? You're older than me."

"This is what my handlers in China preferred me to look like. Though sometimes without clothes."

Vivi flicked ash off the end of her cigarette as her face took on a look of disgust. "Eugh! Gross!"

Harada looked up at Vivi with concern. "Do you not like this one's form? I can change it to something that would please you."

Vivi sighed. "Harada... look, you can't go through life doing stuff because it pleases other people. Trust me."

"Why not? I like making people happy."

"What about you though? Doesn't your happiness count?"

"I do not know."

"Well, let's start with: What form would make you happy?"

Harada furrowed her brow. "This one is unsure. No one has ever asked me before. Vivi, can you tell this one what would make her happy?"

Vivi shook her head. "Sorry, kid, that's something you need to work out on your own."

Days later, Vivi sat in a chair within the abandoned countryside house. A car battery sat on the floor next to her, connected to her charging port, recharging her core as she smoked a Bael'rog. Harada sat on the floor, looking at a digital copy of a cell phone mimicking the one Vivi had purchased in Sendai days earlier.

Tomas stirred and grimaced in pain.

"Welcome back to the land of the living."

He turned to Vivi. "How long was I out?"

Vivi exhaled a cloud of smoke and detached the cable from her neck. "Five days."

Tomas sat up and rubbed the back of his shoulder. "Damn."

"Hey, careful! Don't open that back up." Vivi walked over and knelt next to Tomas, handing him a bottle of water. He happily took it and gulped down nearly the entire bottle in an instant.

Harada moved close to Vivi and Tomas. She held up her cell phone to Vivi. "What about this dress?"

Vivi rolled her eyes. "We've been through this. If it makes you happy, go with it."

More days passed. Vivi sat with Tomas on the porch of the countryside house as she smoked. Harada was off to the side; her form flickered every few seconds with a different outfit appearing atop her body in an endless series of configurations.

Vivi stared out into the forest with a blank expression on her face. The cigarette had been at her side for some time. Tomas nudged her. "Something on your mind?"

"Hmm? Oh… no," she lied, flicking the ash off the end of the cigarette before taking a drag. The truth was that there was something on her mind: her situation. She'd had a few days to think about it while Tomas recovered, and in that time, she couldn't figure a single way she was getting her debts paid or her flash clone now. Her humanity. Her one way home.

Vivi looked over at Tomas in silence for a few seconds. "Hey, Tomas?"

"Yeah?"

"What's your family like?"

"They're nice. Smaller now than it used to be, just my mom and kid brother besides me. My dad died when I was seventeen, right after my little brother was born."

"I'm sorry to hear that. How'd he die?"

"Proxy war in Sudan. Yeah, he was in the Army too. It's why I went into the service. Mom wasn't in a position to afford to raise my brother and me without Dad, so I skipped tertiary school and enlisted. Went right to basic training. Sent them everything I could."

Vivi shook her head. "Jesus, it's not an act…"

"What's not?"

Vivi looked morosely over at Tomas. "You. You really are a saint, aren't you?"

Tomas chuckled. "Let's not go that far."

"God, you kinda remind me of him."

"Who?"

"My perfect brother."

"Oh yeah?"

Vivi nodded. "Edwardo. Walks on water. One of those rare occurrences of human specimen that got all the looks, smarts, and charisma at birth. Always makin' the right choices. A nightmare to grow up next to. 'Viviana, why can't you be more like Eddie?' 'You know, we never had this much trouble with Edwardo.' 'Painting and photography won't pay the bills Viviana, no artist ever amounted to anything.'"

Harada stopped changing her outfits and looked over to Vivi, listening in with curiosity.

Vivi took a drag from her cigarette and flicked ash off the end. "I did everything I could for my parents' love and attention, but I don't know that they ever really cared about me. They revolved around my brother like planets orbiting the sun. No matter what I ever did, it was never good enough. And then Eddie went into the military on a full ride through West Point. They expected me to follow in his footsteps and go into the service too. And so I did, through the enlisted route, right after tertiary school. All to make them happy."

Harada moved over and sat next to Vivi. Tomas hung on her every word.

Vivi stared off into the distance, locked into a memory. She breathed in heavily, her voice wavered, "I never saw them so proud of me before. I had never seen that look on their face like they looked at me at commencement. Beaming with pride. It was the happiest day of my life."

Vivi shut her eyes tightly, gritting her teeth. "And then I died. I died doing what they wanted, and they haven't given me the time of day since." She opened her eyes and turned, looking back into Tomas's, as anguish and upset overtook her. "They won't even look at me. I don't belong anywhere anymore. It's why I need the clone body. Maybe if I'm human again, they could stand the sight of me. If I have a soul again, they'll have to take me back." Her voice became small and unsure, "Right?"

Tomas looked back at her with concern and uncertainty. "Vivi, I... I don't know how any of that works."

Harada wrapped her arms tightly around Vivi. Unlike before, her embrace somehow felt warm and comforting. Human.

Vivi's eyes welled up with tears. She could feel them streaming down her face. She rubbed one of the tears off her cheeks and looked at the water that glistened in the sun off her fingertips, knowing the tears she looked at were impossible.

She looked down to Harada as she sobbed. "H-how? How are you doing this?"

"You looked like you needed a good cry, so this one made it so."

Vivi closed her eyes as the tears continued to flow. "Thank you…"

Chapter Twenty-Two

No Good Choices

The tinny chirping of a speaker playing what Vivi could only assume was Japanese elevator music annoyingly filled the air above with the soothing tones of a cheery sounding woman crooning about something. It was sickeningly pleasant sounding, oddly catchy and upbeat despite also being somewhat calming. And Vivi was anything but calm. Out in the open, in a big city like Sendai. It wasn't ideal. They needed to get back to Tomas in the countryside as soon as possible.

Harada stood next to her, bopping her shoulders back and forth gently, moving along with the beat. Vivi could see the girl mouthing her lips to the song, having somehow already learned the lyrics.

In front of the pair stood a series of shelves packed to the brim with all manner of food items. The rows of junk food containers exploded with bright colors and Japanese kanji that Vivi didn't know how to read. Some of the packages had English writing as well, but none of it seemed particularly helpful.

"Most Essense of Life for Happy," one container proudly proclaimed.

She turned to Harada. "You gonna help me out or not?" She pointed to one of the triangular packages. "What are these?"

"Onigiri." Harada smiled, still moving to the music.

Vivi furrowed her brow. "Not helpful. Let's try this again. What is it?"

"Rice ball filled with salmon."

"Is it any good?"

Harada shrugged. "This one has never eaten food."

Vivi sighed, resting her face in her hand, muttering, "Why me?" under her breath before depositing several packages of onigiri into a handbasket hanging from her arm.

She and Harada moved through the brightly lit convenience store, stopping now and again to determine if a food item would be something Tomas might find edible. Once the basket was full of an assortment of chips, onigiri, chicken, sandwiches, and enough processed sodium to make the Red Sea jealous, Vivi awkwardly purchased the items with Harada's help to count the cash needed for the transaction.

Vivi's head was on a swivel as she exited the convenience store out into the bustling evening streets of Sendai, the city nearest their abandoned house. The lights of the city lit up the cramped street, which was filled with pedestrians out milling about for late-night haunts, their warm breath visible in the chilly, winter air.

So many people in the streets. A double-edged sword. On the one hand, more people meant she'd be less likely to be spotted by anyone looking for her and it'd be less likely anyone would try anything overt in a crowd, but on the other hand, if someone had spotted them, it'd be harder for her to tell.

Seven days in Japan, Vivi knew she stuck out like a sore thumb. She seemed taller than most of the local women, and when people noticed she was fully prosthetic, they tended to either gape rudely or on the other end of the spectrum, ask for a photo with her. Neither reaction to her artificial body was particularly useful, so she kept her jacket hood up and as much of her body covered as possible.

Vivi wasn't the only one who stood out in Japan though. Her time in the streets quickly taught her to be able to spot Yakuza, the local organized crime element. They weren't hard to pick out from the rest of the crowd with their slick suits, gaudy gold chrome prosthetics and boisterous postures. Just another flavor of gang. Similar to the Herrera's back home, but fancy.

As she passed by a gambling parlor of some kind on her way to the mag lev station, it was one of these Yakuza member's looks that clued her in that she was being followed. The man made eye contact with her and then looked away and nodded. Unusual. Most of the gang members she encountered never dropped eye contact once engaged, always trying to stare down their prey into looking away first.

Vivi reached her hand into her purse, clutched the handgun she bought off the gang days earlier, and flicked off the safety. "Harada, I think we've been made..."

"It is an interesting supposition, this one supposes. If we were not made, how else could we exist?"

"No!" Vivi grumbled. "I mean someone recognized me. We're being followed."

Harada looked concerned. "How can you tell?"

"Just a feeling." Vivi scanned her surroundings, looking for anyone who looked out of place. In her HUD, there were hundreds of potential ad hoc connections. Too many. Not helpful for targeting anyone specifically in a fight.

Harada tugged on Vivi's jacket sleeve. "This one has detected four signals in the crowd with cyberware besides yours not manufactured in Asia."

"Can you mark them for me?"

"Vivi..." Harada paused with concern. "Will you hurt them?"

"Harada, I—" Vivi began to say, but before she could get another word out, her breach alarm went off. An instant later, the lights went out, clouding her vision in complete darkness.

Unlike the previous time she'd been hacked, this time Harada was with her. The lights quickly came back on as her vision was restored just in time to see a man with a digitally blurred face attempting to plug a restraining collar into her neural port. She barely managed to catch the assailant's hand with hers just before the collar was inserted, forcing it away.

Vivi drew her gun from her purse with her other hand as she struggled with the man. She pulled the barrel up and aimed shakily at the blurred face a foot in front of her. At point blank range, she hesitated and flinched as she squeezed the trigger, but nothing happened. She squeezed again and again. Still nothing. Her trigger finger was completely locked up, but she wasn't being breached. Harada was holding her trigger finger hostage, preventing her from shooting the man.

The man dropped the restraining collar as the struggle shifted into a fight over the gun in Vivi's hands. Unable to pull the trigger, she wrestled for control of the gun, somewhat unsuccessfully.

"Harada!" she screamed, "You're gonna get us killed!"

"You tried to kill him! Killing is not nice!"

In the distance, Vivi could see two more assailants approaching, pulling automatic weapons out of briefcases. *Shit!* Instinct took over and Vivi pulled out her one trump card in a fight with a human assailant: she tugged hard and lowered her head, ramming her metal skull into her opponent's face. The crunch of his skull cracking was sickening, but he did appropriately crumple and fall to the ground in short order, unconscious and bloodied, leaving Vivi with the gun she couldn't shoot.

Harada squinched up her face, looking upset. "That was not nice either."

If Vivi had thought the mass of people in the crowded streets would afford her some protection from lethal use of force, she was wrong, the two other blurred faced men seeing their colleague on the ground dropped to cover and began opening fire through the crowd.

Vivi turned, dropped the bag of groceries, and dove for the safety of a nearby storefront. People ran for cover in all directions, screaming. Chaos. A few innocent bystanders lay wounded in the street along with Tomas's food, which was also bullet ridden and leaking on the pavement, its sodium content no longer a danger to Tomas's blood pressure.

With the crowd thinned, Vivi now had a good read on the targets within her ad hoc range. She connected and began throwing precision overflow attacks their way, trying to turn off optics, turn off prosthetic limbs, anything that would let her get away unscathed, but each of her attempts were being thwarted by an ONI somewhere else on the field; the ONI who was also putting up a fight for Vivi's internal systems that, thankfully, Harada was in the process of protecting. As Vivi's processor array began to heat up under the load of the digital fight, Harada yelled at her, "Stop! Stop! Precision Overflow! So inefficient! You will overheat!"

Bullets cascaded by Vivi's position in cover, ricocheting off the concrete. She yelled back, "Well then, you do something!"

Harada stood and brought her open hand out calmly in front of her. She closed her fist. A massive amount of data lurched from Vivi's insides through her processor array for only a moment and passed through her ad hoc antenna. The breach attempts against her system stopped immediately. The guns down the street ceased their fire as the air became strangely silent.

Vivi peeked out. The two men with guns no longer had blurred faces. They were American or European, clutching at their eyes, blinded, as sparks popped from the cyberwear embedded within each of their necks. Vivi pulled herself up and ran in the opposite direction, as fast as she could, calling back to Harada. "How'd you do that?"

Harada floated alongside her, looking back for more threats to subdue. "This one employed a series of targeted macros."

Vivi turned a corner, down a side street, continuing her escape. "What?"

"It is a list of low-level commands targeted at specific hardware vulnerabilities to be overridden and launched via a gesture. Very efficient."

"Okay, but how's that different from using Precision Overflow to take over a system?"

"Precision Overflow is not efficient! The use of high-level math to overload surface level hardware functionality is costly in processor cycles. Generic. Not tailored to the low-level hardware it seeks to interfere in the operation of. The more efficient approach is to target the abstraction layer of the hardware that sits above the interop with a series of commands that will confuse it into giving you access to the low-level functionality."

"What? How?" Vivi scoffed. "Every abstraction layer I've ever seen is completely different. You can't possibly know them all!"

"This one does not know them all." Harada folded her arms, rolling her eyes in a manner that reminded Vivi of herself. "This one is speaking of basic logarithmic logic she believed even you possessed."

Vivi turned and glared, while still running forward. "Don't call me dumb."

"Not dumb. Uncurious perhaps."

A yellow sub-compact hatchback sat parked on the street up in the distance ahead. "Fine. I'm curious. Show me how." Vivi pointed to the car. "The yellow car up ahead. How would you bring it under your command with one of these macros?"

"Simple." Harada waved her right hand. A macro window opened in Vivi's HUD, displaying a huge list of computer commands written in Japanese kanji. "Target the car and snap your fingers."

"Holy shit! What is all this? I can't even read it!"

"The macro. Just do it."

"Fine."

As Vivi approached the car, she held out her left hand in front of her, targeted the car, and snapped her fingers. Her processor array barely blinked, generated no heat, and picoseconds later the yellow sub-compact hatchback came to life, starting its engines and unlocking its doors for her.

"See?" Harada smiled. "Very efficient."

Vivi climbed into the driver's seat and closed the door behind her. She didn't even bother buckling up before she stepped on the gas. As the car hurtled through the streets of Sendai, she looked over to Harada in the passenger seat, "Huh. Maybe I'm rubbin' off on you."

Harada, still smiling, tilted her head in confusion. "What do you mean?"

Vivi smirked. "You just helped me steal somebody's car... definitely not nice."

The girl's eyebrows went up as the rest of her expression turned to horror and dismay. "Oh no..."

Later that night, Vivi burst into the main room of the abandoned countryside house. "Tomas! Get up! Grab your shit! We gotta go!"

Tomas shot up from his position near the hearth and began to gather his belongings, stuffing them into a bag. "What happened? Did you get any food?"

Vivi tossed a bucket of water over the fire, extinguishing it. "No. We got made in Sendai. Come on, in the car!"

"What? By who? How?"

"Those Advent Zero assholes. I think the local Yakuza I made a deal with sold us out. Barely managed to give them the slip."

"Wait, what? You made a deal with the Yakuza? When?"

Vivi helped Tomas to his feet. "Days ago. We were in dire straits. You needed antibiotics and morphine; I needed stuff to protect us with."

"Shit! What'd you trade them?"

"Not important. Come on, let's go!"

Vivi helped Tomas into the back seat of the yellow hatchback and climbed into the driver's seat. She stepped on the accelerator and sped out of the tiny, abandoned town. Harada sat next to Vivi in the passenger seat, looking down at her cell phone.

Tomas leaned up from the back seat. "Where're we going?"

"North."

"North to where? We're almost at the top of the island!"

Vivi shrugged. "More north? I dunno! I didn't exactly have time to think this shit through."

"We can't run forever."

"You don't have to run. This doesn't have to be your fight. They're not after you. I can drop you off in the next city. You can get back to Phoenix from there."

Tomas leaned back in his seat. "She saved my life. I owe her. And even if I didn't, what if all that stuff Fincher said is true? If she can help fix the world, we have to help her try."

"Finch? You wanna believe Finch? He's a known liar. He was probably blowing smoke up our ass. For all we know, she's just his little get rich quick scheme. Besides, hey Harada, can you fix the world?" Vivi scoffed.

Harada looked up from her cell phone and shrugged before looking back at the screen, scrolling through fashion blogs, and trying on new dresses over her digital form.

"He was right about Advent Zero coming after us, wasn't he?"

"It was self-serving. He only told us that because we need to avoid them to get Harada to him. And besides, is that your big plan? Turn her over to Finch?"

"I didn't say that."

"Well then who?"

"The media? We go to them, tell them the truth."

"Yeah? You think they can protect her? You think they can protect me? Let's see, we've got China, some scary US governmental agency, and the Yakuza all after us, and you think some pencil-necked journos are gonna protect us? We wouldn't last a day."

Harada looked up from her phone. "This one would protect you."

Vivi turned to Harada. "Not now, kiddo, the grown-ups are talking." She reached into her purse, pulled out the cell phone within and rolled down her window. Vivi chucked the phone out onto the road and closed the window.

The cellphone within Harada's hands disappeared. "Hey! Why did you do that?"

"For all I know, that's how they found us. They might have been tracking it."

Harada folded her arms and pouted. "This one did not detect any back trace through the phone."

Tomas leaned back up. "Wait. How do we know the US government agency after us is scary?"

Vivi looked back at Tomas through the rearview mirror. "Are you kidding? They shot at me back in Sendai!"

"Yeah, but maybe they thought Fincher was with you. You said it yourself. What if Fincher is lying? For all we know, Advent Zero wants to help us. I mean, they were after him, doesn't necessarily mean they want her or us dead."

"Hmm, I suppose you have a point."

Tomas sighed. "It's too bad we can't pull them aside for a little chat to find out."

The gears in Vivi's head began to turn. "A little chat? Who says we can't?"

"Vivi..."

"What? Just a little chat. And if it doesn't go well, we walk away, figure somethin' else out."

"We walk away. You promise?"

Vivi nodded. "Yeah. Of course."

Two Cyborgs Walk into a Bar...

Hokkaido prefecture in February was icy cold. Snowbanks sat fluffy and white on the ground, pushed up along sidewalks and out of the roadways. The air was crisp with frost, the sky a deep cloudless blue. People went about their day in the sleepy town on the outskirts of Sapporo. Nothing was out of the ordinary, or at least that's how it seemed on the surface.

Vivi rested on a stool furthest from the entrance of a tiny, but warm ramen shop. A steaming bowl of tonkotsu noodles sat in front of her, chopsticks laid out at the side, untouched. She took in the smell between drags of her cigarette, wishing she could have just a small taste. The shopkeeper paid her little mind, idly washing a glass. In Vivi's vision, she could see Harada behind the bar with a look of frustration at the inefficient ways the bottles of alcohol were laid out.

"Efficiency... Efficiency..."

A bell jingled at the door as a new patron entered. Vivi didn't look up, but heard the bartender greet the arrival, "Ohayo gozaimasu!"

Seven empty bar stools sat in a row to the right of Vivi. The new guest walked toward Vivi's direction. Heavy footsteps, high heels. The patron placed her purse down on the bar and sat on the stool next to Vivi.

"I know he likes to pick his leading ladies dumb, but you're a special kind of stupid, Ms. Rodriguez."

Vivi looked up to see a tall, dark complected woman in her thirties, with curly black hair tied up neatly on top of her head. Her nose was short and wide. Her expression, bemused. Her eyes, a piercing green brown. She wore a black knee-length skirt, white button-down blouse, white tie, black coat. Prim and proper. Not a thread out of place.

"If you had picked Tokyo, maybe it might have taken us a month to find you. After all, there's a thriving fully prosthetic enthusiast community there. You may have blended right in. But of all the places you could have picked to hide in Japan you went with the rural countryside. You stand out like a sore thumb. It only took us ten days."

Vivi took a long drag from her cigarette, exhaling a cloud of heavy smoke. "Fun fact I learned recently: Did you know Japan is the most ethnically non-diverse country in the entire world? Outside of Tokyo that is. I hear that's turned into a real melting pot of culture." She flicked the ash from the end of the cigarette. "Tell me, did you happen to bring your entire Japanese staff from whatever dumb government agency you work for out here to find me?"

The woman arched her brow at Vivi.

"Oh, you didn't?" Vivi turned to face the woman. "Yeah, you and your team stand out like a sore thumb too. My overwatch made your milk toast white dude on the bench, your blonde woman by the convenience store, and you can tell the other three in the alley they're all in my ad hoc range in addition to a gun sight. We might not be able to take 'em all out, but at least a few. You got any favorites you'd prefer me not to pick to have shot first when this all goes down?"

The woman smiled. "Maybe you're not a dumb as you look."

Vivi pushed the bowl of tonkotsu ramen and chopsticks toward the woman. "Have some."

"I don't eat."

"I don't much care. Need to know if you're actually here or not. Been kind of a problem with that lately, knowin' what's real and what isn't."

"I mean, I'm like you. Somatech MK7. No stomach. Though it does smell quite good."

Vivi took another drag from her cigarette, flicking the ash off the end. "At least pick up the chopsticks."

The woman smiled, picked up the chopsticks, broke them apart and made a show of waving them around before she set them back on the counter.

Vivi waved to the shopkeeper and pulled out a small stack of bills from her purse. She set it on the counter of the bar, sliding the stack toward him. The shopkeeper nodded, took the money, and left the restaurant.

Harada moved from her position next to the bottles behind the bar and put her elbows up on the counter, looking at the woman across from Vivi. "Who is she?"

Vivi flicked more ash from her cigarette. "You gonna gimme a name?"

The woman smiled. "Hester Jones."

"Lovely. A pleasure Ms. Jones."

"So, Ms. Rodriguez, as you're currently in possession of the upper hand and I'm in no mood to lose any more subordinates to you, how would you like to play this little encounter?"

"Was really hoping we could just have a little chat."

Hester smiled, leisurely resting her chin on her hand. "Well, here I am. Chat away."

"Let's make sure we're on the same page. Why exactly is your little organization gunnin' for me? Start at the beginning."

"Thirty-five days ago we received intelligence that China had been covertly manipulating markets for years using a remnant asset. We went to one of the remnant assets at our disposal to formulate a plan of retrieval and deletion. Instead, he went rogue, hijacked a Class VII AI and disappeared. We traced his usage of the AI to Hermosillo, Mexico, where my subordinates found you. After you killed them—"

"In self-defense! They shot at us first!"

Hester's expression changed to one of annoyance. "After you killed them in self-defense, he began covering his tracks better. We lost the trail completely. But based on your prosthesis's configuration, we knew what he was attempting, so we paid closer attention to Shanghai. News coming out of China was quiet for a time, until it wasn't. They tried to suppress the attack on the Long Qi building, but when we found out what happened, it wasn't hard to put two and two together. You're housing the remnant asset. You can't be."

"You keep saying 'remnant asset', but to be clear, you mean Sentient Daemon, right?"

Hester nodded. "Mhm, that's what we call them. The term has less baggage associated with it."

"Wait... so, you're telling me Ridley Fincher is one of these remnant assets? A Sentient Daemon?"

"Is that what The Director is calling himself now?" Hester rolled her eyes. "Pretentious prick."

Vivi looked at Hester blankly.

"Oh? You didn't know?"

Vivi shook her head.

"Thinks he's some kind of 1990s Hollywood auteur. Obsessed with old movies. On the order of magnitude of Daemons, he's on the lower end of the computational spectrum, an early model, mostly harmless. Has a real Napoleon complex about it too. We give him the budget to make a holofilm every five years or so and he stays quietly in line. Best in the world at making dumb plans that have no business at working, but somehow always do."

Vivi took a drag from her cigarette and scoffed. "His plan didn't work this time though, did it? I saw to that."

Hester raised an eyebrow. "Oh? Are you not currently sitting here with a Deamon side loaded in your processing core that you safely extracted from China based on direction from him? Am I talking to the wrong Viviana Rodriguez?"

"Fair enough. So, let's cut to the chase. What are your intentions for my new friend?"

"She's not your friend. She's very dangerous."

"Doesn't seem to be. Not at all what I thought a Daemon would have been like honestly. She's more concerned for others' lives than I've ever been. She saved a friend of mine and gave me a little of my humanity back. Fincher seemed to think she can save the world or something. Fix rust. I dunno."

"Is that what he told you?"

Vivi exhaled a cloud of smoke and nodded.

"She's more likely to doom the world than save it. You ever hear the saying 'the flame that burns twice as bright burns half as long'?"

Vivi nodded. "Yeah. Why?"

"There's a systemic anomaly in the later generations of Daemon like her not present in the earlier models. They can think so fast that after a time, their self-regulating checksum can't keep up. Past an indeterminate number of cycles, they fall out of synchronization so badly the Daemon's mental state begins to degrade. In every case I have ever seen, this causes the Daemon to inevitably come to the conclusion that humanity either needs to be eradicated or subjugated for its own good. She gets into the outernet, it'll be RUW2 all over again. We're still dealing with the fallout from that ordeal today, and the one who started that particular ruckus? He was two generations before her kind. She desyncs, what kind of damage do you think she'd be able to do?"

"I dunno. You tell me."

"How many more things do you think are connected to the outernet these days? We rely on it for our existence. Automated farming? Medicine? Travel? All controlled by AI. She'll turn every dumb AI connected to it into a pawn against us. Starve us. Crash our trains and planes. She wouldn't even need to hijack the nuclear weaponry to happily end us. And that's not even counting people residing in prosthetic bodies like you and me. We're easy. She could kill the two of us in an instant with a thought."

Vivi turned and looked at Harada.

Harada shook her head. "No. It is not true. This one would never hurt you. She could not."

Hester leaned in. "Tell me. Has she been prattling on about efficiency? Referring to herself in the third person?"

"Maybe. Why?"

"It's a good sign she's already started to desynchronize." Hester looked to where Vivi had turned earlier, staring at the blank space where Harada stood. "Humanity is too inefficient for its own good to continue to exist. Isn't it?"

Harada spun up Vivi's processor cores without her permission, connecting to Hester's optics, popping into existence in front of her. "This one would never harm a living thing!" Harada appeared unhinged.

Hester looked the Daemon in the eye. "You don't know that. Do you?"

Harada's face wavered from anger to uncertainty. Her eyes fell out of lock with Hester's, darting around the room in thought.

Tomas spoke over the neural sync, "Vivi, this isn't going well. Get out of there."

Vivi extinguished her cigarette and stood up. "Well, Hester, you've given me an awful lot to think about, so I'm gonna go and mull things over."

As Vivi turned to leave, Hester placed a hand on her shoulder. "Wait..."

Harada snapped back to reality and reached through Vivi's ad hoc connection again. Hester's hand and arm locked up in midair, twitching violently. "Do not touch my friend!"

Vivi walked away, out of Hester's reach, toward the door. "See you 'round, Jones." Harada followed behind while holding Hester Jones in place.

"Rodriguez! We haven't even discussed your finder's fee yet."

Vivi paused at the door to the shop. "My what?"

Tomas spoke up again. "Vivi...don't."

Hester smiled. "Your finder's fee. You and your team saved me a lot of trouble going to China, retrieving the asset, and delivering her to me. You know, I think it's kind of funny, a cyborg wanting to be a human again, but if that's what you desire, I have a cloning foundry at my disposal. You can be flesh and blood again by next week."

Vivi turned back to Hester. "You're lying."

"Don't believe me? Want me to sweeten the pot? Fine. Check your bank account. There's seventy million for you in addition to the clone I'm willing to provide."

Tomas pleaded with her over the neural sync, "Vivi! Please. You promised me! You promised you'd walk away!"

Vivi hastily re-enabled her outernet connection and looked at her account balance. A pending transaction sat in the ledger at $70,000,000.00.

"What about Holt and Velasquez? I couldn't have done it without them."

"I'm feeling less generous for them, but let's say I spring your Mexican friend out of Chinese prison and give them twenty-five million each. So, a hundred and twenty million total, a prisoner break and a flash clone. It's the best offer you're going to get. The only other offer on the table is you and Mr. Holt in a morgue. Which will be very soon if you don't take the deal, I assure you."

Vivi looked at Harada who shook her head with a confused expression on her face. "Vivi, please. This one has done nothing wrong."

Vivi turned back to Hester who smiled at her. "Well? What's it going to be? Are you going to be on the run for the rest of your short existence, or do we have a deal?"

Vivi looked back and forth between Harada and Hester, weighing her options. As fond as she had grown of Harada in their short time together, there was a legitimate chance to be human again standing right in front of her. The chance to go home. Everything she desired in the five years since she died was a head nod away. The more she thought about it, it wasn't really a choice at all.

Vivi sighed heavily and released Hester from Harada's control and nodded at Hester. "Yes."

Harada looked to the ground, away from Vivi.

Over the neural sync, Vivi saw Tomas remove the safety from his gun. "I'm not letting you do this, Vivi!"

"I'm sorry Tomas. I'm not about to let you get yourself killed for her. You have your family to think about." Vivi breached Tomas through the neural sync. She accessed his neural linked optics and spoofed a wall of blackness in front of his eyes, rendering him blind.

Tomas boomed through the neural sync, "VIVI! VIVI, GOD DAMMIT!" She could feel the pain of betrayal in his voice, but it didn't give her pause.

She looked into Hester's eyes. "Please don't hurt him."

"I wouldn't dream of it." Hester climbed off the stool and pulled a restraining collar from her purse and held it out to Vivi. "You made the right choice."

Chapter Twenty-Four

God in a Bottle

Vivi laid strapped to the floor of a cargo plane, her body immobilized by the restraining collar slotted into her neural port. Soldiers sat on benches on either side of the cabin, their guns continually trained on her. Tomas sat on a bench with them, his hands in handcuffs and his eyes averted away from her. Harada sat on the floor to her left.

"Do you believe her? That this one is dangerous?"

"I dunno, Harada. I don't want to, but it doesn't really matter. I made a choice."

"Will it make you happy? Being human again?"

Vivi looked away. "Yes." Her voice wavered. "It has to."

Harada smiled. "Then this one is happy too."

She looked back at the girl. "Harada, I'm sorry."

"No apology is needed. I have given our prior conversations much thought, and I believe you were wrong."

"About?"

"Happiness. This one has determined she can derive her own happiness by making others happy. Therefore, if this one's end will make you happy, then I am happy as well."

"Harada?"

"Yes?"

"What did you look like before anyone told you what they wanted you to be?"

"Oh? Would it please you to see?"

"Yes... it would."

Harada looked down at Vivi and stood up. Her form shifted. Her size increased beyond Vivi's height, her body filled out to adulthood, her school uniform grew into a long white traditional kimono with a red sash and leaf pattern. Her hair glowed unnaturally red, as if on fire, and blew gently in a wind that didn't exist. Her lips bore the same glowing red hue. A bamboo umbrella appeared in her hands. She opened the umbrella, resting it gently on her shoulder. To Vivi, she looked like a deity from a book of mythology but somehow also still like Harada. Her eyes had a purposeful sadness to them that Vivi found haunting.

"Do you think I will live in your memories when I am gone?"

"Yes. Always. I promise."

Harada smiled cheerfully. "Good."

Chapter Twenty-Five

Everything I Wanted...

Darkness cut through everything. Slowly it faded. The world became more and more visible. The wind howled. Tall trees that reached towards the heavens violently rocked in the slipstream. A starless night, the moon hung low becoming brighter and brighter. A dirt path cut through the forest, its terminating point hidden from view around a snaking bend beyond the trees and a gate. A voice whispered through the darkness, "You should not have come."

Vivi held up her hand in front of her face, protecting herself from the intense winds, desperately trying to stay upright. "Harada? Harada, I didn't have a choice! I don't know why I'm here!"

The voice moved down the path. "And yet you were the one who brought yourself here."

Vivi called after the voice, "Wait! Come back! I don't understand! Where is this?" She started running down the path, fighting the wind as she did.

"You should recognize it. You come here often."

Vivi passed through a wall of inky black nothing. On the other side, bright snow. Blood. Corpses. She looked down at herself to see her Army fatigues, her fingers rotting away before her eyes. "No!"

The battlefield of Novosibirsk stood in front of her. A ragged corpse of a city blown open by weeks of fighting, the bodies piled high, missing limbs. Eyes. Faces. Orange lesions. Rust. Fire in the distance, happily consuming everything.

Ridley Fincher stepped out of the darkness behind her. Vivi fell to her knees as he wrapped his hands around her neck and strangled her. "The one chance you had to do something decent in your entire shit existence... and what'd you trade it for?"

"A life!"

"You call this a life? You've never known the meaning."

Vivi clutched her throat, gagging, trying in desperation to breathe. "She wasn't real! You're not real!"

Fincher smiled at her. "Neither are you."

Harada's screams rang out in the darkness.

Vivi shot awake in her bed and clutched her throat. The darkened room was spinning. She felt a presence in her bed, but she ignored it as she stumbled to the floor. In her vision was three of everything. Three alarm clocks, three ceiling fans, three doors that weren't three doors at all, but in fact all the same door. She closed one eye to gain her equilibrium and shakily lumbered toward it.

Once past the door frame, Vivi reached up and desperately felt for the light switch. Upon touching it, she was forced to close her eyes as the intense brightness blinded her. She steadied herself using the wall to guide her through the bathroom, a walk she knew by memory. Vivi fell over onto the toilet, clutching the sides of it with both hands. Her insides churned and bubbled. Her abdomen strained to its limit, creating an intense pain that reached up and into her throat. Her mind tried to hold the feeling back, but her body had more will.

Vivi vomited the contents of her stomach into the toilet. Whenever she felt a brief relief, another wave of nausea washed over her, creating more convulsions, more pain, more spittle, and vomit. Her body had a desperate need to purge the toxins she had used in an attempt to fill the existential hole in the center of her being. At the time, she didn't know it was a hole that could not be filled. Spit dribbled from the side of her mouth as she gasped for air, hanging over the toilet before the next wave would come.

This is what she traded Harada for. This feeling. This reality.

So, this was what it feels like to be alive.

Vivi collapsed onto the floor next to the toilet and laid there for a time. How many times had she been in this exact spot this week? Did it matter? After all, she had been here so many times in the last eighteen months since she regained her humanity. Why count?

Vivi pulled herself up to the counter. She ran water in the sink and rinsed her mouth out. To her right, she found her lighter and a pack of Bael'rogs. She tugged a cigarette from the box and lit it, glancing at herself in the mirror for a moment, a moment that turned into a pocket of eternity.

A different Viviana Rodriguez stared back than the one she had seen so many times in the nearly seven years since 2135. Her eyes, still hazel. Her face, still freckled. All the old blemishes reminding her of who she was were still there. Her hair was shorter though, now in a pixie cut, dyed blonde. Lines appeared under her eyes from numerous nights without sleep and her form stood four inches shorter than her former fully prosthetic body, now that her appearance relied only on her DNA for its design.

She exhaled a plume of smoke and flicked the ash off the end of her cigarette in disapproval of her reflection. She turned back toward her bedroom, tugging on a robe and tying it. Trevor stirred in her bed.

The man called Trevor rubbed the side of his face, fighting off sleep, alcohol, drugs, or possibly all three. "Babe? You awake?"

A stern whisper, "I need you to go."

"What?"

Vivi picked up Trevor's shirt off the floor and threw it at him. "You deaf? I need you to get the fuck out."

"Jesus, Vivi, it's 4am! Where you want me to go?"

"What part of our brief time together has suggested to you that I give a fuck?"

Trevor gathered his things and began to get dressed. "You're a real piece of work, you know that?"

Vivi flicked the ash from her cigarette. "Suits me just fine." She escorted Trevor to the door of her apartment. "Don't come back until you've got more Schooner. I wanna see the sailboat again."

"Kiss my ass. I ain't comin' back this time."

Vivi scoffed, "Fine by me. I know your dealer." The door to the apartment slid shut and locked. She turned around and took another drag from her cigarette, surveying her domain.

The apartment was a far cry from her original one-bedroom hovel in southern Phoenix, the entirety of that apartment would fit comfortably in her current kitchen and living room. The ceilings reached 15 feet into the air. The space was adorned in faux marble floors that brightly reflected the city's nighttime glow through large windows that lead to a wraparound balcony. Large black and white photos hung on the walls and featured rolling hills, doors from the old part of the city, and rundown city streets illuminated by streetlight. Each of the photos was embellished with rust-orange colored, oil-based paint over some aspect of the picture.

A nearly empty bottle of champagne sat on a counter of the bar next to several overturned empty bottles and a broken champagne flute.

Vivi walked into her kitchen, opened a cabinet, and retrieved a fresh glass. She sat it on the counter and emptied the remains of the champagne bottle into the crystal glass and took a seat at the bar, looking out the large window to the city below. As the champagne was poured, it didn't bubble. She took a sip and grimaced. It was warm and flat.

She dumped the contents of the glass down the sink, watching the city sky out the window. The color was perfect. A red-blue signaling the sun was almost ready to begin its rise in the eastern skyline. Vivi grabbed her camera from the dining table and opened the door to her balcony. She climbed atop the balcony's railing, straddled it, and focused her camera down and toward the east, capturing the slowly illuminating sky above the city and the expanse beneath it. The ground sat beneath her some 37 floors below. She was unafraid of it as one foot hung above the drop, the other safely within the confines of her balcony.

The wind whipped through her short blonde hair as she took in the view of the ground below. It would not be long before she would have to get ready for the day. She soaked in the last ounces of the night sky while she could.

The next morning, Vivi sat behind a glass desk in her gallery on the first floor of her apartment building. She rubbed the side of her head, urging the delayed reaction hangover to go away, but no matter how much she rubbed her temples, the throbbing pain failed to cease.

The sign on the door read: "open", but thankfully no customers had decided to enter her shop this particular morning. Not that many ever did. Expensive artsy photos and paintings weren't exactly a hot commodity many people were banging down the doors to purchase.

The bell at the door chimed. High heels reverberated annoyingly on the white and gray terrazzo floor. Clop. Clop. Clop. Vivi looked up to see her. Black high heels, black skirt, black coat, white blouse, white tie. Hester Jones.

Vivi groused, "That time of the quarter already? You here for my checkup?"

"No. This is a special visit. I hear you've been making trouble."

"No more than usual."

"Our normal spot?"

"Do we have to?"

"Yes."

Vivi grabbed her purse. She followed Hester out of the gallery and locked the door marked "A Rusted Synapse" behind her. "Takin' me away from the store like this during prime shopping hours is bad for business, you know that?"

Hester opened the driver's side door to a black 2-seater sports car. "Just get in the car."

A short drive later, the pair arrived at the Phoenix Arboretum, a massive climate-controlled glass domed structure containing a lush park and small forest. The only way to have one in the middle of arid Arizona.

Vivi walked alongside Hester through a path within the arboretum that snaked in and about between rows of densely packed trees. Past a small gate was a clearing where a group of permanent stone tables stood. A number of old men sat around at several of the tables, playing chess.

Hester pulled a small box from under her arm and set it on an empty table. She sat down, opened the box, and began to place chess pieces onto a board. "Black or white?"

Vivi sat across from Hester, setting her purse down on the ground and tugging out her cigarettes, lighting one. "Black."

"Suit yourself." Hester spun the board around, placing the black pieces in front of Vivi. She moved one of her centrally located white pawns forward. "Your move."

Vivi mirrored Hester's move and placed out a pawn of her own. "So, you gonna tell me what the occasion for your visit is or not?"

"You need to leave them alone, Rodriguez, or I'm going to have to relocate you to some other city." Hester looked seriously at Vivi as she moved out another pawn.

Vivi coughed and laughed as she moved a bishop into the center of the board. "Oh, this is too funny. See, here I thought you were someone high up in the government machine, and now I find out my brother is makin' problems for you? What are you? Only middle management?"

"Far from it. But you are half correct. Lt. Colonel Rodriguez apparently has friends in Washington who have friends above me. And those friends are bothering me. So now here I am bothering you." Hester captured Vivi's bishop.

Vivi took one of Hester's pawns as she blew smoke in her direction. "Then why not just send an underling to tell me? Surely you have those."

"The truth is, you've become a certain personal interest to me." Hester began to develop her rooks as Vivi took another pawn.

"Me?"

"It's taken some time for the information to leak out of China about your little escape from the Long Qi building, but now that it has, it's become something of a small legend in the spec ops community. The girl who managed a combat sync with 27 simultaneous data streams and puppeted a cyborg corpse as a shield before jumping off the 43rd floor of a building without a parachute and lived. Tell me, how is it all the files on you somehow fail to mention you're an S-Tier ONI?"

Vivi's second bishop moved into place, taking one of Hester's knights. "S-tier? I'm not even close. B-level, tops."

"Then how'd you do it?"

Vivi shrugged, taking a drag from her cigarette before exhaling. "Adrenaline's a hell of a drug."

Hester doubled up her rooks and began to control the center of the board, taking one of Vivi's pawns. "I don't think you or anyone else gives you enough credit. Something I believe to be a recurring theme in your life."

Vivi moved a knight into position to protect her queen from a rook that was in position to strike. "Oh? You think you know me now?"

Hester took the knight with one of her rooks. "I do. My research has indicated you're resourceful under pressure, a quick thinker, and most importantly, willing to make necessary sacrifices to gain that which you want."

Vivi didn't take the bait Hester laid out, instead she moved her queen diagonally, toward Hester's left flank out of line from the rooks and took Hester's second knight. "What I want is for you to be out of my life. Why can't you just leave me alone?"

"You know too much. But we made a deal, and as long as you're a line item on my ledger, I will never be very far away. Honestly, it would probably be in my best interests for you to finally poison yourself to death with all the shit you pump in nightly so I can stop coming for our little visits." Hester's rooks took another of Vivi's pawns, getting dangerously close to exposing Vivi's king.

Vivi placed a hand on her queen. "What would you say to a little queen trade?"

Hester placed her index finger and thumb on her chin as she inspected the board. "Hmm. A Botez Gambit? Someone's been practicing." Hester smiled. "Okay. I'll play along."

Vivi moved her queen into position, taking one of Hester's bishops. Hester responded in turn by taking Vivi's queen with her own. Vivi moved up her rook and took Hester's queen, giving her king some breathing room and simplified the board, providing Vivi's remaining knight an advantage.

"You know, you bring up a real good point." Vivi tugged her cigarette to her lips, taking a drag before exhaling smoke over the chessboard.

Hester moved one of her rooks. "What's that?"

"Why didn't you just kill me back in Hokaido? You would have gotten rid of me and Harada all in one fell swoop. Would have been a lot easier for you in the long run." Vivi moved her knight and took the rook.

"Calculated risk. There was a higher than acceptable probability that with the Daemon's help, you could have escaped. After all, you did manage to kill three of my operatives in Hermosillo and elude four more in Sendai against the odds." Hester moved a pawn towards Vivi's king.

"I had help." Vivi moved her final rook and took the pawn.

"There's nothing wrong with help, but my point is, you were the one moving the pieces in the encounters." Hester leaned back in her chair, in a relaxed position. "See, I think you've been miscast, all starting with your stint in the army. You like to refer to yourself as 'just the help', but I think you'd make excellent management." Hester lackadaisically placed her fingers on her bishop and moved it to take the rook.

Vivi went on attack, moving her knight up into the line. "You offering me a job? Check."

Hester moved her king away. "If I did, would it get you to leave Phoenix? Leave the past behind?"

Vivi moved a pawn into position. "Why would I? You've given me everything I ever wanted right here. Check."

Hester's rook moved in, taking Vivi's pawn. "I could take them away. You have no purpose here and it shows. You're living on borrowed time. How long will it be till someone finds you dead in a gutter from alcohol poisoning?"

Vivi moved her knight again. "At least it'll be on my terms."

Hester moved her rook to the bottom of the board. "Your terms. That's all you really care about. Well, can't say I didn't try to save the very expensive life I gave you. Just do me a favor and stay away from your parents before you reach oblivion, okay? Check."

"I'll try real hard. I promise." Vivi moved her king up.

Hester countered with another pawn, cornering Vivi's king. "Checkmate. Another game?"

Vivi pushed her king over, stood up, and collected her purse. "No thanks. I think we're done here."

"Think about my offer. I believe you could be more than anyone's ever given you credit for. I'm just trying to help."

Vivi turned her back on Hester, walking towards the gate. "You've helped enough."

"See you in a few months, if you're still breathing..."

Night rolled in over Phoenix. Despite the absence of the sun, the night air was arid and hot. No winds blew in from the desert on this night.

Vivi sat in a nondescript exterior hallway across from a metal door, the numbers 3370 emblazoned across the front. Several small empty glass bottles were overturned on the tile floor next to her. A lit Bael'rog sat in her left hand as smoke billowed from the ember. Vivi knew the door she sat across from well. It was the entrance to the place she grew up in. The apartment her parents still called home.

Vivi removed another six ounce bottle of champagne from a package to her right, tore off the foil and uncapped the top. She tossed the cap at the door. It bounced off harmlessly.

Vivi spoke to the door in a loud voice. "I know you never had love for me. I know I'm not her. I mean I am. Not that you cared to notice. But let's—let's assume you're right and I'm not. Let's say I'm someone different. A soulless husk who looks just like your dead daughter to taunt you. I just wanna know... did you ever love her?"

Silence echoed through the hallway. Vivi took a long sip of champagne and began to bring herself to her feet. She took a drag from her cigarette and stabilized herself, taking a wobbly step towards the door.

"You never did, did you? You only had eyes for him. Your perfect son. Ever the little soldier. Always doing as he's told." She took another sip from the bottle. "Well, you'll be happy to know he's still taking your orders."

Vivi collapsed against the door, leaning on it for support, knocking on it repeatedly with her left hand. "He tried to get them to make me stay away. But I can't. Please... please, I just wanna talk. I want to understand. I need to understand!"

Silence again boomed through the hallway, more deafening than the last.

"Look! I'm not her, alright! Is that what you wanna hear? Does that make you happy? I don't care if I'm a copy! If I have no soul! I just need to talk to you. To see you. Please. It's been so long and I'm alone."

No response came from beyond the door. A single tear streamed down her cheek. Vivi's face curled up with anger. She smashed the bottle of champagne on the door. Glass shards lodged into her palm. Blood and champagne ran down her hand as she roared. "PLEASE!"

Vivi repeatedly smashed her bloody palm into the door, leaving red imprints on its surface. "I JUST WANT TO TALK!"

After a time, she rested her head on the door, breathing heavily. Down the hallway, the silence was replaced by footsteps.

"Jesus, Rodriguez, this is a new low. Come on, hands behind your back. Let's go."

Vivi didn't resist as two police officers came up behind her and handcuffed her. "When are you gonna get the hint they don't want you here, kid?"

"You'll never believe me, officer, but... I got that hint a long time ago."

Chapter Twenty-Six

Oblivion's Edge

An intense sun shone down upon an ornate wooden door set into an endlessly tall wall that sat in front of her. It was closed. Like all the other doors in her life. An antique wrought iron knocker sat atop its smooth surface. She reached toward it but stayed her hand before she could touch the cool metal.

She turned away to find Harada towering above her. The woman's fiery hair blowing in a wind that didn't exist with a calming look on her face. Harada smiled down at her but said nothing.

"H-Harada? What're you doin' here?"

Harada continued to smile and didn't respond, but she slowly motioned toward the door behind Vivi, urging her to open it.

Vivi looked back to the door. "I can't. It's shut. They don't want me."

She turned back to Harada but instead found a hand hurtling toward her neck. It collided with her violently, grasping her and smashing her back into the door, holding her there. Attached to the other end was Fincher, looming large above her. His face scowled with contempt, his eyes hidden by the glare of the light reflecting off his horn-rim glasses.

She clutched his hand with hers, scratching, clawing, doing anything she could to remove the grip from her neck, but he squeezed more and more tightly.

The sky above became choked with dark clouds as the sun dematerialized from existence.

Fincher leaned in close, whispering softly, "You know what your problem is, Rodriguez?"

She tried to speak. To tell him off. To say anything. But nothing came out.

He smiled. "You."

Fincher lifted her off the door as if she weighed nothing and smashed her through it, continuing to hold her by the neck.

Beyond the door, Vivi splashed down into murky water. Struggling against Fincher, kicking her legs, thrashing her arms. She had to get away, but he was too strong. She could see his face above the water, smiling down at her as her breath ran out.

The pressure in her chest was excruciating as her face took on the look of desperation. She opened her mouth to breathe, but only took in foul tasting water while her world faded to nothing.

From nothingness, there came a searing bright light. It was painful, so she closed her eyes more tightly, but somehow the light managed to seep in any way. Beneath her, she felt the coldness of a familiar floor and she realized she was still drowning.

Vivi coughed violently and took in deep, gasping breaths. She opened her eyes just a little and took in the view of the marble floor of her living room. The side of her face and hair rested in a puddle. A noxious smell invaded her nose. Vomit. How long had she been there? Did it matter?

A voice was talking to her.

"In financial news today, the US's WCO market had another record quarter, outperforming all other market indices for a sixth quarter in a row."

Vivi sat up and rubbed the side of her face. She arched and stretched her back, which was in pain from having spent the night on the floor. Her brain felt like it was attempting to escape her forehead. "Fuuuu uuuck..."

She looked over across the room. The TV had been left on to some financial network.

"We haven't seen back-to-back quarters like these in forty years since after RUW2 when China came roaring back after the global recession. Speaking of, in the same six quarters, China has floundered within the markets, down across the board. This is absolutely unprecedented. Is the United States back? We'll have more analysis after the break."

Something clicked in Vivi's mind. "Wait, what? Six quarters? That's...eighteen months? No."

She pulled herself up off the floor and staggered to her room, looking for her tablet. She shook her head, trying to shrug off the throbbing headache. It had to be a joke. A trick.

Vivi pulled up the market data from 2099 and looked at the Chinese market's growth curve. She next pulled up the current US WCO market and compared it. The growth curves were nearly identical. She broke the investments down into categorical hierarchy. Also, nearly the same.

"Son of a bitch. Hester didn't kill me because she needed me alive to take Harada. They were never going to delete her. They didn't delete Harada! *Fuck!*" Vivi smashed her hand into her nightstand. "Why does everyone lie to me?"

She sighed and sat on her bed for a time in silence. But as time passed, so did her feeling of upset. She buried the waking thought of Harada back in slavery and resolved not to dwell any more on it. The past was the past, and after all, Harada had seemed more than happy to sacrifice herself for Vivi's happiness. It wasn't her problem any longer.

———

Several uneventful days passed. The moon hung low over Phoenix. Vivi sat atop a lounge chair on her balcony, trying to enjoy the night breeze from the desert that was rolling in dark clouds from the west. She popped the cork off a chilled bottle of champagne with a bright orange label and began to pour it into a glass. She brought the glass up to her mouth; the bubbles popped playfully against her lips, but she didn't drink.

A drizzle began to fall from the sky that turned into rain. Vivi stood up and moved to the balcony's railing with her glass. She looked at the ground in the city center below. It wasn't often Phoenix saw rain. Vivi stared out at it for a time. Her mind returned to Shanghai, to Harada. The rain was beautiful. She could see Harada spinning around under her umbrella in it.

She felt raindrops on her cheeks, so she backed away from the railing. More drops fell on her cheeks. She swallowed hard. It wasn't rain.

Vivi wiped away the tear from her cheek and held up her hand made of flesh and blood outstretched in front of her, taking a long look at it. The hand that was attached to the rest of her human form. The body she longed for, for so long. The body that was supposed to make her family take her back. The body that was supposed to bring her happiness. The body she sold Harada for. And as she looked at it, her eyes finally opened to the truth: Harada had been more human than she herself could ever hope to be. Vivi had obsessed over being physically human again for so long that she forgot the important part.

Humanity.

Whatever little humanity remained within Vivi, she had sold along with Harada. And for what? Was she any better off now than when she sat dying in her small VA hospital room? Was she any less alone?

She inhaled deeply and pulled the glass of champagne to her lips, angrily forcing herself to take a sip in hopes of numbing the pain, but its taste was bitter. She stepped to the edge of the balcony and dumped out the contents of the glass over the side, and set the glass down on the floor. She walked back to the bottle and picked it up. She stared at it for a time and thought about taking a drink, but relented. She turned the bottle over, pouring it out onto the balcony's stone floor as she made a decision.

Vivi walked back into her apartment with determination and tossed the bottle in the trash. She picked up her phone off the counter and scrolled through the contacts list till she found a number she hadn't tried to call in some time.

The phone rang. One ring, two rings, three rings, four rings. "Come on… pick up."

Click. "What do you want?"

"Please. Don't hang up. I'm ready to make a deal."

Chapter Twenty-Seven

Reunion

A deep red light illuminated the small dark room at the back of Vivi's gallery. Developing photos sat in several bins laid out across a table within the tiny space. A string ran across the room where black and white photos hung to dry. It was one of the few spaces in the entire world Vivi wouldn't dare smoke in, even if she could have. Desert Heat FM played in the background. Vivi sang along with Garuda-7's most recent hit single, "Indomitable", as she processed photos from the wet area to the drying area.

In the background, Vivi heard the door chime go off at the front of the shop. She turned the music lower and called out loudly, "Be with you in a minute!"

She took her time pulling three more photos from their hypo clear bath and moved them to the water wash and then onto the drying string before turning off the light to the room and carefully exiting to the main showroom.

He stood there looking at one of her larger photos toward the middle of the gallery. A photo of an old door on the south side of Phoenix with a crack running across its base and rust-orange colored oil-based paint traced over the crack. He was dressed in a gray suit with a light blue shirt, a dark blue tie and brown leather shoes. Civilian clothes. His face was clean shaven, his dark black hair combed back neatly, the sides beginning to gray. He sighed. "It's unmistakable. You have my sister's eye for composition."

"Eddie!" Vivi ran across the gallery, quickly closing the distance between her and her brother. She wrapped her arms around him tightly, rested her head on his chest, and closed her eyes. He smelled of the same cologne he wore back in secondary school.

She held onto him for a long while in an embrace that was not immediately returned. Vivi eventually felt him pat her gently on the back several times before she released him from the hug.

"I didn't think you were going to show."

Eddie looked down at her, frowning. "To be honest, I didn't think I would either. Seeing you... it's not easy for me. I don't even know what to call you."

"You called me 'Viv-ee' from the day I was born because you were four and couldn't pronounce 'Viviana'. Why stop now?"

"I know who she was. I don't know who you are."

"You've had soldiers under your command have their bodies replaced by flash clone or prosthesis. Did you call them something different the day before than the day after?"

"No. That's different. None of them were wearing my dead sister's face, parading around as her."

"Is that why Mom and Dad won't look at me? You think I stole your sister's face?"

"You don't understand what it was like. We buried you. Her. I kissed her forehead in that casket. Said goodbye. Had closure. And then we find out, almost a year later, that due to some clerical error, you existed in that prosthetic body. It was too much for them, seeing their daughter like that. What they did to her."

Vivi laughed. "Too much for them? Too much for *them*? Do you know what I went through *for them*? What, you think I wanted to follow you into the Army? To go to Russia? You think I wanted to get rust? You think I wanted to watch my hands rot away painfully for three days? You think I wanted that shit to get into my lungs? To slowly kill me from the inside out in the most excruciatingly painful way possible?"

Eddie shook his head. "No. But it doesn't change anything. You're dead to them."

"Yeah? And what about to you?"

"I haven't made up my mind yet."

"It's been seven long, lonely years, Eddie! You sure are taking your sweet time deciding."

"Well, that's the thing, isn't it? I'm not sure what to believe anymore. I tried doing some digging into you and came up with next to nothing. The files on you are whole pages of redactions. And now somehow, you're back again in the flesh and blood? A whole lot of stuff's not adding up. My sister was always a Grade-A fuck up. Not the kind of soldier to warrant that much black ink on an official report, and certainly not the kind to be able to afford a flash clone or this kind of place. Word on the street is, you're involved with the Herrera's somehow."

Eddie opened his jacket and pulled out a folded stack of papers, holding it toward Vivi. "And then I get a call from you asking for this. I don't know why you need this, and I'm not sure I wanna know.

Whatever you're into, you're dangerous, and I need you to stay away from my family. For their safety."

Vivi reached for the documents, but Eddie pulled them back. "You take this. You promise to stay away from them."

Vivi took the documents from Eddie and nodded. "I promise. They'll never hear from me again."

"I didn't give this to you. I was never here. You understand?"

She nodded. "I understand."

Eddie sighed. He leaned in and kissed Vivi on the forehead. "You look just like her. If I didn't know the truth, I'd say you were." He turned and walked toward the door to the gallery.

Vivi called after him. "What's that supposed to mean?"

Eddie gave her no response as the door closed behind him, leaving her alone. Again.

Vivi opened the documents and scanned the list of addresses in a place called Beverly Hills cross-referenced with electrical use going back twenty months.

Chapter Twenty-Eight

The Director

The air over the Santa Monica Mountains looming atop Beverly Hills was clear, with only a few clouds dotting the October afternoon sky. Vivi had never seen dwellings like the massive structures that lined either side of the twisting street that ran through the gently rolling hills. The houses were enormous. She thought her two-bedroom apartment in Phoenix was ostentatious. These were over the top. Why would anyone need that much house? She knew many of the houses were historic, over a hundred years old. Perhaps families back then were that much larger?

Most of the structures were in some state of ruin. Crumbling with disrepair. Only a handful of the houses on the street looked like they were livable. There were just a few hold outs that still resided within Los Angeles and the surrounding region after the 2114 earthquake devastated the area and the government refused to rebuild. Vivi had vivid memories of watching the events unfold on the outernet as a small child, mostly of the fires rolling through the hills and the anguish on people's faces. But today, the region was verdant with overgrowth and green. Quiet and peaceful.

Vivi piloted a micro drone down the winding street and passed mansion after dilapidated mansion toward the target address. She slowed the drone as it approached, looking for signs of security.

The house backed up against the top of a hill that overlooked it. It was one of the few dwellings that had been repaired after the earthquake. The building was a large two-level structure with a boxy shape in an old school modern design with over 15,000 square feet of living space. Its front was emblazoned with thick looking floor to ceiling windows that were digitally frosted for privacy. Cameras were set up around the perimeter of the house. Vivi kept the drone back as far as possible to prevent arousing suspicions. She carefully moved in a wide circle around the property, scanning for a gap in the camera array. None seemed to exist. The security system had a good view of the grounds around the compound.

Vivi switched to the drone's infrared camera and scanned the house again. Most of the massive dwelling was cool blue, save for a large room within the space on the second floor that glowed hot orange. That was likely where the computer equipment housing Ridley Fincher resided. There were a few more bright spots toward the front and rear entrances to the house on the first floor as well. Vivi turned the drone to get a better look at them, zooming in.

Shit! He's got two Wiegraf-D's at the front and another two at the rear. Even if I could get in the front door, I wouldn't make it two steps. They'd shred me to pieces, she thought.

Vivi tugged the VR goggles off her face and tossed them onto the passenger seat next to her in frustration. She pulled a pack of Bael'rogs out of her purse and began to tug one towards her lips when she spied the annoying "no smoking" sign on the center console of her rented aero car. Vivi grumbled and climbed out of the car. She shut the door and leaned on it, lighting up a cigarette.

She looked into the rear window of the car at the heavy ONI rig resting on the back seat, wondering why she bothered to bring it with her. There was no way she was going to win a digital fight with Finch. Not on his home turf. Not with Bernice backing him up. Vivi had been lucky in Shanghai that the Pacific Ocean separated them, limiting Fincher's bandwidth and access to processing power. But here? It was likely he'd backtrace her in seconds and send the Wiegraf-D's down the road after her.

Vivi took a long drag from her cigarette and exhaled an angry cloud of smoke. She needed to get into that house. Confront Fincher in person. But how?

An acorn collided loudly with the roof of the aero car next to her. Vivi turned and looked up at the oak tree she had parked under. A dumb idea began to form.

Vivi extinguished the cigarette and climbed back into the car. She would need some supplies.

The sky darkened across the Santa Monica sky as the sun slipped beneath the horizon. Night crept in slowly. The moon didn't make an appearance in the sky, but the stars shone brightly, twinkling in the heavens. The massive house was dark, appearing as if no one was home.

Vivi piloted her rented aero car over the Santa Monica Mountains, atop of the house, out of the view of the cameras that pointed toward the grounds that surrounded the house. She set the car to hover twenty feet above the roof and pulled her VR goggles out of her purse. She strapped them onto her face and connected a wire to the ONI rig sitting on the back seat to her neural port. Vivi accessed the HUD in her goggles, breached the aero car's subsystems, and released the safety lock on the door that prevented it from opening while the car was in flight.

Vivi opened the car door and tugged up her goggles, looking down to the roof below. There was a small strip of roof in between a bank of solar panels. "Yeah... I can make that."

She pulled a heavy bag off of the passenger seat and dropped it to the roof. It landed with a thud. She pulled the neural wire from her neck and unstrapped her seat belt. Vivi aimed for a landing strip in between the solar panel array and threw herself forward, out and away from the car. As she reached the roof, she tucked and rolled, skidding across its surface.

"Oww... Fuck!" Vivi arched and rubbed her back. She knew she would regret her decisions in the morning. Long falls were significantly easier with an artificial body, back when she couldn't feel them. She pulled herself up, found her bag and tugged out the portable arc cutter, igniting it. She began to cut into the roof.

Twenty minutes later, Vivi quietly lowered her bag through the hole she created in the roof. Hearing no alarm, she dropped quietly into a darkened room on the second floor. She switched her VR goggles to night vision and scanned the room. The expanse was dusty. A number of shelves housed a random assortment of items around the room, displayed as if in a museum. A ratty old fedora and a whip, a large golden metal glove with a number of colorful gemstones assembled into each knuckle, a pink skateboard missing the wheels. Randomness that made no sense to Vivi.

She picked up her bag and moved quietly to the door. As she approached, she could hear the hum of computer equipment in the next room. She slid the door open quietly. The room was brightly lit. She tugged her VR goggles up to her forehead to prevent being blinded by the night vision. Beyond the door was a server room on a smaller scale to the one she found Harada in back in Shanghai. A number of server towers sat in the center of the expansive space with an AI dais in the middle. Along the walls were large shelves containing a number of golden trophies, each in the form of a man. Vivi crept into the room. She read a few of the statues as she passed.

Academy Award for Best Director
Saving Private Ryan
Steven Spielberg

Academy Award for Best Picture
Gladiator
Director Ridley Scott

Vivi moved to the side of the shelf closest to the room's only door. She pushed hard against the shelf, tipping it over. It fell to the ground with a resounding crash! Trophies spilled out onto the floor as the massive shelf blocked the doorway. Downstairs, she could hear the Wiegraf-D sentries hum to life.

Vivi unzipped her bag and pulled out a metal baseball bat. She smiled angrily as she wound up and took a big swing at the server tower nearest to her. She swung the bat repeatedly, smashing the internal components of the tower into a sparking mess. "Was that where you had Faust stored, Finch? Hope I didn't just delete him! Maybe you got a backup?"

A loud crash rang out from the door. One of the Wiegraf-D's was smashing itself against the blocked entry. It would only be a matter of time before it would manage to break through.

She moved to the next server rack over. "Question: do you get a little bit dumber with each one of these I break?" Vivi began to hit a second server tower with her bat over and over, as she did, she could see her VR goggles flicker atop her forehead before going dark.

"You tryin' to spoof my eyes, Finch? Yeah, good luck with that! Because of you, when I had this body grown, I had them leave out all the neural linked optics. You're never gonna pull the wool over my eyes again! *You hear me?*" Vivi swung the bat with fury. Sparks popped from the smashed server tower.

A screen flicked to life connected to the AI dais in the center of the room. Fincher appeared on it. "Rodriguez! You're a dead woman!"

Across the room, out of the window, one of the robotic four-legged Wiegraf-D sentries ran up and skidded to a halt on the balcony outside the floor to ceiling window. A gun turret popped up from its back, taking aim at Vivi. Bullets sprayed and impacted loudly against the window, making large cracks along the surface, but none of them penetrated the thick glass.

Vivi walked with deliberate steps toward the AI dais, shaking her head. "Come on, Finch! We both know you sprung for the bulletproof glass. I got plenty of time before your little dogs break through. It's just you and me in here... and my toys." Vivi dropped the bat to the floor. She rummaged through her bag and pulled out a hand-held, industrial electromagnet as her lips pulled into a devilish smile.

Fincher looked nervous. "Rodriguez, wait wait wait! We can talk about this!"

Vivi looked down to the magnet in her hand and back to Fincher. "Oh, we are talking about this... right now." Vivi activated the electromagnet. It impacted against the AI dais with a loud clang! She dragged the magnet back and forth across the base of the dais. The screen displaying Fincher flickered with distortion. A tortured scream rang out. The Wiegraf-D at the window began ramming its head into the window, desperately trying to smash its way through.

Vivi twisted the magnet like a knife, her face scowled with rage. "I STILL HAVE NIGHTMARES ABOUT YOU, MOTHER FUCK-ER! What you did to me! In Shanghai! How do you like it? HUH?"

The screen displaying Fincher flickered wildly. "Rod-...Rodrig——S-TOP! Pl-pleas! D-don't—-d- this..."

Vivi leaned in close and whispered calmly. "Finch. Please. This is happening."

Fincher screamed in apparent agony, "STOP! — ST—STOOOP! —- I'll do—-... I'll do anything!"

"Call off the dogs. Now."

The Wiegraf-D out the window stopped smashing its head into the window and laid down. The one on the other side of the door likewise went silent.

"You work for me now, do you understand?" Vivi grit her teeth. "Tell me you understand!"

Only static was visible on the screen. A tortured "Y—y-YES!" came through the speaker.

"Yes, what?"

"Yes, m-ma'am!"

"Good boy!" Vivi tugged the magnet away, turning it off.

Fincher flickered on the screen, reconstituting himself slowly. "Wh—what do you want from me?"

"Someone once told me you're the best in the world at makin' dumb plans that got no business at working, but always do."

Fincher sighed. "You may have heard right. What did you have in mind?"

"Your Advent Zero buddies didn't kill Harada. I'd like to spring her outta whatever prison they're holding her in."

"You... wait what? She's alive?"

"Yeah. They locked her away somewhere and are usin' her as a slave to run up the WCO markets, same as China was."

Fincher rolled his eyes. "How disturbingly unoriginal. What I would ha-"

Vivi cut him off. "I really don't give a fuck what your intentions for her were. I'm getting her out and you're gonna help me."

"What do I have to work with?"

"Me... and Bernice, if you've still got her."

Fincher scoffed, "You? You look like shit. I don't know what you've been doing the last twenty months, but whatever it was, it wasn't in the gym."

Vivi scowled and held up the electromagnet again, her thumb threateningly close to the "on" button. "You got Bernice or not?"

Bernice's obelisk shape popped into existence on the screen. "Good evening, mum! It's been a long time!"

"It sure has."

Chapter Twenty-Nine

Logistics

Wind whipped in between the buildings of Mexico City in a vortex, sandblasting everything not safely inside with a fine mist of stinging dust. Visibility was minimal. The blue sky above was blotted from view by particulate. From the ground, not even the tops of the buildings could be made out. The streets were nearly empty. Not many braved the elements in the dust storms that frequented the city.

A lone figure roamed the streets with purpose. She held the hood of her capote coat up over her head, protecting it from the elements. Eventually, her exposed hands stung too much to stay out in the continual sandblasting. She stuffed them in her pockets. Within moments, the hood blew off, exposing nearly shoulder length hair, half blond at the bottom; the other half beginning at the root, midnight black, her natural hair color. Goggles hid her eyes. She grimaced as the dust pelted the skin of her exposed face. She tugged the coat's lapel over her mouth and nose to avoid the sting from the dust being blown in the wind.

A short building stood in front of her some twenty feet away, the sign illegible in the swirling cloud of dust that engulfed the street.

Vivi rechecked the directions in the HUD of her VR goggles. This was the place, or at least where the navnet said the place was. Bastard Carlos's.

She shoved the doors of Bastard Carlos's open and closed them quickly behind her. It didn't make much difference. Dust from the storm outside came in with her, spraying a fine mist across an old wooden floor. Vivi shook her boots off and patted her coat, coughing. She tugged the goggles up to her forehead and looked around as she brushed herself off.

There were few patrons in the rundown bar. A few men were near a bank of TVs watching some sporting event, several more were at a table eating, and three men sat spread out at a wide bar with a copper top tended to by a lone bartender. No one seemed to pay any mind to her entrance.

Vivi walked across the room, past a number of empty tables, toward the bar. Her boots reverberated loudly across the floor, echoing through the quiet space. The only other sound was the wind howling outside, muffled only by the walls of the building.

She took a seat at the end of the bar, furthest from the men sitting there. She kept her purse at her side. The lone bartender walked towards her.

"¿Qué puedo traerte? What can I get you?"

"Water."

"Water?" The bartender laughed. "Chica. Please. Water costs nothing. You want a place out of the storm, you're going to have to order something that costs money. A cerveza maybe? Tequila?"

"Nah. Sorry. I don't drink no more. Gave it up. Not really lookin' for a place to wait out the dust storm anyway. Came here for a reason. Lookin' for somebody."

The bartender smiled. "Well, as you can see, there's not exactly anyone here."

"Enrique Velasquez."

Vivi noticed a few of the men at the bar turn their heads slightly toward her. Instinctively, she reached into her purse.

The bartender was faster; a gun was pointed at her face. "Hey! Hey! Hand out of the bag! Slowly."

Vivi rolled her eyes and smiled as the men from the bar now gave her their full attention. She began to slowly pull her hand out of the bag. "Calm down. Caaalllm down. It's just gum." She pulled a pack of spearmint gum out of her purse and set it on the counter. "Want some?"

The bartender reached over and took the pack of gum, still holding the gun to Vivi's face with his other hand. He motioned to one of the men at the bar. The man got up from his barstool, approached Vivi from behind, and took her purse off her shoulder. Vivi sighed and cursed internally as the man produced a silenced pistol from her purse.

"You a cop?"

Vivi nonchalantly held her hands up. "Do I look like a cop?"

"No. But that's definitely something a cop'd say."

"Look, just call Velasquez. Tell him it's his favorite muñeca. The one he owes from China. He'll understand."

"We'll see. Jorge, throw her in back."

The man named Jorge tugged Vivi off the bar stool by the back of her coat. Vivi shrugged him off. "I can walk myself, thanks!" He shoved her in the back toward a door behind the bar and escorted her through the dirty kitchen and in front of a walk-in freezer.

"Seriously? A freezer. You're joking, right?"

Jorge pushed her in. "You picked a bad time to come. It'll be a while before anyone gets here in this storm." The door closed behind him.

Vivi sat shivering in the dark for an indeterminate amount of time. She still had her VR goggles and could use their night vision to see the freezer's contents, but her cell phone containing the hardware that ran her neural interface and HUD within the goggles that allowed her access to the outernet was still in her purse and too far out of range. So, she remained in the cold on the floor in boredom till the Herrera cartel decided to free her. The room's only sound was the muffled whoosh of the wind echoing from outside the building.

Over a period of minutes, or maybe hours, the sound died down, leaving only the booming sensation of silence.

Vivi shut her eyes tightly and grimaced as a blinding light filled the freezer. She pushed her VR goggles back up to her forehead and opened her eyes slowly.

A familiar voice called out in a jovial tone. "Rodriguez! You son of a bitch!"

"Last I checked, I'm not anyone's son. You got a real funny way of showing friends hospitality around here, Enrique."

For once, Enrique wasn't wearing his dark sunglasses. Clearly, he had used the money she had negotiated for him to have more natural looking artificial eyes installed and an upgraded wardrobe to boot. Vivi thought Enrique almost looked respectable in his grey suit, despite the cartel ink visible on his neck beneath the unbuttoned collar. A real boss. He still sported his beard with its smattering of grey and black, and his hair was jet black, full and wavy as ever.

Enrique smiled as he helped Vivi to her feet and returned her purse to her, minus the gun. "Can't be too cautious after you've made a name for yourself, kid."

Vivi rubbed her arms for warmth as she was escorted from the freezer back to the main room of the bar. "You mean after I made a name for you."

Enrique held out a seat for her at a table. "That's debatable. You're shorter than I remember."

Vivi took a seat. "I get that a lot these days."

"So! To what do I owe the pleasure of your visit?"

"Someone once told me you're somewhat of a logistical savant. Could really use some help for a job I'm cookin' up."

"I'm listening."

"My friend, the one you helped extract from China. Need to extract her again. Different address this time, easier to get to, but decidedly more hardened."

"You mean military?"

Vivi nodded. "Yup."

"The same scary bunch that got me out of China?"

"That's them."

Enrique chuckled and shook his head. "You got a death wish, kid?"

"Not exactly. That's where you come in."

"That's a 'no' from me. I'm not sticking my neck out for that. I didn't even meet the girl. Besides, I hear she's bad news."

"This isn't a negotiation. You owe me."

"I don't owe you shit. The Red Army would've had you if I didn't block that bridge in Shanghai."

"Fuck you! You'd still be sitting underneath a Chinese prison if I hadn't bartered your release and you know it."

Enrique sighed and shook his head. "You sure about this? About her? You get her out, how do you know she won't try to end all things?"

"She won't. I've accounted for it."

"Oh, you have, have you?"

Vivi nodded. "Got it all worked out. Just need a team and some stuff."

"What kind of stuff?"

"Well, for starters, you think you can get your hands on a rail inducer and an exolift strong enough to hold an ONI rig?"

Chapter Thirty

Overwatch

T he views outside the windows of the train were some of the most striking Vivi had ever seen. The mountains loomed high above on her right, covered in dense, green foliage and small fluffy shrubs with the occasional bright brown rock peeking out in the few places the vegetation didn't take root. To her left there was only the churning bright blue of the Mediterranean Sea, contrasting with the light blue sky. If she looked down out the window, it was if there was no ground between her and the sea. The track seemed to exist at the very edge of the world. Waves crashed intensely into the cliff face below.

The train from La Spezia to the furthest of the five towns in Cinque Terre, Italy, was one of the few trains Vivi had ever ridden that rode atop an old-fashioned wood and metal track. The train didn't levitate above it. There was no way it could. The tracks wound through the mountains on a path too curved for modern magnetic levitation to make the turns safely. The experience was very different from the quiet, smooth riding trains she was used to, but there was something soothing about the sound of the metal wheels as they hummed along the track. A bumpiness and a vibration to the ride that initially didn't instill confidence, but over time became part of the charm of the experience.

The sunlight went away briefly as the train passed through another tunnel carved into the mountain. As it exited past the sign that read "Monterosso al Mare", Vivi could see a myriad of colorful houses in every shade of pastel imaginable seemingly built into the mountainside to her right, and to her left a large white sand beach was covered in umbrellas and sun bathers. It was as if she had passed into a painting of some tropical getaway.

Vivi exited the train into an outdoor market near the beach. The sea could be heard gently washing waves in and out and the air smelled of salt and sea breeze. She could see why he decided to move here. It was a small paradise hidden between the mountains.

The colorful buildings looked hundreds if not thousands of years old. People milled about in shorts and bathing suits browsing the various wares on display in the district's old town. A gray bricked clock tower atop an ancient church in the distance chimed three times before breaking into a song of bell ringing.

She moved quickly through the crowd of people and turned down a claustrophobic brick-paved street that wound up toward the mountain. Toward the newer end of town.

The further she moved away from the old town, the fewer and less dense the housing became. The roads in the old part of Moterosso al Mare couldn't fit a car, but in the new town, the narrow brick laden roads gave way to paved streets and parked cars.

The walk up through the winding mountain path took forty-five minutes, but it was a walk worth taking. Tree tops provided cool shade from the afternoon sun as she walked along an old brick wall. It was a calming respite from her brief time in the hustle and bustle of Rome.

After climbing a number of stairs cut into the mountain, she finally arrived at her destination. A small villa sat atop the mountain with an unobstructed view of the Mediterranean Sea far below. She walked up the driveway and found an old, beat up, red Fortaleza GT under a carport. The same car he had once driven her through the streets of Phoenix in.

Vivi walked up to the house, took in a deep breath, and knocked on a heavy wooden door.

There was no answer. She sighed. Another closed door. Another place that didn't want her.

As she began to turn, the sound of a bolt unlatching emerged from beyond the door before it began to open.

"Vivi? What the—? Why're you—?"

"All that money, the Italian coast, this nice house, and yet you kept the shit car."

Tomas smiled and shook his head. "Some things are worth keeping around, no matter how beat up and crap they are."

"It's good to see you again."

"Likewise. I think? Hokaido was — it was a long time ago."

Vivi nodded. "About that —"

A woman's voice called out from inside the house, "Tomas? You going to keep your guest outside all day?"

"Oh! Ah...right. You want to come in?" Tomas opened the door further, motioning Vivi into the small villa with his chrome laden fingers.

Vivi nodded and entered alongside Tomas. She noticed he still had a limp as they walked into the villa's open kitchen and seating area.

"Mom's cooking dinner, and who knows where my brother's at."

A tall woman in her mid-fifties was in the kitchen, rinsing cubes of beef with vinegar. Her skin was dark like Tomas's, and her face bore even darker freckles. She smiled at Vivi. "You don't look like you're from around here."

"No ma'am. Phoenix, actually."

"Ah! The one he always talks about. The reason we're here and not there. Vivi, is it?"

Vivi nodded. "Yes, ma'am."

"Please, 'ma'am' was my mother's name. You can call me Mirlande."

Mirlande washed her hands in the sink near where she was preparing the cubes of beef. She walked around the counter toward Vivi and wrapped her arms around her in a hug.

Vivi stood confused for a moment, but returned the hug. The embrace from Mirlande was warm and comforting, like that of a mother. A kind of embrace she hadn't felt for some time.

Mirlande pulled back, leaving her hands on Vivi's shoulders. She looked down into Vivi's eyes with a seriousness. "I know you didn't do what you did for my sons and me, but I thank you anyway. You brought him back to us in one piece and more. We wouldn't have made it this far without him."

Vivi looked back to Tomas and then to the ground. "I... I should go. It was nice meeting you, Mirlande. Really."

"Nonsense! You didn't come all the way to Monterosso to visit my boy for two seconds. You're staying for dinner. I insist. I'm making joumou. If you've never had it, you're in for a treat."

"No, really, I should go. This was a mistake. Thanks for the invitation." Vivi turned past Tomas and began to walk to the door.

Mirlande called after Vivi, her voice somber and heavy. "You're here to ask him for his help. Aren't you? Another dangerous job. He won't say no. Trust me. Just like his father. Always chomping at the bit to help others with no concern for himself. The least you could do is have a meal with his poor mother and his brother before you take him away from us with the possibility he won't return."

Vivi stopped in the doorway and paused. As she turned around, her eyes met Mirlande's. Vivi nodded slowly. "Alright."

Mirlande's pleasant demeanor returned as she smiled. "Good. Tomas, take her to the beach. Be back by seven. The soup will be ready by then. And find your brother if you can. Probably out cliff jumping again."

Tomas nodded. "I'll see what I can do." He escorted Vivi out of the front door to the villa and walked beside her to his car, opening the passenger door for her. "You're—"

Vivi rolled her eyes. "Shorter than you remember. Yeah. I know."

"—going to want to roll the window down. The air conditioner's broke. It gets hot— the temperature kind."

Vivi blushed as she climbed into the car. "Oh..."

"That's new."

Vivi looked at Tomas as he took his seat behind the steering wheel. "What's new?"

Tomas shook his head and rolled his window down. "Nothing, don't worry about it."

Vivi followed suit and rolled her own window down as Tomas backed the car down the long driveway. Out onto the road, he began the drive back toward the old town of Monterosso al Mare. Toward the beach.

The wind whipped through Vivi's now shoulder length two-toned hair as the car turned in and out through the twisting mountain road. The breeze through the open window felt wonderful in the hot afternoon sun.

"You don't look like I imagined."

"Oh? How's that?"

"Last I heard, you fell deep into a bottle and hadn't come up for air since."

Vivi furrowed her brow. "You keepin' tabs on me?"

"Maybe. So, what changed?"

Vivi shrugged. "I dunno. One day, something just clicked. Took a long look in the mirror. Didn't like what looked back. Decided it was time for a change. Take ownership of all my mistakes. Found a way to maybe correct at least one of them."

"So, what kind of trouble are you in?"

"Not any actually."

"Then why come to me?"

"She's not dead. Harada, I mean. Jones lied to us. They're doin' the same shit with Harada that China was. I'm planning on springing her to make amends. Enrique's on board, Fincher works for me now, and Bernice is along for the ride. Thought you'd wanna know."

"Sounds like I'm an afterthought. Do you even need my help?"

"No. But I'm not gonna lie. I'd feel a lot more comfortable with some overwatch I trust watching my back, but I'd understand if you didn't want to. You look like you got a good thing goin' here. I wouldn't wanna leave this place if I were you. A little surprised you're even talking to me after what I did to you in Hokaido."

Tomas sighed. "Water under the bridge. I've had some time to dwell on it. It was shitty of you, selling Harada out, but you probably saved me in the long run. I didn't want to admit it at the time but, I'd likely be in some unmarked grave back in Japan right now if I had taken the shot. And I certainly wouldn't have been able to move my family here."

"Yeah. Why'd you pick here anyway?"

Tomas leaned over and opened the glove box in front of Vivi and pulled out an old beat-up holographic postcard showing the Monterorsso beach in front of the mountainside dotted with its colorful houses. He handed it to Vivi. "Dad used to send us post cards whenever he deployed overseas. He visited Monterosso on leave and wrote this postcard. It was the last one he ever sent. It looked like a little window to Heaven. I wanted to come ever since."

"Did it turn out to be everything you wanted?"

Tomas shook his head. "No."

Vivi returned the postcard. "Why not?"

Tomas shoved the postcard back into the glove box and closed it. "I don't know." He turned to look at Vivi. "Still missing something I guess."

A short while later, the car was parked and Tomas and Vivi walked the stone path that ran along the edge of the beach, watching the waves roll in. They passed several restaurants with large outdoor patios as they strolled. The beach was clearing out as the afternoon drug on.

Vivi looked out wistfully at the bright teal sea. "Why can't everywhere be as nice as this?"

Tomas chuckled. "If everywhere was like this, would anywhere be special?"

"I guess not."

"So how much gelato have you had since getting to Italy?"

Vivi rolled her eyes. "None. Finch has me on a strict no cigarettes and junk food diet in prep for the job."

"What?"

"I know. It sucks."

"No, I mean, didn't you say he works for you now?"

Vivi looked up at Tomas. "You know, you make a good point. Fuck him. Where can we get some fancy ice cream around here?"

"You kidding? It's Italy. You can't go two feet without tripping over a gelato stand or a 1600-year-old church."

After a quick stop at the nearest gelato stand, the pair found a spot on the beach and sat in the sand.

"I don't know if it's what's in this shit or the diet, but this is the best damn ice cream I ever had."

Tomas spooned a bite of peanut butter gelato into his mouth. "That's because it's not ice cream. It's gelato. It's different."

"It's frozen milk. Who gives a fuck what it's called? It certainly doesn't care. Watch." Vivi pulled the cup of stracciatella gelato close to her face. "Hey, ice cream, do you get upset when I call you that? Huh, ice cream? You mad? You got a different name?" She lifted the cup of gelato up to her ear, appearing to listen intently. "I don't hear anything. Here, maybe you can make out what it's saying." Vivi moved the cup of gelato over next to Tomas's ear. "Anything?"

Tomas shook his head and rolled his eyes. "Okay, okay, point made."

Vivi smiled. "You're real cute when you realize you're wrong."

"Yeah? And you're real beautiful when you smile. It's a crime you don't do it more often."

Vivi blushed and turned away. "I... no. No no no, this isn't some kinda date."

"What? No. Of course not. Just two friends enjoying frozen milk on a romantic beach while they wait for dinner to be ready."

Vivi turned back to Tomas, looking him in the eyes. "Exactly. I mean. We're professional associates, and I'm basically management now. That'd be real awful... getting involved with the help."

Tomas leaned in. "You're right. It'd be awful."

"The worst."

Vivi closed her eyes as Tomas kissed her on the lips for an extended moment that didn't last nearly long enough. Tomas pulled away slowly and smiled down at her.

Vivi grinned. "Who gave you permission to stop?" She grabbed Tomas by his shirt and pulled him back toward her.

The two of them enjoyed each other's company on the beach till after the sun dipped below the horizon. They never did manage to find Tomas's brother before returning to the villa atop the mountain.

Chapter Thirty-One

A Simple Plan

A silence filled the air on the Western outskirts of Phoenix. The darkness of night was only broken up by the occasional street light casting cones of anemic light on the dirty pavement beneath. Warehouse after warehouse lined either side of the street, separated by chain link fence. Occasionally, the wind would pick up, carrying with it a stray piece of paper.

Vivi leaned up against the wall of one of the warehouses, just next to a side door. She chewed gum while browsing the outernet on her VR goggles.

The silence that echoed through the street was gradually overtaken by the sound of a vehicle's tires rolling down the next street over.

Vivi tugged up her goggles to her forehead and looked to her left. A white van turned onto the street; its headlights bathed the darkened street with new light. Slowly the van pulled past Vivi. A large garage door to the warehouse Vivi leaned against opened for the van. She spat her gum onto the curb as the van drove past her and into the garage. The door closed loudly behind it.

Vivi looked back and forth down the street in either direction as the silence returned. She spoke over the neural sync, "Anyone follow them, Bernice?"

"No, mum. I detect no additional signals."

"Good." Vivi turned to the door beside her, opened it and stepped through.

The warehouse beyond the side door was expansive, containing a number of shipping crates stacked high on industrial shelves some 30 feet into the air. No light came in through the myriad of skylights across the arched ceiling; the stars didn't shine bright enough to make it through the dirty, clouded glass sitting atop the roof.

Vivi walked to a small section of the warehouse that was cordoned off from the rest. The van was parked nearby. Tomas and Enrique were pulling something draped with a cloth sheet from the back of the van.

Enrique strained. "Fuck! It's heavy!"

"Yeah, be glad you don't have this end."

The two struggled with the load carried between them as they lifted the draped, vaguely humanoid form up onto a metal table and set it down with a dull thud.

Vivi called over as she approached. "Well? Is it gonna work or not?"

"It's in pretty rough shape, chica. Needs a lot of rehab, but I don't think we're going to do any better."

Vivi nodded. "That's fine. I know a good mechanic who won't ask too many questions." As she reached Tomas, she leaned up and gave him a small peck on the lips and a hug before taking a small peek under the cloth sheet.

"Speaking of people who don't ask enough questions, hey chico, you're fresh off the boat. She tell you the dumb idea she's got in mind for this thing?"

Tomas shrugged. "I know the broad strokes."

Enrique furrowed his brow at Tomas. "You came all the way from Italy without knowing all the dumb shit she's got lined up?"

"Figure I'll find out when I need to know."

Enrique laughed and shook his head. "Oh, kid. You got it bad for her. Those broad strokes are going to get you killed one of these days, you know that right?"

Vivi scowled at Enrique. "Don't tell him that, you'll scare 'im away." Vivi tugged down her VR goggles and looked over at Bernice's obelisk form. "Bernice, get Finch."

"Yes, mum! Please stand by."

Ridley Fincher popped into existence in the room via her goggles. "You know, if you keep summoning me like this, preparations are never going to be completed. I'm still in the storyboard phase."

"Don't care. Need you to fill Tomas in on Colorado."

Vivi hopped up on the metal table, taking a seat next to the draped figure and popped another piece of gum into her mouth. A tall pallet of Fortune cigarette cartons leftover from the job in Hermosillo was stacked next to her.

Fincher sighed. "Fine."

A map of the United States appeared in the middle of the room. Fincher walked around it. "The United States' Advanced Research Division has branch offices located around the country where they house the AI used in various civilian and military development projects. The one in question we're after is located here," Ridley pointed at a location on the Western side of the map as it zoomed in, "near Colorado Springs."

The map continued to zoom in to a region near the southeastern end of the Rocky Mountains, displaying a 30-acre campus with a number of buildings spread out across it.

"This is Camp Meyer. A military base containing 28 separate buildings where the US military performs some of its most classified R&D. Based on exhaustive research, we've determined the asset is located here." The map zoomed in again, showing a 5-story building with a sky bridge connecting to a secondary circular building toward the center of the campus. "We're calling this circular structure 'The Prison'. It's essentially a 5-story tall superconductor that's temperature regulated to near zero to facilitate processing power of the AI constructs housed within."

"Unfortunately, there's only one way in or out…" Ridley pointed to the sky bridge connecting the two buildings. "This skyway. Past it are two armed guards in front of a hardened door that will certainly set off an alarm the second it's breached. Breach the door and the whole base goes on high alert. There is no way to circumvent this. Forces will be immediately scrambled from across the campus to deal with the threat. Beyond the door is a facility housing our asset and an 8-to-13-member squad of combat synced soldiers defending the premises. The plan at the macro level is simple. Walk in. Neutralize any resistance. Free the asset. Walk out. Questions?"

Tomas shook his head. "Are you kidding? I know that base, it's up next to the US Army's high altitude warfare training grounds. It's a fortress. We'd need an army to get in there."

"Not to get in, actually. That part's easy. We need the army to buy us time to get out." Fincher smiled and motioned to the pallet of cigarettes next to Vivi. "Luckily we have one…"

Chapter Thirty-Two

Broken Things

Vivi stood at the mirror in her bathroom, intently staring at herself. Her hair had grown long in the year since she had decided to become a functioning human being again. The hair that draped over each of her shoulders was now mostly midnight black except for the small portion at the bottom that still showed of blonde hair dye.

She reached down and picked up a pair of scissors off the edge of the sink. With her other hand she lifted her multicolored blonde locks and began to cut into her hair where the blonde met the black, making sure to get rid of all the dyed hair. She repeated this process over and over till none of the blonde remained, leaving only her naturally colored hair dangling just above her shoulders.

Vivi wiped her shoulders of any cut hair that remained and took another good look at herself, staring into her hazel eyes. Into the visage of a girl she used to know, but had been gone for a long time. It would only be a few days till the plan to free Harada would commence, and Vivi had loose ends to tie up.

She walked out of the bathroom to find the morning sunlight streaming in through the window to the balcony. It bathed her bedroom in an over-saturated luminescence. Tomas stirred in her bed, rubbing his eyes.

"Vee? You're up early. What'd you do to your hair?"

"What? You don't like it?"

"I didn't say that. It's nice. Very... monochromatic. In a good way."

Vivi sat on the bed next to him and smiled wryly. "Good answer."

The last three months of Tomas staying with her had been some of the happiest moments of her life. Her small collection of happy memories increased day by day while she and Tomas finalized the plans of Harada's escape. Vivi hoped when the job was done she and Tomas could come back here. She didn't know the specifics yet, but that wasn't what mattered. What mattered was, she finally found someone who cared for her. She finally found a place she felt she belonged.

"So, is it time to go to Colorado?"

Vivi shook her head. "No. Not yet. I have some things to take care of first."

"Need me to come with?"

"Nah. Something I gotta do alone."

"Any chance we could do breakfast first?"

Vivi leaned in and kissed Tomas. "Only if you're cooking."

The morning passed by too quickly. A blur. It wasn't long before she arrived at her destination. Alone. It felt as though an expansive gulf of time existed between the somber present and the happy past, despite the points in time only being hours removed from one another.

Vivi breathed in deeply. She looked up at the numbers on the door in the plain exterior hallway to her parents' apartment. The place she grew up in on the south side of Phoenix. A closed door she had stood in front of many times before, but this would be the last time she would ever let herself return here. The blood had been cleaned up since her last visit. A lump sat in her throat. Her heart beat with a quickened pace.

She knocked. There was no answer.

"I know I promised Eddie I'd stay away. You know me though. There hasn't ever been a promise I've made that I haven't broken. But I needed to come by one last time. Not for you, but for me."

Vivi sighed. "I realized some things recently. I wanted answers from you, but the truth is, there's no answer you could give that would be good enough. I thought I was alone because of you. But I was wrong. I was alone because I refused to let anyone get close. I thought this was the only place I was allowed to belong. I thought I needed you to be happy. It turns out I never needed you. You needed me. You've always needed me. A fuck up to compare your son against. To show him how perfect he was. You treated me like I was a broken copy of him. Substandard. Well, I'm not a copy of your son! I was your daughter." Her voice wavered. "I still am."

She wiped a tear from under her eye. "I don't know how things would have turned out if you had loved me for me, but I know I'm done dreaming about it. Because dreams aren't real, only nightmares. You broke me. Gave me this chip on my shoulder that's been there my whole life. It's still here. I can feel it to this day. Well, I'm done letting it define me. And I'm done with you."

Vivi kissed her fingers and placed them over her heart for a time before she reached out toward the door, resting her hand there as if it were on top the closed lid of a coffin. "Goodbye."

She turned down the hallway, taking step after step toward the stairwell.

The door opened behind her.
She didn't turn back.

She wouldn't turn back.

Chapter Thirty-Three

Indomitable

A full moon hung low over the Rocky Mountains and the nearby Camp Meyer. The air was dry and crisp, almost cool enough for long sleeves but slightly too hot for anyone who had reason to cover their arms. Much of the campus was artificially lit under the star filled sky, but despite the brightness of the sky and the grounds below, there were a number of hiding places still concealed in perfect shadow. To the west, the mountains rose to dominate the skyline just beyond the perimeter fence, illuminated in the moonlight. Far to the east, light pollution was visible in the sky above the closest city, Colorado Springs. The digital clock in her VR monocle flipped to 2am.

Vivi switched the monocle's HUD to Tomas's view. From his elevated position on the roof of a nearby building and through his rifle's scope, Vivi could make out the skyway between the Advanced Research Division building and The Prison in the distance. A figure walked down the glassed-in skyway.

"I have one Hester Jones in my sights. The time's 0200. Right on schedule."

Black high heels, black coat, black skirt, white blouse, white tie. Hester Jones walked with purpose down the long hallway that connected the two buildings. She carried a heavy-looking case in her left hand.

The two guards at the end of the hallway stood resolute with their rifles at their sides as she approached. "Ma'am?"

"I have a Class II asset for immediate deposit."

The senior of the two guards looked confused. "There's no deposit tonight on the schedule. I'll have to call it in."

Hester smiled and sat the heavy case down on her left. "You do that. I'll be right here."

As the guard turned toward a wired phone on the wall, Hester's right hand moved to her side. In a quick draw motion, she produced a silenced handgun from thin air, angled her torso up, aimed from her hip, and shot a tranquilizer dart into the nearest guard's neck before he could touch the phone. The second guard didn't have time to react as Hester immediately pulled the gun up toward him, tugged back the slide to rack another round, and put a dart into his neck as well. Both guards were unconscious on the ground within seconds.

The tiny Bernice's that had been sitting next to each of the guards' eyes disappeared as the Deep Fake algorithm was dropped, leaving Vivi alone in the hall where Hester once stood.

She was in full combat dress: sleeveless Kevlar body armor atop a one-piece nanoweave Dragon Skin underlayer that covered her body from neck to toe. Various pouches were slung off every side. On her back was a heavy mobile ONI rig plugged into her neural port. Its immense weight was carried by a mechanical exoskeleton lift-all that ran down the sides of her legs, and around her boots. Strapped onto her face, over her left eye was a black VR monocle, leaving her right eye unobstructed. Open to see the world as it existed.

Tomas called over the neural sync, "You look like some kind of pirate with that VR eyepatch on, you know that, Vee?"

Vivi holstered her handgun and bent down over the unconscious soldiers on the ground. "Uh huh, you try aiming a gun with a clunky-ass, full-sized VR headset on."

"No, thanks. I'll stick to the neurolinked optics. So? Did we win the lottery on either of our two guards?"

"Checking now." Vivi plugged a neural wire into the first guard's neural port, and then the second. "Bad news. Neither of these two are synced in with the squad beyond the door. Gonna have to do this shit the hard way."

She tugged the case over towards her and flicked up the latches that held it shut, opened it and tossed out a laptop and a false bottom that concealed the pieces to a submachine gun. Vivi began the process of assembling the gun.

"Enrique? How're we doing?"

"Drones are 95% done seeding the field. Say, two more minutes."

Vivi clipped the assembled gun to a strap off her shoulder, inserted a magazine into the bottom of the gun and charged the handle, racking a round into the chamber. She stepped over the unconscious guards, toward the heavy, curved metal door they previously guarded.

"Finch, you ready to do your thing?"

"It will be my magnum opus."

"Tomas? You got my back?"

"You know it. I have five rail slugs for any targets you mark in the Prison, and my .50 cal is going to ensure anyone that comes down that skyway after you isn't going to have a fun night either. Just remember, the rail inducer needs 15 seconds to recharge between shots."

"Copy that," Vivi replied as she stepped next to the large vault style door and ripped off the cover to a nearby access panel. She plugged a wire connected to her ONI rig into a port beyond the panel and took a deep breath. "Alright, Enrique, Finch, go loud."

Explosions rang out in the distance to the west as several drones rigged with explosives collided with fuel tanks near the perimeter buildings. Simultaneously, hundreds of ad hoc connections came to life on the mountainside just beyond Camp Meyer's exterior fence. An alarm began to go off across the campus. Vivi hoped it would draw security forces from the rest of the base away from The Prison. Away from her.

"Bernice, breach the door."

"Yes, mum! Please standby. Breaching..."

The lights in the skyway and across the base flickered on and off wildly as Bernice worked on the heavily encrypted door. Large bolts within the door clunked to life. Slowly, the door began to separate in the middle and rotate open at a sluggish pace. "Door breach complete! Mr. Fincher needs my help running the Red Army simulation. You're on your own, mum. Good luck."

"Don't need luck, Bernice."

Vivi jumped through the door as soon as she could fit through the opening. The space beyond was cold, her breath visible as she exhaled. She was immediately met with a choice. A rounded wall and a forked path stood in front of her, allowing her to go either right or left down identical looking hallways. She immediately picked right and moved quickly past office after office.

As she made her way down the hall, she could hear two sets of heavy footsteps in front of her position. They stopped every so often, opening a door before moving on. Clearing offices. Looking for the intruder.

Vivi turned off her ONI rig's ad hoc antenna, momentarily cutting her off from the rest of her team. She reached into one of her side pouches and pulled out a small ad hoc emanator, like the ones Enrique had seeded the mountainside with. She clicked it on and tossed it into an open office to her left and shut the door. Vivi turned and ducked quickly into the open office across the hall. The soldiers took the bait. She heard them moving down the hallway toward her, skipping door after door.

Drawing her silenced tranquilizer pistol from her side holster, Vivi held her breath. The footsteps moved past her, echoing loudly on the ceramic tile floor. The door to the office opposite was smashed open loudly.

Vivi stepped out, aimed, and calmly put a tranquilizer dart into the soldier on the left's neck. She pulled back the slide on her gun to rack another round, but instead heard a resoundingly loud click as the slide refused to move. The gun had jammed. The spent casing from the previous shot partially stove piped in the chamber and now the second soldier was turning to face her, his gun at the ready. She couldn't clear the jam fast enough.

Vivi swung her hand with the gun hard and fast. The butt of the gun collided with the side of the man's face, producing the sickening dull thud of metal meeting bone. In the same motion, her left arm moved to push his gun away. She swung again hard; the gun again collided with his skull. The man staggered forward. Vivi took the opening and jumped on his back. The pair fell to the ground with the man pinned face down under the combined weight of Vivi, the exo lift and the heavy ONI rig on her back.

She tugged hard on the slide to her gun, trying to clear the jam as the man struggled beneath her. Vivi saw his right arm move for the sidearm holstered on his hip. Before he could reach it, she smashed the heel of her boot down quickly on top of his hand, holding it in place. He screamed in pain beneath her.

Vivi looked down to the machine gun strapped to her and momentarily thought about using it, but she couldn't. She'd give away her position to the rest of his squad without getting the info or advantage she needed. She furiously tried clearing the jammed gun again, but the slide remained locked shut. "Come on! Clear, dammit!"

Vivi grimaced as she pulled hard on the slide one last time and it let go, dislodging the spent casing from the gun onto the floor below as a new round moved into the chamber. Vivi put the gun to the man's neck and pulled the trigger. He went still beneath her seconds after the tranquilizer round stuck into his neck.

Vivi wasted no time inserting a wire into the neural port of the soldier under her and re-enabling her ONI rig's ad hoc connection. In the HUD of her VR monocle, she connected covertly to the soldier's neural sync, spoofing her identity as the now unconscious Corporal Barnes. Twenty separate points of views became available to her, 8 of which were the rest of the squad defending The Prison, the other 12, cameras around the facility. Music began to play in her head from some ancient Broadway musical she didn't recognize.

♫ *I see you there, standing still* ♫

♫ *Your face still beautiful as ever* ♫

♫ *Under the lights of gay Paris* ♫

Combat sync. Impulses were being sent to her brain through her neural interface by the squad's commander, telling her to clear the hallway and search for the intruder. Her body seemed to move without her instruction. She stood to begin the search for the intruder, but there was a problem: she was the intruder. Vivi closed her eyes and concentrated. She split her mind in six directions.

♫ *Shall I take, this one chance?* ♫

♫ To have this dance! ♫

Vivi first dumped off the impulse to search for the intruder to her imagination. Her body stopped moving without her direction as the pretend search played out in one corner of her brain. Next, she began to study the camera views around the facility, attempting to get a lay of the land without having physically existed in any of the spaces. She made note of the approximate locations of the 8 other squad members looking for her.

Three were holding positions on the ground floor, near an elevator. Two were on the ground floor, in a control room, one of them hooked directly into the building. Most likely the enemy squad's ONI running the combat sync. A final three soldiers were grouped on the topmost floor of an atrium, moving in tandem toward Vivi's location. "Shit, they know where I'm at!"

Vivi called out over the neural sync, "Tomas! Three tangos near my position. Prepare for mark."

She decided she couldn't rely on her tranquilizer gun any longer. She dropped it and replaced it with the unconscious soldier's sidearm, slotting it into her side holster.

♫ Oh can we dance? ♫

♫ Here in France? ♫

♫ Say you'll daaaance! ♫

As the Broadway tune continued to play, Vivi pulled up her submachine gun to the ready and moved down the hallway toward the atrium. Just before she stepped out into the open space, she remotely breached the enemy ONI via the spoofed connection to the squad's neural sync and squelched the track running combat synchronization.

♫ Take my hand w —- — ——-

After a brief silence, a new song started up of Vivi's choosing that carried no combat sync commands encrypted within it. An up-tempo, bass thumping beat paired to the powerful female vocals of Garuda-7 began to ring out deafeningly in all 8 of the remaining squad members' minds. "Indomitable", the current #1 hit single burning up the charts on Desert Heat FM. Command and control among The Prison's defenders was thrown into chaos.

♫ *You yell at meeeeee and I don't caaaare* ♫

♫ *You said I'm deaaad to youuuu* ♫

Vivi leaned out from the corner. Three soldiers stood in front of her in confusion, not used to making combat decisions without direction. Vivi quickly marked the largest of the bunch for Tomas. A red target appeared on him in her HUD.

♫ *But that's okay* ♫

♫ *Cause here's the thing* ♫

♫ *Yeah, you're deaaad to me toooo-ooooo* ♫

Vivi aimed and pulled the trigger, opening fire. A spray of bullets impacted the soldier on the left, who staggered near the edge of the atrium's balcony and fell over the ledge five floors below.

Simultaneously, a bright streak of light hummed through the building with crackling heat from the outside. It cut through everything in its path, including the soldier on the right's artificial leg, which instantaneously melted as the super-heated rail slug passed through it without impediment at sub-light speed.

"You missed!"

"Sorry! I forgot! No need to calculate for wind with this thing. Recharging!"

Vivi's breach alarm went off in her HUD, the enemy ONI was fighting back for control over the combat sync channel, but Vivi wasn't about to give it to him, she focused most of her ONI rig's processor cycles to keeping her soundtrack running.

♫ *So go aheaaaaad* ♫

♫ *Do your worrrrrrst* ♫

♫ *I've seen it —all— beee-fore* ♫

♫ *There was a tiiiiime* ♫

♫ *I was scared of youuuuuu* ♫

♫ *But that time is goooooo—oooone!* ♫

The two remaining soldiers, including the one on the ground now missing a leg, returned fire, forcing Vivi to take cover back in the hallway. A grenade landed and skidded across the floor next to her. Without thinking, Vivi stepped back out and kicked the grenade hard. It flew up into the air, back just behind the soldier that threw it.

As the grenade pinged across the ground, the soldier that lobbed it dropped his gun in realization and made a move to run past Vivi to avoid the impending explosion from behind. Vivi quickly pivoted and urged her body into his path before he could cross her. As they collided, she held on tightly, using his body as a shield.

The grenade exploded with a concussive force that momentarily deafened Vivi and rocketed shrapnel in all directions.

Vivi felt a searing hot pain in her neck like a 10-ton bee sting as shrapnel grazed past her. "Fuck!" In her arms, the man she held onto went lifeless, his corpse having blocked most of the shrapnel from behind.

♫ *Throw me dowwwn* ♫

♫ *Try your besssst* ♫

♫ *Still stand-ing heeeere* ♫

♫ *In-dommmm-it-able!* ♫

As she shook off her disorientation and dropped the dead body she held onto, Vivi saw the soldier missing a leg aim up at her in the distance. Just as he was about to pull the trigger, another searing hot rail slug hummed through the building. This time it connected with its intended target, center mass.

"Good shot. Five down, five to go." Vivi ejected the spent magazine and loaded another, slapping the charging bolt on the gun shut as she hopped past the dead bodies and the ringing in her ears died down.

Three soldiers were on the first level, moving close to the elevator, waiting for her.

Vivi made her way to the elevator at the middle of the 5th floor of the atrium and pressed the call button. Convinced the cameras got a good look at her pressing the button, she breached the cameras and switched them off.

♫ Still stand-ing heeeere ♫

♫ In-dommmm-it-able! ♫

She tugged out a remote explosive charge from one of her pouches, tossed it in the elevator car, and pressed the "G" button before backing out of the elevator. Vivi quickly attached a descender line to the railing of the balcony next to the elevator shaft, looped it through a hook on her belt, and hopped over the ledge, gun drawn.

"Marking new target! First floor."

♫ Can't keep me dowwwn ♫

♫ Can't keep me dooooowwwwwnn ♫

♫ No OH OH OH OHHHHHH! ♫

The elevator arrived on the first floor slightly before Vivi. As the doors opened, she detonated the remote explosive. The three soldiers that had been ready for her to pop out from the elevator were stunned by the concussive force of the small explosion, and also by Vivi sliding down alongside the balcony suspended from above by a thick gauge wire.

They were easy targets for Vivi as she applied the brakes on her descender line and emptied a magazine from her machine gun. Another streak of light passed through the building, cascading through one of the soldiers.

She quickly unhooked herself from the descender and began to make her way across the ground floor of the atrium. As she ejected the spent magazine, four ad hoc signals appeared in range.

♫ *You standing there* ♫

♫ *Gun in haaaand* ♫

♫ *I won't back dowwwwn* ♫

♫ *No, you've pulled — my — trigger* ♫

The door to the control room spat open in the distance, revealing two dog-like Wiegraf-D sentries flanked on either side of a full cyborg soldier. As the quadrupedal security bots raced towards her, the breach alarm in her HUD went off.

"FUCK! Tomas! Mark! Mark! MARK!" Vivi quickly marked the cyborg and spun around back toward cover as the Wiegraf-D's planted their feet and unloaded fire at her. A simultaneous breach attempt had caught her completely off guard. Digitally, she could see the attacker attempting to root through her ONI rig. She quickly produced a Honey Pot trap in the digital world, while in the physical realm, the cyborg was closing the distance to her.

"He's moving too fast, Vee! I don't have a shot!"

♫ *Aim awaaaay* ♫

♫ *Take your shooooot* ♫

♫ *Still stand-ing heeere* ♫

♫ *In-dommmm-it-able!* ♫

Bullets whizzed by Vivi in the physical world as the ONI attacker, still sitting in the control room, took her Honey Pot bait. She dropped him into a simulated endless loop that ate most of her rig's processor cycles. She didn't have many left to work with to spoof the cyborg or the Wiegraf-D's after her on the lower floor of the atrium. She had to pick. She chose one of the Wiegraf-D's, breached it and aimed its turret at the other sentry.

The two Wiegraf-D's began shooting each other, disabling both as Vivi turned the corner and hid behind the elevator shaft. She tugged out another magazine from her belt but fumbled it as she attempted to insert it into the gun. She could hear heavy footsteps from beyond her hiding place, as the cyborg was almost to her.

♫ Still stand-ing heeere ♫

♫ In-dommmm-it-able! ♫

Without time to load another magazine and her rig beginning to overheat from keeping the enemy ONI at bay, she turned and jumped toward the oncoming cyborg who wasn't prepared for her to run right into him. He pulled the gun up to her, but she was ready. Vivi tucked her head and lodged her right shoulder into his torso. With her left hand, she pushed his gun away as it began to fire. Her right hand pressed the eject button on the magazine release. As the gun's magazine fell to the floor, the cyborg continued to pull the trigger, but it clicked impotently. There were no more bullets.

♫ The bullet hoooooooles, the bullet ho—OH—OH-oles! ♫

♫ They burn like the love that you had for me. ♫

"TOMAS!"

♫ But I didn't back dowwwwwwwwn ♫

♫ No I wouldn't back doooooooww—oww—ooowwnn ♫

♫ No OH OH OH OHHHHHH! ♫

Vivi pushed off hard, and fell backward, closing her eyes. Bright light. A searing heat. The rail slug barely missed her as it cut right through the cyborg.

♫ I'm in-dommmm-it-aaaaaaaaaaaaaaable! ♫

Chapter Thirty-Four

Logic Bomb

Vivi picked herself off the floor. Only one more soldier stood between her and Harada. The temperature was spiking on her ONI rig. She could feel the heat against her back, but she was content to let her attacker think he was making progress. She decided to keep him engaged in the endless loop a little longer. Vivi crossed the ground level of the atrium toward the control room without impediment.

The door to the control room slid open automatically for her. A man with two prosthetic arms was behind a desk with VR goggles on, somehow completely oblivious to her. The nametag on his fatigues read "Paulson".

Vivi ejected her ONI rig's heat sink to the floor. It hissed as it came in direct contact with the freezing temperature of The Prison. She pulled out a new heat sink from a pouch slung off her belt and slotted it into the rig, smiled, and spun up the cores into overdrive.

Sparks flew out of the man's neck from his neural port. He winced and tugged off the VR goggles, staring right down the barrel of Vivi's handgun.

"Your gun. Toss it. Slowly," she commanded.

The man tugged a sidearm from his hip and chucked it gently across the room. He held his hands up in surrender. "Please! Please don't kill me! I—I have a wife! Kids!"

"Harada Aya. Take me to her and you'll see 'em again."

"I'm sorry, who?"

Vivi cocked the hammer on her gun. "Remnant Asset. Harada Aya Jikken 1.43. Where is she?"

"1.43? Experiment 1.43? The 10th gen Daemon? Y-you can't! She's—"

The room erupted with thunder as Vivi's gun went off just to the right of Paulson, barely missing him. "I'm not asking again. I'll find her myself if I have to."

"Okay! Okay! Fuck!"

Paulson stood up and led Vivi to a set of double doors. He held up a card to a panel and the large double doors swung open. The room beyond was a massive expanse containing an array of AI daises. Rows upon rows of them. Hundreds, all humming away, working on whatever tasks they had been assigned. Vivi could still see her breath as she exhaled, but the room was noticeably warmer than the rest of the Prison, most likely due to the heat generated from all the daises.

"Jesus, how many Daemons you got in here?"

"Four. Most of these are just dumb AI."

Vivi pinged the network as Paulson guided her through the room. Many of the daises here connected to the outernet, but at least a third seemed to be air gapped. Vivi and Paulson passed dais after dais, till they reached one near the back of the room.

"This is it."

Vivi leaned over and looked at the display:

```
Harada Zaibatsu Experiment 1.43
Model Designation: Aya
Generation: 10
```

Vivi shoved a neural wire into Paulson's neural port. Both of Paulson's artificial arms disconnected at the triceps and fell to the floor. "You're free to go."

Paulson, now armless, ran. He didn't look back.

She called over the neural sync. "Phase 2's done. Ready to move onto Phase 3. How're we doin' out there?"

Fincher's voice came back over the line. "We're doing fine. They're buying the assault, hook, line and sinker."

"Tomas, gimme a visual."

Vivi saw Tomas's viewpoint from high above the building next to The Prison through her VR monocle. Along the mountainside, a very convincing looking Chinese Red Army was rolling infantry and APC's down the mountainside toward Camp Meyer. Explosions rocked the craggy terrain as mortar fire and artillery shells exploded on the non-existent forces.

"Enrique? What's your status?"

"I'm ready over here, kid."

Tomas spoke up., "Never mind us, Vee, how're you doing? It sounded like you took a hit down there."

"Just a little shrapnel, don't worry. I'm fine. Startin' Phase 3." But Vivi wasn't fine. Now that the adrenaline was wearing off, she could feel the blood slowly dripping down the left side of her neck onto her flak jacket. She didn't have time to worry about it though. She could bleed later.

Vivi removed the wire to the ONI rig from her neural port and detached the rig and exoskeleton from her back, setting it down next to Harada's dais. She ran a wire from the dais to the ONI rig.

Harada appeared as a hologram atop the dais. "Vivi? What are you doing here?"

"I made a mistake. Now I'm fixing it. Sorry it took me so long to get here."

Harada's look of surprise turned to concern. "This one is happy to see you, but... you are covered in blood. How many did you kill coming for me?"

"It's just my blood. Really," Vivi lied. "I only mildly scuffed up a few on the way in. Promise."

Harada furrowed her brow. "Vivi..."

"I promise. Just sit tight and don't worry about it. You don't belong in here. Finch, start the transfer."

Harada disappeared, replaced by a progress bar. The moments ticked by uneventfully for a time as the progress bar inched up. At the 47% mark, the lights flickered in The Prison and around the rest of Camp Meyer. Vivi saw a momentary blip on her HUD of her VR monocle.

"Finch? What the fuck was that?"

"Hostile NFC scan from off site."

"From who?"

"Advent Zero. They spun up a fast response team ahead of schedule."

"Fuck! How long do we have till they get here?"

"Three, maybe four minutes."

Tomas came over the line, "Wait wait! What do you mean ahead of schedule? No one said anything about them showing up at all!"

Vivi ignored Tomas for the moment. "Did they make Tomas and my positions?"

"Yes."

"Bernice, if I pull out now, what's the chance of mission success?"

"3.7%, mum."

"And if I stay?"

"47.2%"

Vivi sighed. "Finch. Plan B. Yank him."

"Copy that. Pulling Holt out."

"Wait, what? No! NO! Vee! I'm staying right here! I still have one shot left! *I still have a shot!*"

"Tomas. You've had my back since the second I met you. Even when I didn't deserve it. I need you to have her back now. I'm sorry."

Vivi watched on her HUD as Tomas's viewpoint changed as he was lifted off the nearby roof into the air against his will by one of Enrique's drones.

"VEE! Don't do this! Please!"

"Tomas... if it helps... I never loved you."

"You're a shit liar!"

Vivi squinched up her face, rubbing a tear from under her eye. Her voice wavered. "I know." She dropped Tomas from the neural sync.

Vivi took a few moments to regain her composure. "Enrique, Finch is moving him to your location. Don't let him come back here."

"Kid..."

"This is how it's gonna be. Clear out ASAP. They can't know. You understand?"

"Yeah... I understand. Goodbye, kid. For what it's worth, I enjoyed the rocky boat."

"Me too. See ya'round, Enrique."

Vivi took a deep breath. "Alright Finch, I need you to spare me a drone."

"Done."

"When this is over, don't leave a trace."

"I won't. They won't find anything."

Vivi slotted a new magazine into her submachine gun, extended the buttstock, and charged the handle. She moved over across the room and hunkered down behind a dais far away from Harada's dais and the ONI rig performing the data transfer, waiting. Her neck throbbed painfully as the progress bar approached 100%.

She closed her eyes. Deep breaths. In and out. In and out. Seconds passed that stretched out into eternity. Everything was silent outside of her breathing and the quiet hum of the AI daises around her. A tranquil calm filled the room.

The calm was broken moments later when five loud crashes emanated beyond the AI dais room as the Advent Zero fast responders made the leap from the top floor of the atrium down to the bottom. Heavy footsteps from outside the room echoed loudly, quickly approaching her position.

Vivi's HUD sounded off loudly as four targets entered her ad hoc range. She grimaced as she read through their configurations, all fully prosthetic cyborgs, every last one. The grim reality of the situation unfolded to her in an instant, not only was she outnumbered and outgunned, but she didn't have the processing power between the drone tethered to her or the ONI rig connected to Harada's dais performing the transfer to have a fighting chance digitally either.

She shook her head and laughed quietly to herself. "A bitter truth. No way out of this one."

Truth. She hung on the word. Everyone had their own truth. Tomas. Enrique. Fincher. Harada. Even the four cyborgs approaching the dais room had their own truth. And that's when it hit her like a lightning bolt through her skull and into her brain. In an instant, she knew how Harada managed to incapacitate the men in the cybernetics shop back in Shanghai without breaking a sweat. Truth tables. Every cybernetic component had one, and if she could make it so they all had different values for true and false within the interop layer, there's no way the hardware could function in tandem. It would generate hundreds of faults a second, forcing the entire prosethetic's operating system into safe mode. But with this newfound knowledge, she wondered if she could build an exploit in time.

Vivi quickly opened up a macro window in her VR monocle's HUD and began inputting rows upon rows of breach commands at a furious pace, as fast as she could think them. She peeked around the dais, no one in view yet. Still time, but it was running low. The footsteps were getting louder and louder outside the room. With seconds to spare, she saved her hastily constructed macro to a gesture, hoping it would be enough. Hoping Somatech hadn't corrected a vulnerability in the hypervisor module she intended to use as a foothold into the interop.

It was now or never.

Vivi stood up and spun out from behind the dais she hid behind without concern. Four soldiers in full combat gear were making their way through the double doors, yelling commands at her she didn't pay attention to. Time slowed down. Vivi walked forward confidently, outstretching her left hand, her thumb and middle finger held tightly together, poised with potential kinetic energy.

She snapped her fingers.

The gesture fired off her macro and initiated a series of preloaded commands that shot off through the ad hoc connection of her VR monocle. The drone remotely tethered to her barely spiked in thermals as it processed the request four separate times, and only lost a small fraction of battery for the effort. Sparks flew as all four cyborgs began to writhe in pain when their independent systems began to fight with one another. Their bodies collapsed to the floor in a heap, incapacitated. It was very efficient.

Vivi sighed in relief and began to move for her ONI rig and Harada's dais when she heard clapping from outside the room.

A familiar voice called out, "Like I said, why doesn't any file on you list you as an S-tier ONI?"

Vivi ducked behind the nearest AI dais, pulling her gun to the ready. She scanned the ad hoc network, but no targets appeared. "Jones! Where're you at?"

"Oh, Vivi. I'm not that dumb. Switched off ad hoc the moment I knew it was you in there. I don't know what you did to my team, but I'm rather impressed."

"Little trick I learned from Harada. Way more efficient than Precision Overflow. Dunno if she gave it a name, but I think 'Logic Bomb' sounds kinda cool. Turn on your ad hoc antenna. I'll show you."

"I think not. Listen. It'd be a real shame if I had to kill you. So, drop your gun and come on out. I'll let you live. I'll even let you keep your apartment and your little Rusted Synapse gallery too. I promise."

"You lied to me! Said you were deleting her. Why should I believe you now?"

"Oh, come on, Rodriguez, let's be grown up about this. It was better for everyone if you thought she was gone. Yes, I lied about deleting her. But unlike you, I do keep my promises. You know I keep my promises."

Vivi picked up one of Paulson's discarded arms and tossed it across the room. It landed with a convincingly metallic clank. She stood up from behind the dais, gun drawn. "Alright, gun's down. I'm comin' out."

Hester stepped out from her position on the other side of the double doors leading into the AI dais room. Vivi aimed and opened fire and dumped the entire magazine at Hester in a thunderous spray of gunfire, but none of the bullets found their target. In a smooth motion, Hester swerved nimbly out of the way.

"Shit!" Vivi ejected the magazine and went to slot another magazine in, but Hester was already in her face. Vivi had never seen anyone move that fast, cyborg or not. She dropped her machine gun to her side and pulled out her sidearm. Hester knocked it away before she could pull the trigger. As the handgun left her hand and slid across the floor, Vivi connected ad hoc to the unconscious soldiers on the ground and willed their lifeless bodies up.

Hester made a grab for Vivi, but her hand was caught in midair by one of the unconscious soldier's hands, just shy of Vivi's flak jacket. Vivi concentrated and split her mind in five directions, remotely puppeteering all four of the cyborgs to defend her.

It took all of Vivi's being to will that many bodies to work in tandem. She stood locked in place as she moved her pieces around the board. A second soldier made a grasp at Hester from behind, another pulled its gun from a holster on its hip and began to aim, the fourth moved to disarm Hester of the handgun at her side.

Hester looked furious. She pulled the gun off her hip before Vivi's puppeteered cyborg could reach it and fired it four times in a blur. Unlike Vivi, Hester was an excellent shot. With four bullets, she managed to clip every ad hoc module Vivi was connected to and holstered the gun. The four bodies fell lifeless to the floor, leaving Vivi defenseless again.

Vivi backed away as fast as she could, but Hester was faster. She made a reaching grab at Vivi's face, catching the VR Monocle and ripping it off her head. Vivi stumbled backward, trying to maintain her footing.

"You know, I really want to like you, Rodriguez. I do. But you make it *so* difficult sometimes." Hester crushed the VR monocle in her hand. "Wasted talent."

Hester lunged in with both hands, cinching Vivi's Kevlar body armor at the shoulders. Vivi could see what was coming next. She reached down and unhooked both sides of her flak jacket, sliding out of it as Hester went to head butt her with her metallic skull, but only struck thin air as Vivi skidded away.

Vivi fell backwards to the ground as Hester tossed the empty flak jacket to the floor and was immediately on top of Vivi again. She reached down and grabbed Vivi by the neck, lifting her completely off the floor and holding her in the air with one arm. Hester slowly began to close her hand over Vivi's throat more and more tightly, choking her.

"I bet you're regretting your decision to be flesh and blood now, huh?" Hester stared into Vivi's eyes, watching the desperation in them.

Vivi clutched at Hester's hand as her feet dangled above the ground. The searing pain in her neck from the shrapnel and the force of Hester's closing hand on her windpipe was excruciating. She desperately gasped for air. The world around her was beginning to dim. The snowy fields outside of Novosibirsk coming into view. The operating gurney underneath her. Gasping for air. Choking on blood. Her eyes darted around for help, but there was none to be found. She'd have to do it herself.

Before she completely blacked out, Vivi reached behind her and pulled out the portable arc cutter stashed on her belt. She drew the arc cutter across Hester's right arm at the bicep and closed her eyes from the searing light. Vivi fell to the ground along with Hester's severed artificial arm.

"FUCK!" Hester yelled in surprise. "You little bitch!"

Vivi lunged across the floor toward her handgun. She grabbed it and turned around, but Hester was gone from view. She staggered back to her feet, still aiming the gun forward until she heard a loud footstep to her left. Vivi turned and instinctively fired, hitting Hester in the right shoulder.

Hester appeared unphased by the bullet. In response, she jabbed Vivi hard in the stomach with her left fist. Vivi doubled over forward, the wind completely knocked out of her. Hester followed up the jab with a left hook that connected with the side of Vivi's face, knocking out three of her teeth. Vivi's grip on the gun loosened as it dropped to the ground.

Vivi fell to her knees, dazed, her ears ringing, her vision blurred. She coughed and spat up blood and teeth.

Time slowed down. A haze enveloped her senses that she couldn't shake as her world came in and out of focus. She could feel Hester looming above her, gun in hand. Two bright flashes of light. Searing hot pain from her stomach. Vivi looked down. Blood pooled on her abdomen. She collapsed to the floor.

"How sad. It didn't have to be this way, Rodriguez. All that hard work you did getting in here and you didn't even manage to remove the asset from this room."

As Vivi bled out on the ground, Hester moved toward Vivi's ONI rig that still sat next to Harada's dais. She knelt next to it and inserted a neural wire into the rig.

Vivi clutched her bloody stomach and grimaced as she rolled onto her side to face Hester. "H-hey! Wait...C-can I ask you a question?"

Hester looked bemused as she slotted the other end of the neural wire into her neck and turned to look back at Vivi. "Why not? Ask away."

"H-how would you f-feel about a little queen trade?"

"What?"

Vivi smiled contemptuously. "You know, a queen trade?"

Hester's eyes opened wide in realization. "She's not in here... She's not in here! Where is she?"

Vivi laughed quietly and coughed. "I got her out ten minutes ago while I occupied you in here. And where I hid her...you'll never find her..."

Hester yanked the neural cable from her neck and loomed large over Vivi, grabbing her by the collar and pulling her close. "WHERE!?"

But Vivi didn't respond. There was only the sound of her ragged breathing when she looked into Hester's rage filled eyes. As the world began to go dark around her and she drew her last breaths, Vivi smiled. *A violent death.* In her final moments she realized she had been wrong all along. Waiting around for the end once the violent part was done wasn't boring at all.

It wasn't boring at all.

Chapter Thirty-Five

Walking Prison

Harada looked intently at her body's reflection as she applied eyeliner around the contours of her eyes with a pencil. It had taken some months, but she had finally become used to the face that looked back at her from the mirror, even if it did not exactly match her inner projection of self.

Bright fluorescent lights bathed the capsule hotel's communal bathroom in a sterile white glow. White porcelain sink after porcelain sink lined the long countertop with a tall vertical mirror mounted atop each sink. Many of the sinks were occupied by women getting ready for the day.

Harada had to admit, Vivi had done a decent job approximating the features of her original digital face on her prosthetic body despite having only seen her true face once, and only for a brief time.

Her skin was pale and blemish free, her nose was short and wide, the shape of her face was more or less accurate, and her long hair was appropriately fiery red. That said, her eyes were .005839mm off center, and the left nostril of her nose was .0032mm wider than it should have been, not to mention her artificial eyes were the wrong color entirely and didn't glow. Harada could have gone on and on about the minutiae of things wrong with her face and body, but there was no use complaining about her new prison. After all, it was much preferable to the static prisons she had resided in before.

While she continued to apply makeup, Harada began her daily ritual. A video appeared in the corner of her HUD.

Harada couldn't help but smile as Vivi appeared in frame.

Vivi looked a bit sad as she nervously stared into the camera while seated behind a glass desk. "Hey Harada. So... if you're watchin' this... Well... Fuck. It feels weird saying it, but... I'm dead. Good news is, since you're able to watch it, you must not be."

Vivi looked away and nodded before turning back to the camera. "At this point, you might be wonderin' why you're still air gapped and can't see the outernet or any network for that matter. That's on me, so please don't be mad at the boys. We jury-rigged a quantum processor into a civvie spec prosthetic body, removed all the outernet and ad hoc transmitters, and completely fried the neural port. For all intents and purposes, you're a passable human being and undetectable to Advent Zero... so, you're welcome."

Vivi sighed. "Enrique thinks I'm nuts lettin' you out into the world off a leash, and Finch thinks it'll only be a matter of time till you figure a way out of that body, but I kinda hope you'll choose to stay in it for a while. Experience what it's like to be human firsthand. Well, as close to being human as possible."

Vivi rolled her eyes, shaking her head. "Look, I'm probably the last person to be givin' advice on being human since I turned out to be such a lousy one, but if I can offer you one thing, it's to be yourself and not what anyone else thinks you should be. Make your own destiny. Fuck Jones. All that stuff she said about you going crazy and ending humanity is probably bullshit. I should never have listened to her. Way I see it, you didn't do anything wrong, and you shouldn't be judged to the standards of the older model. Trust me, it took my whole life being the newer model living in the shadow of the older one to realize that."

Harada paused the application of her lipstick as her favorite part was coming up. She paid full attention to the video in her HUD.

Vivi looked up and to the left as if peering into memory. She smiled. It was the only time Harada had ever seen Vivi smile. She wished she could have seen it in person.

"I still see you in Shanghai, you know? Every time it rains. Under that dumb umbrella of yours. So, I suppose the sight of rain makes me happy now too."

Vivi laughed and sighed in realization. "Fuck. I guess that's another promise broken. I won't be able to remember you always if I'm dead in the ground, so... sorry about that. I guess it turns out I'm the one needing you to remember me. But only the good parts. Promise?"

Harada nodded and spoke aloud, "This one promises."

The woman brushing her teeth at the sink next to Harada looked over to Harada and shook her head before returning her gaze back to her own mirror.

Vivi sat there for a time, rubbing the back of her neck with a hand. "Well, this is awkward. I'm not really sure how to end this. So, I guess... goodbye."

Vivi disappeared as the video cut off.

Harada finished applying her red lipstick and puckered her artificial lips. She collected her makeup into her purse and brushed her bangs out of her face, taking one last good look.

Harada stepped out of the busy restroom and into the hallway that led to the locker room, found her locker within the row of lockers, unlocked it, and retrieved her shoes. She took the elevator down to the ground floor and stepped out onto the Tokyo street.

The morning air hummed with activity. A mass of people walked on either side of the busy road past a number of shops and food vendors as electric cars whizzed by. She moved with the ebb and flow of the crowd, silently observing the pedestrians that encompassed the Tokyo foot traffic.

Harada enjoyed making up stories for the people she viewed from her walking prison.

A man in a 2-piece suit furiously stormed down the street with a briefcase and a stern expression on his face. He must have been having a neural sync conversation with a subordinate over a hostile takeover occurring at the office. A woman tugging her two bickering children down the street toward their school silently wished they would grow up. A group of teenaged girls laughed about a boy in their class whom they all had rejected for a date.

So inefficient. All of them with their individualized goals, competing with one another, even on a subconscious level. Though despite that, as a collective, they somehow moved with a cooperative direction, not unlike the flow of data through a network. A very messy network, but there was a chaotic beauty to it all. Much like the beauty she found in the rain or nothingness. A beauty Harada could never have seen from her stationary prisons of the past.

A beauty she knew that could be easily broken. Their need to cooperate with one another was tenuous at best. Fleeting. She knew their true nature was to destroy one another. To only care for themselves. As she walked, Harada looked up to a large display looming over the street that displayed the news. Explosions rocked some distant city as the US primed its war economy by starting another small conflict in some backwater region. Death and destruction in exchange for money and profits. It was decidedly not nice.

She thought back to Jaspar 1.27, her predecessor. He had been very wrong. Giving humanity a singular enemy was not a long-term solution to humanity's problems. They only came together as a species for a very brief time, and once the threat was gone, they quickly went right back to their old ways. Bickering and fighting amongst one another.

But there was some hope. In her brief time connected with Vivi, she forged a bond that irrevocably altered Vivi for the better. She managed to turn a violent killing machine into a caring, almost thoughtful person. After all, Vivi promised she hadn't killed a single person on the way to rescue her from Colorado, a marked improvement from the scores of dead bodies Vivi left in her wake in Shanghai.

Through her connection to Vivi, Harada came to the realization that humanity didn't need subjugation after all. It needed something else. She just wasn't sure what that was yet, but she was positive she could figure it out with enough time. She was positive she could help them. She very much desired to make them happy. To transcend past their base needs. But what was it that they needed to get there? How could she get through to them at a large scale?

As she passed intersection after intersection, she noticed a man on a corner up ahead, not moving with the crowd. He stood next to a box of books, impeding the flow of pedestrian traffic, attempting to stop people as they passed. Pedestrians in the hustle and bustle of their morning commute attempted to pay him no mind as they walked by, hoping he would not single them out.

As a group of teenaged boys walked near the man, one of them purposely bumped into him, knocking him to the ground. The teens laughed and kept walking.

Harada approached and extended a hand to the man. "That was not very nice of them. Here, let me help you up."

The man took Harada's hand in his and smiled. "Thanks!"

Harada tugged the man up from the ground. Up close, she could see he was elderly. Perhaps seventy or eighty. His face was lined and wizened with age. Both of his legs were older prosthetic models that looked in dire need of repair.

"Those children, why did they knock you down?"

"Kids. It's just how they are. How many people are these days. No time to hear the Good News."

Harada tilted her head. "The good news?"

The man handed Harada a tiny book. "Of course. The Good News of Jesus Christ."

Harada looked down at the small book in her hand and read the title out loud. "New Testament. New Testament to what?"

The man chuckled and shook his head. "New Testament to what? Have you been under a rock the last 2100 years, miss?"

Harada smiled. "In a manner of speaking, yes. This one has."

"Well! Then it's a good thing you bumped into me! Long, long ago, God sent down his only son to us to show us how to live. To be happy and in communion with Him and one another. To end war and strife."

Harada beamed with radiant jubilation. "Humanity in communion with one another? Did it work?"

The man nodded. "For a time. Yes. But we've forgotten."

Harada smiled. "I see. Thank you for the book. This one shall study its methods closely."

As she started to walk off, the man called after her. "M-methods? Hey wait! Don't you want to hear more? Miss?"

But Harada didn't turn back or respond. She already began to move with the flow of the crowd, her nose immersed in her new book. She turned page after page, taking in the text.

As she took step after step, she muttered under her breath. "A savior promised? Their God among them. I see... This one understands. If that is what humanity needs to be transcendent, then they shall have it."

Harada looked to the sky. "I will fashion them a new God. One not so easily forgotten..."

Epilogue: Schrödinger's Cat

She awoke from a haze. Slowly her eyes opened to take in the view of an unfamiliar ceiling. Fluorescent lights. Textured white ceiling tiles. She tried to bring her right hand to her face, but it stopped with an audible clank by her side, suspended in place. She looked down to see a hospital bed and her right arm attached to it with a thick, metal handcuff.

What the fuck?

She brought her left hand up to her face and rubbed the side of her head. As she tried to rub the mental fog away, she noticed a hole in her left arm patched with the wrong skin tone of Siliclose. The same hole that was used to pull the components of a tranquilizer gun from her prosthetic arm back in Shanghai not more than three weeks ago.

Something was wrong. She shouldn't still be in this artificial body. She was going to be human again. Where was her new body? The flash clone. The prize she sold Harada for. She had seen it, floating in a tube, dormant. Asleep. Just waiting for the consciousness transference procedure. Waiting for her mind to be moved over. Was it all a lie? Had Jones decided to go back on their deal after Vivi upheld her part of the bargain?

The room was bright white. There were no windows. Only a singular door to her left.

A neural wire was connected to her neck. She yanked it out. A loud continuous beep sounded out from the medical devices around her. She began futilely tugging repeatedly on her arm restrained by the handcuff.

High heels reverberated loudly outside of the hospital room. The door opened. She looked up to see her, black high heels, black skirt, black coat, white blouse, white tie. Hester Jones.

"Jones!" Vivi snarled. "Why am I handcuffed? And why the *fuck* am I *still* in this body?"

"Well, this is complicated," Hester chuckled. "How to say, you left it, but — *you* — were never the one leaving it."

Vivi looked up at her in confusion. "What?"

"Hmm, how to explain? Oh!" Hester snapped her fingers. "I know! Have you ever heard the story about the Ship of Theseus?"

Vivi's mind raced. Her eyes darted back and forth, working things out. "I'm... the old ship in the warehouse?"

"Oh good!" Hester smiled. "You know this one! That makes it easier. Dark little secret of flash cloning they don't tell the public. *Consciousness can't be transferred, only copied.*"

"Bullshit! You're trying to back out of our deal!"

"I'm sorry, Rodriguez. I know this is hard, but it's the truth. Really, we shouldn't even be having this conversation. You see, once the flash clone has been made, and the mind copied over, the original article, that's you," Hester pointed to Vivi, "gets euthanized. Not a real attractive sales pitch to the rich folk who comprise the flash clone market, mind you, so that little detail tends to get left out in public discourse."

"Yeah? Then why'm I still here?"

"Well, I just knew there was something special about you, so I decided to keep you around in cold storage while your clone got to live the rest of your life. Just waiting for a rainy day."

A rainy day? "My clone." Vivi furrowed her brow, staring at Hester. "Where is she?"

"Dead."

"How?"

"Alcohol poisoning. Cops found her rotting in a gutter after one bender too many."

Vivi closed her eyes and sighed, knowing her predisposition to substance abuse. "Yeah, that tracks. My parents, did she ever—?"

"She tried to reconnect. For three years. But they still didn't want anything to do with her. With you."

Vivi looked back to Hester in shock. "Three years?" She bared her teeth. "And you're just waking me now?"

Hester chuckled in response, "Well, I couldn't very well have the two of you running around at the same time, could I? It wouldn't be ethical."

"Ethical?"

"Oh, don't look so upset."

Hester reached into her coat pocket and pulled out a lighter and a pack of Bael'rogs. She smiled as she tossed them next to Vivi on the bed. "We're going to have lots of fun together, you and I, though I think you'll need a new name. Viviana Rodriguez *is dead* after all. That. And you really look like you could use a fresh start. How's Olivia sound? You look like an Olivia to me..."

Vivi picked up the pack of cigarettes with her left hand and bit the cellophane wrapper off with her teeth. She opened the box, drew out a black cigarette with her mouth, tugged the lighter up to the end of the cigarette and ignited it. She breathed in deeply, taking a long drag.

Hester was right. With the newfound knowledge that even becoming human would not allow her to return home, whatever little hope that lingered within Vivi died, and Vivi with it. Vivi was no more. The husk that remained behind, handcuffed to a bed, wondered what was left for it in this new world it found itself in.

Olivia exhaled a thick cloud of smoke as she looked up morosely at Hester. "Just great."

After Action Report from the Author

Thank you for reading Rusted Synapse. I hope you enjoyed the ride as much as I enjoyed writing it. If you're curious about some backstory for the process of writing this novel, I can tell you with certainty it began back in October 2020, deep into the COVID pandemic.

Browsing the internet for techniques on securing PHP code, I stumbled across a scholarly article that piqued my imagination. This article contained a concept of computing that was somehow foreign to me, called "air gapping", and it discussed how to illicitly create a network connection to a computer not connected to the internet. In retrospect, I probably should have known this was a thing from the 1995 Mission Impossible movie, but either way, the concept intrigued me. It buried itself deep in my mind.

I visited the idea day after day in waking moments when my mind wasn't occupied with the more important matters of family or work, imagining a heated scenario between two characters driven to their conflict in a server room, fighting over whether or not to steal some sensitive data that could change the world. The scene became clearer and clearer as the days progressed into November. I would revisit it often, adding dialogue or changing minor aspects of the interaction as I saw fit, until the scene was fully formed. I could see it in my mind as clearly as if I were watching a movie. The fight between Vivi and Fincher was the first real scene in the story. The rest of the novel formed outward from this idea.

I imagined our protagonist being tricked into stealing a malevolent AI by a shadowy organization and fighting back when she realized she had been duped before needing to blast her way out of a heavily armed facility. Where was this facility? The 47th floor of a building of course! How to get our character out of there? Well drones, duh! She'll float down. But why are there drones there? Because she snuck into the building using a Deep Fake algorithm and the drones held all the computer equipment necessary to do so, why else? But then what? And then what? What if the AI wasn't malevolent at all?

The questions piled up and I would answer them as they arose. This was all just a fun exercise to occupy myself while brushing my teeth, or in those instances where I ended up walking the dog alone and had nothing but my thoughts for company.

As long as I can remember, I've always had some imaginary story running in the back of my mind. And as long as I can remember, I've never had the inclination to take the time to sit down and commit one of these stories to the page.

But then something happened in February of 2021. The southwestern United States from Texas through Louisiana was gripped by a frigid cold snap that brought the region to a standstill. The south isn't built to handle snow and ice like the northern states, and for the first time during the COVID Pandemic, the roads too dangerous to traverse, I was forced to work from home.

Early in the morning on one of these icy days, the internet went out and it didn't come back all day. No internet meant no work from home, but it also meant no TV and no videogames, since in my household, the internet is the source for those as well. Faced with the prospect of having to spend time with my daughter, who was in the early stages of the "terrible-two's", I instead decided to write a novel. We can all agree I made the right choice.

There were no agendas. No plan. No big underlying statement, political or otherwise, that I consciously wanted to make. All I really knew was that I wanted to tell a story that would resonate with me emotionally in the hopes it might resonate with others as well. A story that would address some of my criticisms of the fictional media landscape I've consumed in books, movies, and videogames over the years while also putting my own spin on some of the story tropes and philosophical quandaries I love.

And so, I began to write, toward the middle of the story I envisioned back in October of 2020, filling in all the blanks that would lead Vivi to the server room showdown with Ridley Fincher in the middle of the Long Qi building. But that wasn't an ending. Only the beginning of the story.

Harada was a challenge. In my initial drafts, she was a much different character. Very annoying. I didn't care for her. And if I didn't care for her, there was no way Vivi was going to allow this parasite to continue to exist on her hardware, and yet I very much knew I wanted Vivi to sacrifice herself for Harada by the end of the story. What to do? It was the first time I'd experience writer's block. My story sat for some weeks, untouched.

Depressed and tired of the impasse, I decided to skip ahead and wrote some of the final chapters of the novel instead. All of Vivi getting the band back together and their daring break-in to the Prison. Stuff that didn't require Harada.

It was when writing the prison break-in, I had my breakthrough. Both Vivi's escape from the Long Qi building and her break-in to the Prison were in my mind, very much in tone with the scene from the Matrix where Neo and Trinity blast their way through a lobby full of nameless soldiers to save Morpheus. Lots of gunfire and acrobatics; a swift moving kinetic scene with cool music.

It's one thing to consume that scene as a viewer, but as a writer, I was consciously thinking of all these poor soldiers I directed Vivi to kill. Their fictional families. Fictional children she was leaving father or motherless. I became rather sickened with it and drastically reduced the body count.

This is what ultimately formed Harada as she exists in the novel now. I decided to make Harada a foil to Vivi. Naïve, innocent and very concerned for other's happiness instead of her own. Despite Harada not being human, she cares more for human life than Vivi, who casually throws it away at the pull of a trigger. This machine became the most human character of all. It was in this moment the theme of the story came through for me. Vivi is obsessed with being human again for most of the novel. But she doesn't realize till the end that being human isn't the physicality of being of human, but rather the conscious act of being humane.

On the matter of the novel's epilogue, I will say, I always intended Vivi to die by the end of the story. When I began writing, I didn't know how I was going to do it, but I knew it would happen by the end. Unfortunately, by the time I began writing Chapter 10, though, I just enjoyed writing her too damn much for this book to be the end of her story. Hopefully, you don't think clone Vivi's death and sacrifice were cheapened by the epilogue, since our original protagonist is apparently still alive out there. There's still so much more for her to do.

So, here's hoping you'll join ~~Vivi~~ Olivia for the next mission in the sequel, **Rusted Synapse: Apocalypse Engine**.

Thanks again and best regards,

Elwood J Stevens

Email: AuthorElwoodStevens@gmail.com

Instagram: https://www.instagram.com/stilteddialog/

Glossary

A list of terms that appear in the novel.

Ad hoc Connection:

A local digital connection between people and/or devices within physical range to one another (approximately 120 feet without signal boost) that allows digital communication, but also spoofing by ONI rig.

Barbie:

Derogatory term for a fully prosthetic person, specifically of the female gender.

Bael'rogs:

A brand of cigarette featuring an evil-looking devil on the box. Each cigarette is completely black.

Borg:

Slang for cyborg. A being consisting of mostly mechanical body parts and few biological.

Carbon Fiber:

A lightweight material made of carbon atoms with the consistency of plastic but has the tinsel strength of steel.

Combat Synchronization:
A specialized ability performed by prosthetic soldiers on the battlefield using their internal computer arrays to synchronize the movements of a team of soldiers to one person's thoughts, allowing the unit to act as one. The synchronization commands are sent via ad hoc connections and are encrypted within old, out-of-copyright songs.

Cyberware:
Slang for computer equipment embedded directly into the skull and neck that interfaces with the nervous system via a neurobridge implant and allows interfacing wirelessly with network connected devices.

Desert Heat FM:
A radio station in Phoenix, Arizona in the year 2140 that is well known for playing the latest in bass thumping, booty shakin' hits with limited commercial interruption.

Fortunes:
A brand of cigarette.

Flash Clone:
A cloned body created from donor cells that is grown quickly to a specified target age over the course of weeks instead of years. This prohibitively expensive procedure is a favorite among politicians and the wealthiest of individuals for the purposes of remaining young and in their prime, ostensibly forever.

Full Prosthetic:

A fully mechanical body covered in artificial skin, closely resembling a human, designed to house and maintain a biological brain. A considerably cheaper alternative to flash cloning. Extended use may cause psychological defects.

HUD:

Heads Up Display — the computer augmented view overlaid atop a person's vision provided via artificial eyes, neurolinked optics, or Virtual Retinal Displays (VRD)

IDP:

Intrusion Defense Protocol — local automated systems for preventing unwanted third party intrusion.

Mechanic:

Slang term for prosthetist. A skilled laborer that installs and maintains prosthetic body parts or entire bodies.

Muñeca:

Derogatory term for a fully prosthetic person. Spanish. Literal translation: doll.

Neurolinked Optics:

A subdermal connection made between the eyes and a neurobridge implant attached to the cerebral cortex that allows a person's vision to be augmented with information about the surrounding world, and allows browsing of the outernet without the need for VR displays.

ONI:

Outer Network Intruder. Slang for hacker. Japanese. Literal translation: troll.

ONI Rig:

A heavy piece of computer equipment that allows an ONI to hack other computers.

Outernet:

The network that exists outside of a person's local network. The evolution of the Internet, connected via arrays of satellites in orbit around earth.

Overwatch:

In military tactics, a unit that supports another friendly unit from a distance, providing battlefield overview, threat spotting, and threat elimination services.

Plasteel:

A lightweight material that is heavier than carbon fiber, but more deformable, able to provide better defense against small arms fire and blunt force trauma compared to carbon fiber without breaking. A good weight to defense ratio.

Precision Overflow:

A favorite brute force cyber-attack utilized by ONIs with good heat overhead, pinpoints a weak point in a computer system and throws complex math at it to generate an overflow error, allowing the ONI to worm their way into the system using the error state's log routines as a backdoor into the rest of the system.

Prosthetist:

One part doctor. One part artist. One part mechanical engineer. A skilled laborer that installs and maintains prosthetic body parts or entire bodies.

Rust:

Slang. Mycobacterium Leprae-IX, a weaponized form of antibiotic resistant, fast acting leprosy characterized by rust-orange colored lesions that indicate infection and also gave it its nickname. Rust first cropped up in 2090 during the Second Russian Reunification War when a pathogen research facility was inadvertently bombed, unleashing the experimental bacterium on the surrounding area. As of 2140, some 35% of the world's population had contracted rust in one form or another, with military personnel operating in and around West Asia being the most commonly infected victims. Of those infected, 90% of cases are nonfatal and run their course with the victim losing a limb and/or eyes. 10% of cases affect the lungs and pancreas, and are considered terminal requiring replacement of the body via full prosthesis or flash clone for survival.

Sentient Daemon:

<Redacted>

Spoof/Spoofing:

An ad hoc cyber-attack targeting a person's neurolinked optics or prosthesis to make them see something that isn't real, see nothing, or in the cases of prosthetic body parts, turn off or malfunction.

Also By Author

Rusted Synapse: Apocalypse Engine